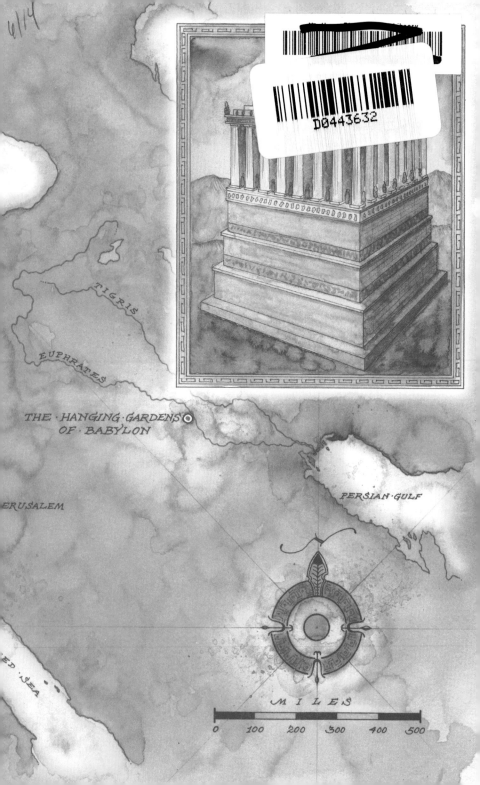

4/4

TIGRIS

EUPHRATES

THE · HANGING · GARDENS ○
OF · BABYLON

ERUSALEM

PERSIAN · GULF

ED · SEA

MILES

0   100   200   300   400   500

THE
TOMB
OF
SHADOWS

In the Underworld

THE
TOMB
OF
SHADOWS

PETER LERANGIS

HARPER

An Imprint of HarperCollinsPublishers

Seven Wonders Book 3: The Tomb of Shadows
Text by Peter Lerangis, copyright © 2014 by HarperCollins Publishers
Illustrations copyright © 2014 by Torstein Norstrand
Map art by Mike Reagan, copyright © 2014 by HarperCollins Publishers

Library of Congress catalog card number: 2014931071
ISBN 978-0-06-207046-3 (trade bdg.)
ISBN 978-0-06-232546-4 (int'l ed.)

Design by Joe Merkel
14 15 16 17 18   CG/RRDH   10 9 8 7 6 5 4 3 2 1
❖
First Edition

FOR DAVE AND ELOISE,
MY FELLOW VOYAGERS INTO WONDERMENT.

CHAPTER ONE

THE VALLEY OF KINGS

FOR A DEAD person, my mom looked amazing.

She had a few more gray hairs and wrinkles, which happens after six years, I guess. But her eyes and smile were exactly the same. Even in a cell phone image, those are the things you notice first.

"Jack?" said Aly Black, who was sitting next to me in the backseat of a rented car. "Are you okay?"

"Fine," I said. Which, honestly, was the biggest lie of my life. "I mean, for someone who's just discovered his mother faked her own death six years ago."

From the other side of the car, Cass Williams slid his Coke-bottle glasses down his nose and gave me a pitying glance. Like the rest of us, he was in disguise. "Maybe she wasn't faking," he said. "Maybe she survived. And had amnesia. Till now."

"Survived a fall into a crevasse in Antarctica?" I said.

I shut the phone. I had been looking at that photo non-stop since we escaped the Massa headquarters near the pyramids in Giza. I showed it to everyone back in the Karai Institute, including Professor Bhegad, but I couldn't stay there. Not while she was here. Now we were returning to Egypt on a search to find her.

The car zipped down the Cairo–Alexandria highway in total silence. I wanted to be happy that Mom was alive. I wanted not to care that she had actually been off with a cult. But I wasn't and I did. Life had changed for me at age seven into a Before and After. Before was great. After was Dad on business trips all the time, me at home with one lame babysitter after the other, kids talking behind my back. I can count on one finger the number of times I went to a parent-teacher conference with an actual parent.

So I wasn't woo-hooing the fact that Mom had been hangin' in a pyramid all this time with the Kings of Nasty. The people who stole our friend Marco and brainwashed him. The people who destroyed an entire civilization. The Slimeballs Whose Names Should Not Be Mentioned but I'll Do It Anyway. The Massa.

I turned back to the window, where the hot, gray-tan buildings of Giza raced by.

2

"Almost there," Torquin grunted. As he took the exit off the ring road, the right tires lifted off the ground and the left tires screeched. Aly and Cass slid into my side, and I nearly dropped the phone. "Ohhhh . . ." groaned Cass.

"Um, Torquin?" Aly called out. "That left pedal? It's a brake."

Torquin was nodding his head, pleased with the maneuver. "Very smooth suspension. Very expensive car."

"Very nauseated passenger," Cass mumbled.

Torquin was the only person who could make a Lincoln Town Car feel like a ride with the Flintstones. He is also the only person I know who is over seven feet tall and who never wears shoes.

"Are you okay, Cass?" Aly asked. "Are you going to barf?"

"Don't say that," Cass said. "Just hearing the word *barf* makes me want to barf."

"But you just said barf," Aly pointed out.

"Gluurb," went Cass.

I rolled down a window.

"I'm fine," Cass said, taking deep, gulping breaths. "Just . . . f-f-fine."

Torquin slowed way down. I felt Aly's hand touching mine. "You're nervous. Don't be. I'm glad we're doing this. You were right to convince Professor Bhegad to let us, Jack."

Her voice was soft and gentle. She wore a gauzy, orangey dress with a head covering, and contact lenses that turned her blue eyes brown. I hated these disguises, especially mine, which included a dumb baseball cap that had a ponytail sewn into the back. But after escaping the Massa a couple of days earlier and creating a big scene in town, we couldn't risk being recognized. "I'm not Jack McKinley," I said. "I'm *Faisal*."

Aly smiled. "We'll get through this, Faisal. We've been through worse."

Worse? Maybe she meant being whisked away from our homes to an island in the middle of nowhere. Or learning we'd inherited a gene that would give us superpowers but kill us by age fourteen. Or being told that the only way to save our lives would be to find seven magic Atlantean orbs hidden in the Seven Wonders of the Ancient World—six of which don't exist anymore. Or battling an ancient griffin, or being betrayed by our friend Marco, or watching a parallel world be destroyed.

I don't know if any of them qualified as worse than what we were about to do.

Cass was taking rhythmic deep breaths. His floppy white hat was smashed over his ears, and his glasses were distorting his eyes. In the lenses, I saw a mirror image of my own disguise, the hat and ponytail, my left cheek decorated with a fake birthmark like a small cockroach. Torquin had been forced to dye his hair black. His ponytail was so thick it looked like a possum attached to his neck. He still wouldn't wear shoes, so Professor Bhegad had had someone paint fake sandals on his feet. You'd be amazed how real that looked.

"You think your mom might have some motion sickness meds?" Cass asked.

"Let's make sure she's real first," I said. "Then we'll take care of the other stuff."

"She's real," Aly said. "Five Karai graphics experts, four coders, and me—all of us examined that photo. No feathered edges, no lighting discrepancies or pixel-depth variations. No Photoshopping."

I shook my head in total bafflement. "So she slips us a cell phone that leads us to the two stolen Loculi. She leaves us a code that reveals her identity, and she helps us escape. Why?"

"Maybe she's a spy?" Cass asked.

Aly sighed, shaking her head. "If she were a spy for the KI, they would know. But they don't. Right, Torquin?"

As Torquin shook his head, his ponytail-possum did a little dance. The car was veering left and right. Someone behind us honked.

Aly peered over the big guy's shoulder. "Torquin, are you texting while driving?"

"Jack mother not spy," he replied, putting down his phone.

"You could kill us!" Aly said.

"Wait," I said. "Your thumb is the size of a loaf of bread.

How can you hit the letters?"

"Make mistakes," Torquin grunted. "But this is emergency. You will thank me."

He yanked the steering wheel to the right, to get into the exit lane.

"No," Cass said, "I won't."

* * *

The afternoon sun was setting on the Valley of Kings, about a quarter mile ahead. Even at this distance we could see tourists flocking to buses. The pyramids cast long shadows toward the Sphinx, who sat there, staring back. She looked pretty bored about the whole thing.

I wished I had her calmness.

Our turnoff—the dirt road to Massa headquarters—was in sight about a hundred yards away. Torquin turned sharply onto a rubbly path. The car jounced at every pothole, and I had to put my arms over my head to cushion the blows against the roof. He slammed on the brakes, and we stopped in a cloud of desert dust.

As we stepped out, three Jeeps appeared on the horizon, speeding toward our location. Torquin's cell phone began beeping.

"Wait—is this the reason we're going to thank you?" Aly asked. "You called for backup?"

"I thought we were going to surprise the Massa," Cass said.

"Dimitrios smart and strong," Torquin said, popping open the trunk. "Must be smarter and stronger."

Aly reached in to hand us each a small backpack with supplies—flashlights, flares, and some stun darts. I slipped mine on quickly.

Before us was a small metal shack with a badly dented side. The entrance to the Massa headquarters looked like a supply shed, but it led downward into a buried pyramid untouched by archaeologists. Deep under the parched ground was a vast network of modern training rooms, laboratories, living areas, offices, and a vast control center, all interconnected. Some of the tunnels and rooms had been built during ancient times to honor the *ka*, the spirit of the dead pharaoh. To make that spirit feel coddled and comfy when he visited the world of the living.

The only spirit down there now was pure Massa evil.

"Moving now," Aly said. She darted ahead of us and reached for the door handle.

With a swift yank, she pulled it open.

"What the—?" Cass said.

"No lock?" I said, staring into the blackness beyond the door. "Weird."

Aly and I peered through the doorway and down concrete steps. It seemed overheated. I remembered this place being cold. At the bottom, a single lightbulb hung from a wire.

"It's so quiet," Cass said.

"What now?" Aly asked.

A soft, plaintive screech wafted upward. A pair of eyes moved erratically toward us out of the blackness.

"Duck!" I said.

We fell to the dirt as a bat flew over our heads, chittering. Torquin thrust his arm upward, snatching the furry creature in midair. It struggled and squeaked, trapped in his giant man-paw. "Not duck," he said. "But very nice breaded and fried, with mango salsa."

Aly's face was white with horror. "That is so unbelievably disgusting."

Torquin scowled, reluctantly releasing the critter. "Actually, is pretty . . . gusting."

The Jeeps had stopped now. Men and women in everyday clothes were filing out, spreading around, surrounding the area. They carried briefcases, heavy packs, long cases. They nodded imperceptibly toward us, their eyes on Torquin for instruction.

"These are all KI?" Aly said.

"New team," Torquin said. "Brought over after you escaped."

"They're armed!" Cass said. "Isn't this overkill?"

Torquin nodded, his brows knit tightly. "Not for Massa."

He had a point. Keeping low, I walked to the entrance and dropped to my stomach. Slowly I thrust my head out over the stairway. A sickly-sweet smell wafted up from below: mildew and rotted wood . . . and something else.

Something like burning plastic.

I pulled the flashlight from my pack and shone it downward. The stairs were littered with broken glass, wires, empty cans, and torn scraps of paper. "Something happened here," I said.

"Need backup?" Torquin lifted his fingers to his lips in preparation for a whistle signal.

"No," I said. "The Massa have surveillance. They've got to be seeing the Jeeps right now. If we go in together, with all the KI personnel, they're likely to react with force. That could end badly."

"So . . . you want just us to go down there?" Cass said.

"I'll do it alone if I have to," I said. "I need to see if my mom is really alive. If she's down there, she won't let anything bad happen. "

Cass thought for a moment, then nodded. "Dootsrednu," he said softly. "I'm with you, Faisal."

"Me, too," Aly said.

"Mm," Torquin agreed.

"Not you, Torquin." I said. No way could we risk scaring the Massa with him. "No offense. We need you out here. To . . . be commander of the KI team."

I began descending the stairs, swinging the flashlight around, trying to remember the layout. I could hear Aly's footsteps behind me. Cass's, too. "Commander?" Aly whispered.

"Had to make him feel important," I said.

"Ah . . . choo!" Cass sneezed.

"Shhhh!" Aly and I said at the same time.

At the bottom was a hallway that sloped downward, feeding into rooms with different functions. As we tiptoed, I flashed the light left and right. The floors were littered with debris. The overhead lights were out. So were the security lights.

I peeked through the first door, a storage area. Metal file cabinets had been pulled open. Some of the drawers were strewn on the floor. A round, old-timey wall clock lay broken among them, fixed at 3:11. Wrappers, newspapers, and assorted garbage had been hastily dropped in piles.

"What the—?" Aly said.

Cass stepped into the room across the hall. He stooped down and picked up a string of beads, which he flipped so that the beads slid up and down. "I think these are called worry beads," he said before slipping them into his pocket.

I shone my light into the room. Tables lined all four walls, with another long table stretching across the middle of the room. Cables lay strewn about like dead eels, chairs were upended, and trash littered the floor. No computers, no files, nothing.

"Looks like there was more hurrying than worrying," I said.

"It's impossible," Aly said, shaking her head numbly. "There were hundreds of people here. It was like a city."

Her voice echoed dully in the silent hallway. The Massa were totally gone.

CHAPTER TWO

VAPORIZED

A TRICK.

It had to be.

No one cleared out of a space this large in such a short time, for no apparent reason. They were up to something, I knew it. "Be careful, guys," I said, ducking back into the hallway.

"Should we contact Torquin?" Aly asked.

I shook my head. "Not yet."

If the Massa were luring us in, Mom knew about it. And Mom would make it all work out. Despite everything, I had to believe that.

As we tiptoed deeper in, the burning stench became stronger, more acrid, until we emerged into a familiar-looking corridor. This one was wider and brighter than the entrance hallway. Like much of the HQ, it had been built in modern times, for a modern organization.

"We took this route when we escaped," Cass said, peering around. "Remember? We went toward an exit to the right. That was where we found the Loculi. To the left was the huge control room . . ."

His voice trailed off as he looked left. The hallway was lit by a dull yellow-orange glow. We stuck close to the wall. I checked my watch—seven minutes since we'd left Torquin. He would be coming after us soon.

We rounded a bend and stopped short. The main control room's thick metal door was hanging open. Days ago, the place had been a hive of activity, Massa workers at desktop consoles and laptops, in consultations, shouting to one another across a vast circular space. An enormous digital message board hung from the domed ceiling, dominating the area.

Now the board was in pieces on the floor, engulfed in flames. Shattered glass lay everywhere, and tables had been reduced to splinters.

"It's like they . . . vaporized," Cass said.

Aly ran to a keyboard of a computer console near the wall. She upended a fallen chair and sat at the desk. "This one's working!" she exclaimed, her fingers dancing on the keys. "Oh, great. It's being wiped clean right now.

13

Military-grade overwrite, every byte replaced with zeroes. They must have started this a few hours ago. I may be able to recover some data. I need a flash drive!"

Cass began rummaging in his backpack. I looked around for surveillance cameras. "Mom!" I cried out, my voice echoing in the cavernous dome. As Cass pulled a flash drive from his pack and gave it to Aly, I ran to the other side of the room, looking for clues. I peered through the doorway at the opposite end, which led to yet another empty corridor.

Numbly, I stepped in. A dim blue light pierced the hallway's blackness. It was shining from a room to my right. I walked closer, focusing my flashlight on the open door.

Its panel said SECURITY. I could hear a soft but insistent beep inside.

Slowly I walked in.

"Faisal?" came Cass's voice from behind me.

I jumped. "We don't need the disguises," I said. "She's not here."

"Who's not?" Cass asked.

"Mom. None of them. They're not anywhere near."

My eyes focused on a flickering light shining from the wall to my left—a rectangular pane of glass with bright blue letters, flashing to the rhythm of the beep.

Beep.

FAILSAFE MODE: 00:00:17 . . .

14

Beep.

FAILSAFE MODE: 00:00:16 . . .

I snapped to and grabbed Cass's arm. "Out—now! The whole place is going to blow!"

Aly was already in the hallway. I pushed her back the way we'd come. Together we sprinted up the hallway toward the exit. At the base of the stairs we ran into Torquin, which was like running into a small building. "Turn around and go!" I shouted. "Now!"

Torquin's face went taut. He scampered up the steps and out the door with the speed of someone one-third his weight.

I felt the floor shake. I smelled sulfur.

The boom shook the walls, its blast hitting me square in the back.

CHAPTER THREE

PURYS ELPAM

"*PKKAAAACCCH!*" I COUGHED and spat as my eyes teared up from the dust.

I was outside, on the ground. Alive. My back rested against Torquin's rented car, which meant I was about thirty feet from the Massa entrance.

I opened my mouth to call out, but instead I sucked in another lungful of sandy dirt. Spitting, I struggled to my feet. Everything hurt. My pants had been torn at the ankle. "Cass!" I finally called out. "Aly!"

"Torquin," a familiar voice rumbled behind me. "Forgot Torquin."

The big guy's silhouette came out of the cloud, coated brown gray from head to toe, as if he'd been created from the dirt itself. With his right hand, he dragged Cass by the scruff of his neck. Cass's face was blackened, his limbs slack. His floppy hat and glasses were gone.

"What happened?" I slumped toward them as fast as my scraped-up legs could take me.

In a moment, Aly was beside me, holding a grimy pair of glasses. "I found these. Is he . . . ?"

"Chest moving," Torquin said, setting him on the ground. "Need to find help."

Aly and I dropped to our knees beside Cass. "Please, please, please, be okay . . ." I whispered, slapping his face gently. "Hey, Cass, come on. Don't forget to be emosewa."

"This can't be happening . . ." Aly said, yanking a canteen from her pack and spilling some water on Cass's face.

No reaction.

A team of KI soldiers surrounded us now. "We've got EMTs coming," one of the KI men called out.

Aly pried Cass's mouth open and dumped water in. "Come on, Cass," she said. "Cass, you can do this!"

Cass's body jerked upward, clipping Aly on the jaw. "Do what?"

"That!" Aly cried out in surprise, falling backward.

Cass turned away, retching a glob of wet sand. "Ewww, that needed a little purys elpam."

Holding her jaw with one hand, Aly managed a huge smile. "I will buy you a gallon of it when this is all over."

17

As two KI operatives approached with a stretcher, Cass's eyes were trained on the Massa headquarters. The entrance shack was a pile of twisted metal.

Another muffled explosion shook the earth. The structure groaned loudly, tilted, and vanished into a widening black hole.

Cass sprang to his feet. We ran for our cars, leaving the stretcher empty on the ground.

* * *

"Corrupt... gibberish... broken..." Aly muttered. She was in the copilot seat of Slippy, the KI retrofitted stealth jet, her fingers flying across the keyboard of the tablet that was built into the arm of her seat. Torquin was our pilot, and for once he wasn't making the plane do barrel rolls. He just focused on flying us back to the KI while Aly tried to get some usable information off Cass's flash drive.

My eyes were fixed on the sea below. The water was silvery and bright on a cloudless day. I don't know what I was looking for, maybe a big ship with a Massa flag blowing in the wind. I was kind of rattled, obsessed with only two thoughts:

We'd gone to find Mom.

We'd walked into a trap.

No warning about the evacuation. No hint about the time bomb. What if I hadn't noticed the readout? What if we hadn't gotten that far into the headquarters? What if we'd been a few seconds late? Did Mom know we would be going back?

How could she have let that happen?

Aly massaged her forehead, sitting back from the tablet. "If only we'd gotten there a few minutes earlier. Those jerks managed to overwrite just about everything. Maybe I can take apart the remaining data packets, but I'll need better equipment."

"You can do it," I murmured. "You're Aly."

Aly sighed, turning away from the tablet. "How's Cass?"

I turned toward the back of the compartment. Cass was lying against the bulkhead just behind my seat, on a narrow platform covered with layers of foam and blankets. He'd been asleep most of the way. Now he was blinking his eyes and grimacing. "What's that smell?"

"No smell," Torquin said. His face turned a slightly deeper shade of its natural red, and he held his arms super-close to his sides.

"Thank you for choosing KI Air," Aly said. "Each seat is equipped with an oxygen mask for use in case of toxic Torquin armpit or fart odor."

"Oow!" Cass groaned.

"What's wrong?" I asked.

"It hurts to laugh," Cass said. "Where the heck are we? And don't say anything funny."

"We're over the Atlantic," I said. "You survived an

explosion with some cuts and maybe a mild concussion. We left mainland ops and now we're headed back to the KI."

"Mainland who?" Cass said.

"The KI has mobile operatives all over the Mediterranean," Aly said. "Their job is to stay there and provide backup when necessary. Torquin has been telling us about them. See all the news you miss when you're asleep?"

"Where were the mainland ops when we needed them in Rhodes and Iraq?" Cass asked.

"We were incognito in Greece, and they had no clue where we were," I said. "But you did see some of them in Iraq. Remember those teams that took those shifts along the Euphrates?"

Aly swiveled in her seat and reached out to touch Cass's forehead. "How are you feeling?"

"Like I was just run over by a knat," Cass replied.

"Knat?" Torquin grunted.

"Backwardish for tank," Aly said. "Which means he's feeling better."

"I'd feel even better with some ice cream," Cass went on. "Actually, any food."

Torquin held up a greasy paper bag. "Iguana jerky. Cajun spice flavor."

Cass groaned. "Any food except that."

I saw a distant, shining, metallic cigar shape on the water below. A tanker, maybe, or cruise ship. It glinted in the sun, sending up sparks of light. For a moment I thought someone was trying to send us Morse code. Rubbing my eyes, I looked away. I needed to get some rest.

"I can't figure it out," Aly said. "How did the Massa escape? Where did they go?"

"And why didn't my mom tell us we were heading into a trap?" I added. "She could have sent a message to her own phone. She knows I have it."

"But she's one of them!" Aly said. "Her mind has been turned."

I glared at her. "I'm her son, Aly! Parents care about their kids. It's . . . it's just built in."

"Well . . ." Cass muttered.

We glanced back to where he was lying.

Cass, who hadn't seen his parents in years. Because they were in jail. Because they had abandoned him to a life of orphanages and foster parents.

I took a deep breath. "Hey, I—I'm sorry."

But Cass's eyes were wide with fright. The plane had begun to shake. We dropped like a roller coaster. My seat belt cut into my gut and I gripped my handrests.

Aly let out a gasp. "Does this mean we're getting close?"

Torquin nodded. "Entering KI territory."

"You're doing that on purpose!" Cass said.

"Magnetic forces," Torquin said with a shrug.

"Something extremely gross will fly out of my stomach

and magnetize to the back of your neck if you don't fly better," Cass replied.

I saw Mount Onyx first, rising like a black fist from the water. In a moment we saw home—our new home, an island undetectable by even the most sophisticated instruments.

"What the . . . ?" Aly said.

My eyes locked on the location of the Karai Institute campus, where I expected to see the lush green quadrangle, surrounded by brick buildings.

In its place was a giant plume of black smoke.

CHAPTER FOUR

TRIANGULATION

THE PLANE BANKED sharply right, away from the campus.

"Where are you going?" I demanded. "The airport is in the other direction!"

"Back of island," Torquin said. "Change in plans."

"It's all jungle on that side!" Cass said. "We'll never land this thing there."

"Airport too dangerous," Torquin declared.

"It'll take hours to hike through the trees," I said. "We need to get there fast, Torquin. The institute is on fire."

Torquin ignored us both, yanking the steering mechanism again.

My stomach jumped up toward my throat. We were out over the water, circling farther away from land. As it vanished over the horizon, Torquin banked again.

We zoomed back in, toward the rear of the island. It was a blanket of green, surrounded by a thin sliver of beach. "The sand is too narrow!" Aly said, her voice rising in panic.

"Banzaiii!" Torquin yelled.

The plane's nose pointed downward. I gripped the armrest. From behind, Cass grabbed my arm. He was screaming. Or maybe that was me. I couldn't tell. As the plane dove, I closed my eyes.

We hit hard. My back jammed down into my hips, like I'd been squashed by an ogre. Cass slammed into the back of my seat. A deafening roar welled up around us as water slammed against the windows.

"Sand too narrow," Torquin replied. "But sea not too narrow."

As the jet's forward momentum slowed to a stop, the windows cleared. I could see the island shore about a football field's length away from us, separated by an expanse of ocean.

Cass's eyes were tightly closed. "Are we dead?"

"No, but I think I sprouted some gray hairs," Aly said, "aside from the lambda on the back of my head. Torquin, what are we doing here?"

Torquin mumbled something in a hurry. He jabbed a button, and Slippy began speeding toward the island on its superlight aluminum-alloy pontoons.

Cass, Aly, and I shared a baffled look. My heart was

racing. As the pontoons made contact with sand, we jumped out. Torquin opened a compartment in the back of the plane and pulled out a huge pack of equipment. I'd never seen him move so fast.

Aly stared, ankle-deep in water. "Torquin, I am not moving another step until you talk to us. In full sentences. With an explanation!"

Torquin handed us each a flak vest, a machete, a lightweight helmet, and a belt equipped with knives and water canisters. "These are for protection," he snapped. "Island is under attack."

"You know that just from that smoke?" Aly said.

"Where smoke, fire," Torquin replied. "Where fire, attack."

His logic was not perfect, but when I saw the furious glint in his eyes I decided not to argue. Aly and Cass clearly felt the same way. We suited up quickly. Weighted down by the equipment, we waded to the shore. The trees formed a thick, impenetrable wall. No paths in sight.

Torquin stopped, carefully looking around. "Wait. Easy to get lost."

"Just follow me," Cass said. "We have the sun, the shore, the slope of the land, and Mount Onyx. More than enough points for geographic triangulation. We don't need a map."

We didn't question him. Cass was a human GPS. He could memorize maps and routes to the inch.

"Need dictionary," Torquin gruffed, as we all started after Cass.

* * *

I didn't know which was worse—the smothering heat of the sun, the bug bites that made my legs look like raw hamburger, the screeching of animals we couldn't see, or the smell of the smoke.

It was all horrible.

I knew Torquin's analysis had to be wrong. The island was shielded by some force that made it impossible to find by anybody. But what had happened? An electrical short circuit? A lightning hit?

I dreaded what we would find.

Cass stumbled and stopped. His face was bright red, his clothes drenched. Setting his backpack down, he sat on a tree stump. "Dry . . ." he said.

"Have some water," Aly said, unscrewing her canteen.

Cass waved it away. "I'm okay," he said. "I meant, the land is dry. The trees, too. If the breeze pushes the fire in this direction, we're toast. Literally."

I nodded. "Let's stay close, in case we have to retreat to the beach."

"We have to help them," Cass said, wiping his head. "We have to be like Marco. He would never retreat."

"Marco," Aly said, "retreated from us."

I helped Cass to his feet. He quickly slipped ahead of

Torquin, taking the lead. We were passing Mount Onyx now. Below us were Jeep tracks, where we'd raced back to the campus when the griffin attacked.

Cass picked up the pace. The smell was pungent and strong. White ash floated down through the treetops. Monkey screeches and birdcalls echoed around us. But I could hear other sounds now. Voices. Distant shouts.

"Stop!" Torquin ordered.

We nearly plowed into each other. Torquin passed us, squinting into the smoky air. I followed closer and saw what looked like an enormous spiderweb, strung between trees. "Security fence," Torquin said. "High voltage."

"Aly knows how to disable that," Cass said. "She did it when we tried to escape."

"From the inside," Aly reminded him. "Not from here. We're stuck."

Torquin crouched silently, grabbed the top of an umbrella-shaped mushroom, and pulled hard. The stalk broke cleanly, revealing a blinking red light, flush with the ground. I heard a soft click. "*Voilà*," he said. "Disables. Thirty seconds. For KI people stuck in jungle."

"You know French?" Cass asked.

"Also *croissant*," Torquin replied proudly.

Cass took the lead again. The scent of smoke was growing stronger. We were practically running now. The sweat on my back felt like a lake against the heavy pack. But up

27

ahead, the dense jungle darkness was giving way to the light of a clearing.

A light made brighter by fire.

Cass stopped first. He dropped to his knees, his jaw hanging open.

"This can't be . . ." Aly said.

We all sank down beside Cass, at the edge of the jungle now. The Karai Institute spread out before us, but it looked nothing like the stately college campus we'd left. The grassy quadrangle was chewed up by boot prints and speckled with glass from broken windows all around. I could see figures moving through the brick buildings, white-coated KI technicians fleeing into the woods. Flames leaped from Professor Bhegad's second-floor collection of antiquities.

Fires raged behind the quad buildings, from the direction of the airport, the dorms, the supply sheds, and support buildings. The tendrils of smoke twined skyward, disappearing into an umbrella cloud of blackness.

"Leonard . . ." Cass rasped.

"Leonard?" Aly said. "All you can think about is what happened to your pet lizard? What about the KI staff?"

An anguished cry from across the quadrangle made us all instinctively duck behind a thicket. I peered through the branches to see a man in a ripped white KI lab coat tumble out the game room entrance. His hair was matted with blood.

As he scrambled to his feet, there was no mistaking

Fiddle, our resident mechanical and aeronautical genius.

"We have to help him," I said, rising, but Aly grabbed me by the collar.

From the building entrance, behind him, stepped a man dressed in black commando gear, goggles, and a helmet emblazoned with a black M.

"Massa . . ." Aly said, pointing him out to me.

"But how?" Cass asked. "The island is undetectable by human means."

"Massa not human," Torquin said.

Now I could see more of them—in the windows of the lab buildings, running across the basketball court. I could see them dragging KI scientists into the dorm, throwing rocks through windows. One of them, racing across the campus, tore down the KI flag, which stood in front of the majestic House of Wenders.

Fiddle staggered closer toward the jungle. He looked desperately around through the broken lenses of his glasses. I wanted to call out to him, but the commando grabbed Fiddle by his lab coat and yanked him down from behind.

"We have to help him," I said.

"But it's four against a bazillion," Cass said.

Torquin crouched. "But this four," he said, pulling a wooden case from his pack, "is very good."

CHAPTER FIVE

COUNTERATTACK

TORQUIN PULLED A long, slender pipe and a handful
of darts from his pack. He moved through the jungle, crab-
walking silently away from the thicket.

Dropping behind a fallen tree, Torquin put the pipe to
his lips, and blew.

Shissshhhh!

Fiddle's captor crumpled downward instantly, felled by a
small, green-feather-tipped tranquilizer dart. "Eye of bull,"
Torquin said.

I scrabbled to my feet and raced out of the jungle toward
Fiddle.

As Fiddle saw me approach, he turned to run away. "It's
Jack McKinley!" I called out as loudly as I dared.

30

He stopped and squinted at me. "I must be dreaming."

I took his arms and pulled him toward the trees. Behind us I could hear doors opening, voices shouting. Torquin's tranquilizer darts shot out from the jungle with impossible speed, each one followed by a groan.

With the sharp *crrrrack* of a gunshot, a tree branch exploded just over Torquin's head. We all dove into a thicket. "Why are we using darts when they're using bullets?" Fiddle screamed.

"KI not killers," Torquin replied. He reached out and lifted Fiddle onto his back as if he were a rag doll. "Go! Deeper into jungle. Hide!"

We followed Cass back the way we'd come. Behind us, an explosion rocked the jungle and we were airborne in a storm of dirt and leaves. I thumped to the ground, inches behind Aly and Cass. A tree crashed to the jungle floor exactly where Torquin and Fiddle had been.

"Torquin!" I shouted.

"Safe!" his voice replied from somewhere behind the tree. "Just go!"

Flames leaped up all along the pathway we'd just taken. As we ran blindly into the jungle, I peered over my shoulder to see Torquin and Fiddle following us. Cass was taking the lead, his head constantly turning left and right. Honestly, I don't know what he was seeing. Every inch of the jungle looked the same to me. But Cass knew. Somehow.

31

Panting, he stopped in a clearing and looked around. The explosions were like distant thunder now, barely audible above the animal noises and the sound of our own breaths. "Did you know this place was here?" I asked.

"Of course," Cass nodded. "Didn't you? We've been here before. We're near the beach where we saw the dead whale. If we have to, we can follow the coast around to the plane."

"Whoa, dismount!" Fiddle said as Torquin stomped into the area. Sliding off the giant's back, Fiddle grimaced. He took off his broken glasses and pulled a tiny shard from his cheek. "This really hurts. That means it's not a dream, right? Which is a bummer."

"Are you okay?" Aly asked.

"Yeah, I think." Fiddle nodded. "Although I should have bought safety lenses."

"What happened here?" I demanded, catching my breath.

Fiddle's eyes seemed drained of life. His face was taut, his voice distant, as if he were recounting a horrible nightmare. "I'm . . . sitting in the airport minding my own business—and these turkeys fly in. No one expected it. We were caught totally unaware. Someone must have given us away . . ."

"Marco," Torquin said.

"Marco doesn't know the way here," Aly protested. "None of us do. It's got to be someone else."

"It is." Cass eyed me warily. "It's . . . Jack."

I looked at him, speechless.

"Not you, personally," Cass said. "Your phone. The one your mom gave you, in the Massa HQ. You turned it on while we were here."

"Wait," Aly said. "And you left it on?"

"Okay, maybe—but so what?" I said. "No signal can get through to the island. It's totally off the grid. Any grid!"

Aly groaned, slumping against a tree. "It's not about location, it's about vector, Jack—meaning direction. When we got in the plane, the signal traveled with us. Once we left the protected area around the island, the Massa could pick up the signal."

I imagined a map, with an arching, beeping signal, traveling slowly from the middle of the ocean toward Egypt. Like a big old arrow pointing where to go. "So they just followed the path backward and kept going . . . until they discovered the island . . ."

"Bingo," Cass said.

I felt dizzy. This whole thing was my fault. If it weren't for my boneheaded move, we wouldn't be in this danger. How could I have been so ignorant? "I—I'm so sorry. I should have known."

Cass was pacing back and forth. "Forget that now, Brother Jack. Really. It's okay. Actually, it's not."

"Need to counterattack," Torquin added, looking back in the direction of the compound.

"You and what army?" Fiddle asked. "You got zombies hidden away? Because the Massa are all over the explosives supply now. I say we run. However you got here, let's get out the same way."

When Torquin turned, his face was lined and his eyes moist, as if he'd aged a few years. "Never leave Professor Bhegad behind."

"Or the Loculi," I said. "Where are they?"

Torquin and Fiddle both looked at each other and shrugged.

"We gave them to Bhegad," Aly said. "He didn't tell you where he put them?"

Cass sagged. "There goes that plan."

"Okay . . . okay . . ." I said, rubbing my forehead as I tried to think this through. "Bhegad probably kept the location of the Loculi to himself—one person only, to avoid a security leak. So we find him first, and he'll lead us to them."

"Unless the Massa get to him before us," Cass said.

"Bhegad tough," Torquin said. "Won't crack under pressure."

"We need to find his EP assignment," Fiddle said. "Emergency protocol. We all get one. It's where we have to go in case of an attack."

"These EP assignments," Aly said. "Are they stored somewhere?"

Fiddle shrugged. "Must be. The assignments are changed randomly from time to time. We're notified electronically."

"I'll need to get to the systems control building." Aly looked up. "The sun is setting. We have maybe an hour before it gets too dark to see outside. That'll help us."

"But the control building will be full of Massa," Cass said.

"We clear it," Torquin declared.

Fiddle looked at him in bafflement. "How? With darts? You guys are out of your minds. We need an army, not a sneak attack with a half-blind geek, a caveman, and three kids barely out of diapers." He looked toward the water.

Aly's jaw hung open. "Did you say . . . *diapers?*"

"Caveman?" Torquin added.

Fiddle backed away slowly. "Oh, I forgot—feelings. Guess you guys want sensitivity. Fine, it's your funeral."

He turned, lurching into the jungle.

"Hey!" Torquin cried.

As he lumbered after Fiddle, I followed. Aly called me back but I kept going. "Torquin, let him go!" I cried out.

After a few turns, deeper into the dense-packed trees, I felt my foot jam under a root. I tripped and landed a few feet from Torquin's pack. I guessed he must have dropped it to lighten his load. But I couldn't leave it there. Not with those tranquilizer darts inside. We could use those.

Wincing, I sat up. I could hear movement—footsteps? I wasn't even sure from which direction the sound was coming. The sky was darkening. I looked over my shoulder, but the jungle was without paths, and even my own footsteps were lost in the dense greenery. "Aly?" I called out. "Cass?"

I waited. High overhead a monkey screamed. It dropped from a branch and landed on its feet, jumping wildly up and down. *Eeee! Eeee!*

"Go away!" I said. "I don't have any food."

It was slapping its own head now, gesturing wildly back into the woods.

"Do I know you?" I said, narrowing my eyes at the creature. During my first escape attempt from the island, I'd been lured to Torquin's helicopter by an extremely smart chimp. Who looked very much like this one. "Are you showing me which way to go?"

Oooh, it grunted, darting straight for the backpack.

So that was its game—distracting me so it could steal the pack! "Hey, give me that!" I shouted.

A loud crack resounded, followed by a familiar scream.

Aly's voice!

Ignoring the branches and vines that slashed across my face, I ran back toward the noise. In moments I saw the dull glow of the clearing.

Silently I dropped into the brush. I had a sight line. Cass and Aly were where I'd left them. Aly's arm was bleeding.

Cass was holding a branch high like a spear. Around them were four helmeted Massa, armed with rifles. They grinned, jeering, taunting my friends in some language I didn't know.

My muscles tightened, ready to spring.

No. No way you can jump in there alone.

Where was Torquin?

I felt something jam into my back and nearly screamed aloud.

Whipping around, I came face-to-face with the monkey. It was holding out Torquin's backpack to me.

I grabbed it and spun back toward the clearing. Shaking, I pulled out the blowpipe. My hands were sweaty. As I reached for a dart, the weapon slipped out of my hand. It clattered onto a rock. Behind me the monkey screeched in surprise.

From the dense jungle, a rifle emerged, pointing directly at my face.

CHAPTER SIX

GOOD-BYE, WILBUR

"YEAAAGHHH!"

Torquin's roar blotted out all sound. He leaped from the brush into the clearing, about twenty yards to my right.

The four soldiers wheeled around. Torquin landed full body on the one who'd found me, squashing the guy to the ground. Behind him, another Massa soldier was trying to take aim at Torquin, but the two bodies were too close. Instead he raised his rifle high and brought it down on Torquin's head. Hard. It hit with a solid thud.

Aly ran toward Torquin to help, but the assailant backed away, the weapon still in his hand.

Its barrel was now bent, forming the shape of Torquin's skull.

Torquin stood, scratching his head in puzzlement. Then, grabbing the rifle, he flung it against a tree, with its owner still holding tight. The guy folded without a whimper.

"Two down," Torquin grunted.

As the other two men maneuvered in the confusion, I snatched up the blowpipe, jammed a dart down the tube, and blew. It sailed into the clearing, nearly hitting Aly and Cass along the way.

Eeee! chided the monkey, holding out another dart.

The men couldn't seem to decide where to point their rifles, at Torquin or me. I aimed carefully, firing once again. Cass and Aly dove to the ground, out of the way. But my shot sailed true this time, catching one Massa in the side of the neck.

EEEEEE! The monkey was jumping up and down now.

"My feeling exactly," I said.

The monkey began gesturing frantically into the trees. I turned to see the remaining commando on his knees, lifting his rifle.

I ducked behind a bush, reaching for a dart. But I had used the last one. The monkey was grabbing my shoulder, leapfrogging over my head. "Hey!" I shouted.

Crrrack!

I flinched as the creature's body jolted backward. It hit me in the face, knocking me to the ground. As I fell, a warm liquid oozed downward onto my neck.

I turned to see Torquin pummeling the last attacker with his massive fists. Cass and Aly were screaming, but I couldn't make out the words.

"Little man, are you okay?" came Fiddle's voice.

I blinked the blood from my eye. Fiddle was kneeling over me, cradling my head in his hand. "F-fine," I said, spraying his face with red dots. "I thought you were going without us."

"I was, until Gigantor got ahold of me," he replied. "Dude, you totally rocked the Massa. I am impressed."

"It wasn't just me," I said, sitting up.

Above, the setting sun had cast the sky orange. The waning light illuminated the small body of the monkey, lying in a twisted position on its back.

* * *

I watched Torquin quickly dig a hole with a bayonet. As he lowered the monkey's body into it, distant shouts and explosions filtered through the thick jungle. The sky was darkening, which would only be to our advantage. By my calculation, the battle for the island had been under way for hours. We had little time and less hope of defeating the Massa. But in that moment all I could think about was the bravery of the little creature.

I felt a tear drop from my cheek onto the dirt. Aly looked at me with concern and put a hand on my shoulder.

"He took one for me," I said with a shrug. "He didn't deserve this."

Aly nodded. As we rushed to cover the hole with soil, Torquin softly murmured, "Good-bye, Wilbur."

"That's the monkey's name—Wilbur?" Cass asked.

Torquin wiped at his cheek with a huge hand.

"Guess he really meant something to you," Aly said.

Torquin shook his head. "Humid today, is all."

With a rustle of leaves, another commando emerged from the bush. It took a moment to recognize it was Fiddle, dressed in a Massa outfit he'd taken from an unconscious soldier. "I suggest we all suit up, guys. No time to lose."

I turned. The four Massa officers were tied to trees at the edge of the clearing, their uniforms piled at their feet. "Four Massa, five us," Torquin said. "I get uniform later."

"Better hope they make them in plus sizes," Fiddle said. "Now, hurry. And take the weapons, in case these guys wake up and break free."

Leaving the gravesite, we each grabbed an outfit and put it on. The guys were all big, so the garb fit loosely over our own clothes.

Cass rolled up the cuffs of his baggy pants, pulled his belt as tight as it went, and grabbed a commando rifle. As Aly picked up another rifle and strapped it over her thin shoulders, her whole body sagged.

Fiddle gave her a dubious look. "You guys are a bigger danger to yourselves than the Massa are."

"Try us," Aly said.

"Follow me," Cass said, stepping to the edge of the

41

clearing. As we fell in behind, dodging our way around vines and trees, the jungle seemed to grow darker by the second. Under the helmet I was sweating like crazy. The noise from the compound had subsided, which meant the battle was winding down. What would we see? My heartbeat quickened with a mixture of hope and dread.

My rifle clanked heavily against my side, but that was nothing compared to the swarm of mosquitoes around my ankles. "Get away!" I said through gritted teeth, bending to swat at the cloud of tiny bugs.

I stopped in midslap at the sight of a flat rock, nearly as big as a manhole cover. On it was a carving of a fierce griffin, a half eagle, half lion. I bent down to examine it. I'd seen it before—back when I'd first tried to escape from the KI.

"Hm," Torquin said, looming up behind me. He picked up the rock and scowled at the carving. "Griffin. Pah!"

The burning smell grew stronger. Through the branches now, I could see the winking lights of the compound. Distant voices shouted. From our left came the sound of painful, pitiful groans. Cries for help.

I looked at the others. They had all heard it, too. We changed direction, moving closer. I knew where we were now—just behind our dormitory.

We crouched behind thick brush. Not ten feet in front of us was a scraggly field, where a guard moved slowly back and forth, smoking a cigarette. "They're using our dorm as a prison," Aly whispered.

"At least they're keeping KI people alive," Fiddle said.

A pinpoint of light shot through the air. Before I could react, the stub of a lit cigarette hit the side of my face.

"*Gggghhh—*"

Torquin's beefy hand closed around my mouth, cutting off an outcry. My cheek stung, and his fingers only made it worse.

The guard stopped in his tracks. He came closer to the jungle's edge. Toward us. I held my breath. His eyes scanned the bushes as he shone a flashlight. From the dorm came a sudden clatter and the muffled voice of a KI captive: "Emergency! Yo, Massa lunkheads—Fritz is having a seizure! Somebody get him his medication!"

Fritz. The mechanic who had been part of my KI training.

But the guard ignored the voice. The beam was coming closer. It would discover my face first. I crouched lower, pressing my hands against the rocky ground. Torquin was to my right. He turned to me and mouthed the words "talk to him." He gestured to my uniform.

I had almost forgotten. We were dressed like them. But what was I supposed to say?

"I see you . . ." the guard said, stepping closer.

Torquin glared. Taking a deep breath, I stood. "Of

course you did!" I said, pointing to the welt on my cheek. "I . . . fell."

Lame, lame, lame, Jack!

A smile grew across the guard's face. He raised his rifle. "Nice outfit, kid. I know who you are," he said. "And your face is going to look a lot worse if you don't tell me where your little friends are."

He lifted his rifle high over his head. I stepped back, shaking.

A dull gray blur shot across my line of sight. It connected with the Massa's face with a sickening thud. Silently, he and his rifle fell to the ground.

The griffin rock was resting by his head.

"Now," Torquin said, stepping triumphantly out of the woods, "we have fifth uniform."

CHAPTER SEVEN

EMERGENCY PROTOCOLS

"HOW DO I look?" Torquin walked stiffly toward us, wearing the fallen Massa's garb. The pants had ripped at the seams, his arms dangled out of the too-short sleeves, and his belly protruded from an unbuttoned shirt.

"Like a bear in samajap," Cass replied. "Too bad it's getting dark. We could kill them with laughter."

Aly and I were poised at the edge of the jungle. Fiddle had raced into the dorm, which was now unguarded. Around us, the compound was in utter chaos. The place may have been a great research institute, but it wasn't built to withstand an assault.

A piercing alarm made us jump. Seconds later, Fiddle raced out the back door of the dorm. Behind him swarmed a group of bedraggled KI people. Two of them were holding Fritz the mechanic by his legs and shoulders. As they disappeared into the jungle to our left, Fiddle gestured toward the escapees. "All of you!" he urged. "Get to MO twenty-one, now!"

"Is Fritz okay?" I asked.

"Diabetic," Fiddle explained, as KI prisoners streamed out of the dorm. "Needs an insulin injection. Fortunately, there are plenty of medical doctors among the KI. We have a couple of hidden shelters on the island. MO twenty-one is near Mount Onyx. There'll be insulin in the emergency supplies there."

I could barely recognize some of the KI staff. Brutus, the head chef, had been beaten badly, his face swollen and red. He had to be helped by two others. Hiro, the martial-arts trainer, was walking with a crutch. They looked toward us, weary and bewildered, as if we were a dream.

Fiddle urged them on, then gathered Torquin, Cass, Aly, and me close. We could hear Massa reinforcements clattering in at the front of the building. "We don't have much time before the goons figure out what just happened. I'll stay here and get as many KI people to safety as I can. You guys get to work finding Bhegad's EP assignment. Aly, you know where to go?"

"Building D," Aly said.

Fiddle nodded. "Right. The systems control center. But

I warn you, the info is encrypted beyond belief."

"Depends on your definition of belief," Aly said with a small grin.

"Radio me when you find him." Fiddle fished a walkie-talkie from his pocket and threw it to me. "The uniforms will give you some cover. Be sure you find those Loculi. Bhegad will know where they are. Do you understand this? Good. I can meet you back at the plane. Where is it?"

"Enigma Cove," Torquin said.

With a nod, Fiddle disappeared in the direction of the dorm. Cass, Aly, Torquin, and I bolted. We followed the perimeter of the campus toward Building D. I was scared out of my mind. The Massa knew our faces. In the light, we were toast. And the baggy uniforms didn't help. But the gathering darkness might help us pass for Massa commandos.

As the alarm blared all over the compound, the chaos seemed to multiply in the quadrangle. Officers were screaming at subordinates, commandos were shoving KI staff toward the dorm. No one seemed to care about four more running people.

We crouched behind the squat, square building and peered into the window. Exactly two Massa were in there, pounding on keyboards. "Skeleton crew," Cass commented.

Torquin stood, gesturing us to follow. He circled the building and strolled through the building's front door, which had been blasted open. "I help, fellow Massa?" he boomed.

The two men turned. One of them nearly spit out his coffee. "Whoa, nice uniform! What have you been eating, dude?"

Torquin grabbed them by their collars, lifted them out of their seats, and butted their heads together. "Pound cake," he said.

Aly slid into a seat in front of a console. Her fingers flew over the keyboard. Code flashed across the screen at impossible speed.

"You can actually read that?" I said.

"Shhh . . ." The scrolling stopped, and the screen filled with random letters and symbols. "Okay, there it is . . . House of Wenders, sublevel seven. That's Bhegad's EP."

"That's the underground lab, where they made Shelley the Loculus shell," Cass exclaimed.

"Where do you read that, Aly?" I asked, staring at the gobbledygook.

"It's in hexadecimal notation," she said. "Those combinations each represent letters and characters."

I stared at her. "You scare me."

"Actually, I scare me, too." She turned from the screen, a concerned look on her face. "I wouldn't have been able to read that even a week ago. Hurray for G7W. Now let's see if we can scare the Massa . . ." Swinging around back to the keyboard, she said, "They will have access to our trackers now, right? So before we get Bhegad, why don't I just zap the KI's tracking machine—along with some other choice equipment . . . hee-hee . . ."

"We can't just run across the courtyard to the House of Wenders," Cass said. "There are tons of Massa. Dark or not, someone will recognize us, just like that guard did."

"Go the long way," Torquin suggested.

"On it." Aly's fingers were a blur. "Overloading the Comestibule circuits . . . disabling the breakers . . . should cause a small explosion there. Okay. On the count of three, the lights should go out everywhere except the House of Wenders. The Massa goons who aren't heading to the dorm will be drawn to the explosion in the Comestibule, buying us some space and time."

"Wait. What if someone is actually in the kitchen?" I asked.

Torquin looked skeptical. "The long way is better."

Aly sighed. "I figure that the kitchen-cafeteria is the one place people *won't* be during a Massa attack. Let's hope I'm right. Ready? One . . . three!"

She leaped from the seat. A distant blast rocked the earth. I staggered and fell to the floor. "I thought you said a small explosion!"

"There goes five fifty-pound sacks of chocolate chips," Cass said mournfully.

Torquin pushed us all outside. We ducked into a shadow, watching smoke rise from the Comestibule.

Together we sprinted across the compound, which was now pitch-dark, save for the lights in the windows of the House of Wenders, directly across from us. It loomed over the campus, as solemn and stately as a courthouse, its wide marble stairs topped by seven columns. The KI flag that flew on a pole in front was now tattered and blackened. As a group of five Massa raced down the stairs in confusion, Torquin called out to them: "Attack! Comestibule! Go!"

They stomped off toward the commotion, and we headed into the grand entrance hall, racing around the statue of the dinosaur that had spooked me so much when I'd first walked in here. The elevator in the back of the hall was empty. We piled inside and plunged downward to sub-basement 7. Torquin held tight to his rifle.

The door opened directly into an enormous domed chamber, lit by a string of buzzing fluorescent lights. Torquin stepped inside, his bare feet slapping on the concrete. The room was full of abandoned workstations, their monitors glowing with the KI symbol.

"Professor?" I called out.

My voice echoed, unanswered, into the dome.

"Empty," Torquin announced.

"I think we all see that," Aly remarked.

"Any other suggestions where to go?" Cass said.

With a soft whoosh, the elevator door shut behind us. As I turned instinctively, the room plunged into sudden darkness.

A low, focused *hissss* came from the ceiling. Three emergency lights flicked on, casting everything in a sickly bluish-white glow. I felt a tickle in my throat. Cass began coughing, then Aly.

Torquin fell to his knees, his eyes red. Quickly he began ripping apart sections of his already ripped pants, then throwing the pieces to us. "Put on . . . nose!" he said, gasping for breath.

"What's happening?" Aly said, doubling over with violent coughs.

Torquin jammed the fabric over his face. "Tear . . . gas!"

CHAPTER EIGHT
LOCATION D

I **SANK TO** the floor. My knees hit the concrete with a sharp crack, my eyes began to water, and I felt as if someone had crawled into my throat with a set of knives.

Torquin was struggling with his rifle, looking toward the back of the room. There, a lab room door was swinging open to reveal a figure wearing a white coat and a gas mask. As the person came closer, Torquin took aim.

I could see a black-and-gray ponytail protruding out from under the mask. As Torquin sneezed, the person bolted to the left.

Aly was wheezing, convulsed into a ball. Cass looked dead. I tried to keep my eyes open, breathing directly into the fabric. I crawled around, following the masked figure, who was grabbing at the wall as if looking for something. I managed to close my fingers around an ankle and pulled. As the person fell to the floor, I reached up and yanked off the mask.

"No!" screamed a voice. "Don't!"

I was face-to-face with Dr. Bradley, Professor Bhegad's personal physician.

And traitor.

"You're"—I gasped—"one of them, too?"

I thought my lungs would ball up and burst. As I fell back, Dr. Bradley sank beside me, red-faced and choking, grasping desperately for her mask.

With a grunt, she yanked it from my fingers. Climbing to her feet, she slipped the mask back on and steadied herself by grabbing the wall.

I blinked like crazy but I was too weak to stand. Dr. Bradley was pulling open a metal panel on the wall, flipping a switch.

She swung around toward me. My eyes were fluttering shut. *Tear gas?* I didn't think so. This was some other poison. I was drifting into unconsciousness, fighting to stay alert.

The last thing I saw before blacking out was Dr. Bradley looming over me like a colossus, reaching down toward my head.

* * *

I awoke next to a corpse.

Or at least that's what I assumed it was—a body draped under a white sheet on a slablike table. I was lying on the floor. Rows of fluorescent lights beamed overhead, buzzing softly. As I tried to sit up, my head pounded.

"Easy, Jack," Dr. Bradley's voice said. "We're not quite done with Cass."

Blinking, I turned. Her back was facing me as she leaned over another table. Her ponytail spilled over the back of her lab coat. I could see Cass's shoes sticking out from one side.

"What happened?" I said.

"Dr. Bradley thought we were Massa," Aly's voice replied. I got to my feet to see her, and my head throbbed with pain. She was sitting with Torquin against the wall near the door. Both of them were red in the face. I figured I was, too, from the aftereffects of the poison gas. "That's why she activated the gas. When she realized who we were, she turned off the jets."

"I meant Cass," I said. "What happened to Cass?"

"Treatment," Torquin replied.

"But—but he's not scheduled to need one yet," I said.

"He's early," Dr. Bradley spoke up. "One possibility is that the poison gas brought it on. That's what I'm hoping."

"Hoping?" I asked.

Aly sighed. "Remember what Professor Bhegad told us way back when we first got here? As we get closer to age fourteen, the effects of G7W start to accelerate. The episodes are more frequent, and the effects are stronger."

"When is Cass's birthday?" I asked.

"He doesn't know," Dr. Bradley said softly. "Even the KI, with all their resources, couldn't get hold of his birth records. They were misfiled in some city hospital and possibly destroyed."

"So he may have less time than we do," Aly said.

Dr. Bradley shrugged. "The good news is that the treatment worked. For now, at least, he will be functional."

"Excellent . . . work," said the corpse.

The voice startled me. It was unmistakably Professor Bhegad's. As I took a closer look at the figure under the sheet, I saw that its head and face weren't covered. But even so, I might not have known the old professor. He was almost unrecognizable, his face chalk white, his eyes watery and small, his hair like a tangled mass of straw. "Good to see all of you," he said, a line of drool dribbling from his mouth as he spoke. "I don't know . . . how this happened."

As his eyes flickered and he drifted off, Dr. Bradley turned away from Cass. "Your friend should be fine for now. As for Professor Bhegad . . ." She took a washcloth from a nearby sink and placed it on the professor's head. "He was thrown to the floor after an explosion. His lung collapsed, and it's quite possible he has some internal injuries; I haven't been able to do a full examination."

"We have access to Slippy on the other side of the island," I said. "Fiddle can help you get there with the professor and Cass, while Torquin, Aly, and I rescue the Loculi."

"Professor Bhegad needs hospital care," Dr. Bradley said.

"Can you bring what he needs—some kind of portable hospital?" I said. "We can't risk keeping him here. If the Massa find him, they'll torture him for information. I can give you a walkie-talkie if you need one."

"I have my own," Dr. Bradley said wearily. "I can reach Fiddle. I suppose this is our only choice."

"Professor Bhegad," Aly said, gently brushing a strand of wispy white hair from his forehead, "Dr. Bradley is going to take you away from here. Have the Massa taken the Loculi?"

"N . . . no . . ." Professor Bhegad shook his head and turned shakily toward Torquin. "They are in . . . location D . . . Go now . . . keep them safe."

"Is that the same as Building D, the control center?" Aly asked.

"Not Building D," Torquin said. "Location D."

"Which is . . . ?" I prodded.

"Dump," Torquin replied.

* * *

The smell and the Song hit me at the same time.

We were in a Jeep that Torquin had stolen at the edge of the compound. Well, *stolen* isn't really the right word. It belonged to the KI, but two Massa guys were in it until Torquin pulled them out and threw them against a tree.

Now we were careening across the airfield toward the Karai Institute landfill, aka dump. My head felt light, as if something had crawled into my brain. Not a sound, exactly, but a vibration that began in my ears and spread throughout my body. "I'm feeling it," I said. "The Song of the Heptakiklos. That means the Loculi are nearby."

"It sbells like subthigg died here." Aly was holding her nose. The stench was acrid, foul, and growing fast as the Jeep pulled up to a smoking hill. "I'll stay in the car."

"Big help," I replied, climbing out the backseat.

I held the end of my too-long sleeve over my nose, but Torquin was breathing normally. "Nice place," he mumbled. "Come here to meditate." We stopped in front of an enormous compost pile, which he carefully examined with his flashlight. Then, barehanded, he began digging out blackened banana peels, hairy mango pits, and globs of wilted vegetables.

The Loculi, it seemed, were buried in a pile of garbage.

Behind us, distant shouts resounded from the jungle. I squinted but all I could see was a small area around me, lit by moonlight and an old, dim streetlamp. Torquin turned, quickly handing me the flashlight. "Pah. Massa. I distract. You continue. Find door. Code is FLUFFY AND FIERCE."

"But—" He stalked away before I could say another word.

I stared at the mound of rotten food and nearly puked. But the voices were getting closer, and they did not sound happy.

There was one spot that looked as if the garbage had been stirred around recently. I hoped it was the right spot, and not just some jungle animal's favorite snack location. Holding my breath, I thrust my hand into the goop. It was clammy and cold. My fingers slipped. I felt a rodent scampering out from underneath, nearly running across my shoes.

Keep going . . .

My wrists were covered now. Liquid dribbled down my arm. Each movement brought a fresh whiff of horribleness. There.

My knuckles knocked on something hard. Guided by my flashlight in one hand, I used the other hand to fling away big gobs until I could see a kind of hatch within:

CHAPTER NINE
EPIC FAIL

"JACK... WHAT ARE you doigg?" Aly cried out, racing toward me from the Jeep. "Torquid's holdigg off sub Bassa. Do subthigg."

I gestured toward the filthy screen. "Torquin said the code was 'fluffy and fierce.'"

"We've seed those words before," Aly said. "Whedd we first got to the isladd, I foud Torquid's pass code id the codtrol buildigg—'all thiggs fluffy and fierce.' How does that help with this—'Epic fail'? How cadd you fail before you evedd try? Add why 'you rodett'? Add what's with the LCD screed?"

"I don't know!" I said. "Maybe it's some kind of code. You're the code person!"

The voices were getting louder. It sounded like Torquin was arguing.

"If it's a code," Aly said, "you should be able to edter subthigg. With a keyboard or dubber pad."

Keyboard. Number pad.

I stared at the message closely. "The letters are in squares," I said. "It looks like a keyboard."

"But it's dot," Aly said, looking nervously over her shoulder. "It's a bessage! Hagg odd. Let bee look at it . . ."

Together we stared at the dumb, insulting thing. I wasn't seeing the words now, just the letters. They were swirling around in my head, arranging and rearranging. There was something about them . . .

I reached out and touched the *F* of *Fail*. The LCD screen changed.

"What did you just do?" Aly said.

"Fluffy and fierce . . ." I murmured, quickly spelling out the words—pressing the *L* of *Fail*, the *U* of *You*, the *F* of *Fail* twice, and so on . . . "I'm just tapping the letters, spelling out the words."

"It would't be that sibple!" Aly insisted.

The door beeped. I jumped back. "It's a keyboard!"

Aly swallowed hard. "Subtibes," she said, "it's a gift to be sibple . . ."

I pushed hard on the door, but it didn't budge.

"You're dot puttigg your weight idto it!" Aly said.

61

"You try," I said.

Aly recoiled. "Doe way!"

I pounded again. I could hear voices getting louder. Aly and I both turned to see Torquin arguing with three Massa. I shut off my flashlight, leaned back, then thrust my shoulder into the door.

A thick cake of hardened, putrid glop fell away, revealing a door handle in the shape of a pull-down lever.

Grabbing it in my slippery hand, I yanked it down. The door creaked open, outward. I thrust my flashlight into the space. It was wider and deeper than I expected—maybe four feet in all directions. I stuck my head inside to see the whole area. And there, resting against the left side, were two canvas bags, full and round and exactly the right size. They were cinched at the top with a rope. One was an olive color, the other brown. Both of them were ragged and full of holes. I guessed Bhegad had hidden these in a hurry.

Quickly I opened the olive sack and saw the glowing, whitish shape of the Loculus of Flight. With a smile, I cinched the bag closed and opened the other. Although I could feel the Loculus of Invisibility, I couldn't see it.

"Yes! Got 'em." Making sure both bags were tightly closed, I pulled them out. I braced myself to run and turned toward Aly. I came face-to-face with a superbright flashlight beam. "Aly, will you please lower that thing?"

A deep, guttural voice answered. "As you wish."

I jumped back as the beam dropped downward, revealing a hooded man, his face concealed by a cowl. In the dim streetlamp light, I saw Aly a few feet beyond him. Torquin was with her now, too. Their faces were ashen, their hands in the air. Behind them stood three Massa.

"What a stroke of luck to find you here," said Brother Dimitrios, pulling back his cowl. "We missed you in Egypt. But how considerate of you to return and find these for us."

CHAPTER TEN

THE ONLY GAME IN TOWN

BROTHER DIMITRIOS HELD out his hand, palm up.
Behind him stood his two favorite henchmen. Brother
Yiorgos was dark and balding, with a round face and a con-
stant creepy smile. Stavros had a mass of curly hair, a thick
unibrow, and a scowl, his chin blackened by beard stubble.

Both of them held guns pointed toward Aly and Torquin.

"I do not like to use such brutish tactics," Brother Dimitrios said, "but I believe we are having some temporary
trust issues. You left us rather abruptly in Giza."

"You kidnapped us!" I said.

Brother Dimitrios chuckled. "We freed you from the
people who had taken you from your homes. That is the
opposite of kidnapping, yes? More like rescuing, I'd say."

He was moving closer now, hand still outstretched. "We extended an offer to you. A lifeline. An opportunity to prevent your own deaths. And instead you fled to your abductors. Tell me, how's that working for you now?"

I took a step backward. "You destroyed Babylon. You brainwashed Marco. You're turning him into some kind of monster. And you promised him he'd be a king! How were we supposed to trust you?"

"Because we are the ones who tell the truth, Jack," Brother Dimitrios said. "We are the good guys."

"You destroyed the Karai Institute!" I said.

"They would have destroyed us if they'd gotten the chance," Brother Dimitrios said. "It has always been part of their plan. But none of that matters now. The KI no longer exists. We are the only game in town. Which is as it should be. I trust we will eventually earn your loyalty, Jack. But for now, you need only give us the Loculi. It is the smartest thing you can do. For yourselves and the world."

As he reached for both sacks, Aly gasped aloud. "Don't!"

I held tight and backed away. Brother Dimitrios chuckled again. "So shy now. And yet you were the one who generously showed us the way to the island, which we'd been seeking for decades."

Once we left the protected area around the island, the Massa could pick up the signal, Aly had said.

"You planted that phone!" Aly accused him.

Brother Dimitrios raised an eyebrow. "You mean, the phone you stole?"

I couldn't read his expression. Was he mocking us? Was it possible Mom had played us?

I thought about what she had done—left us a high-res close-up of her own eye, which we'd used for the retinal scan. That was how we'd gotten access to the Loculi. That was how we were able to escape. She had risked her status to help me. To help us.

At least I'd thought so.

Dimitrios barked a dry laugh. "You know, the timing couldn't have been better. You see, we were looking for a new headquarters anyway, since you betrayed the location of our old one to your Karai Institute friends. So this gave us the opportunity to eliminate the competition, so to speak." He looked around with a satisfied smile. "Not to mention upgrading our location at the same time."

A distant explosion made me flinch. The KI was being destroyed. This reality was squeezing me like a fist. The Scholars of Karai had built the island on centuries of research, on land that no one could ever find. Now all of it—the labs, the healing waterfall, the Heptakiklos, the space-time rift—was under new ownership. Because the Massa had found the one person dumb enough to leave a trail. Me.

"As you can hear, we are already in the process of a . . .

gut renovation," Brother Dimitrios said. "We will rebuild here, more gloriously than you can imagine. If you keep the Loculi, you will die, Jack. Or you can choose to give them to us. And we will save your lives."

I closed my eyes and breathed deeply, trying to shape some kind of plan, something that made sense. I concentrated on the McKinley family motto, which had always gotten me through tough times: a problem is an answer waiting to be opened.

All my life I'd thought that mottoes were dumb. Just words.

Opening my eyes, I stared at the two canvas bags.

There was only one possible answer.

"All right," I said, slipping my hands under the sacks. "You win. Take them."

CHAPTER ELEVEN

WHAC-A-MASSA

"JACK, NO!" ALY cried.

Torquin let out a roar. He turned and lifted Brother Yiorgos off the ground like a toy soldier, but the sound of a gunshot made him freeze.

Brother Stavros stood with one arm raised high, a revolver in his fist. Smoke wisped upward from the barrel, from where he'd shot in the air. His other arm was locked around Aly's neck. "Don't make this hard for us," he growled.

Torquin let Yiorgos fall to the ground.

"*Vre*, Stavros, this is not a movie," Brother Dimitrios said. "Let go of the girl."

Aly pushed herself away from Stavros's grip. Yiorgos

rose, grimacing. They all stood, bodies angled toward me. In the dim light I couldn't see anyone's face clearly, but I gave a sharp warning glance to Aly and Torquin. I did not want them to get hurt.

Lifting the sacks, I curled my hands underneath. The material was worn and ripped, and my fingers felt for the holes.

There.

Quickly I slipped my hand inside the brown sack. I felt the warmth of the Invisibility Loculus. That was all I needed. Just to touch the surface.

I knew I was fading from sight by the look on Brother Dimitrios's face. Utter shock.

He lunged forward. I leaped aside, spinning to the right. I untied the top, pulling out the entire Loculus. Tucking it under my arm, I held tight to the other sack.

Brother Stavros scooped his gun off the ground, where it had fallen.

Anything and anyone you touch becomes invisible.

I grabbed Aly's uniform. With a grin, she turned toward Stavros. "Face, meet foot."

He looked around, baffled at the voice coming from nowhere, and he never saw the swift kick Aly planted on his jaw. As he fell unconscious, Aly hooked her hand into Torquin's belt. "Your turn."

"Time for Whac-a-Massa," he said.

Together we moved toward Brother Dimitrios, angling from the side. He stood, trembling, staring in the direction we'd just been. "This is the biggest mistake you can possibly make. Trust me. Also, striking a man while invisible is ungentlemanly conduct."

"A little to the left," Torquin replied.

As Brother Dimitrios flinched, the red-bearded giant delivered a haymaker to his jaw. Dimitrios's feet left the ground. He flew back into Brother Yiorgos, and both men hurtled backward, smacking into a tree.

The three men lay there, inert. Torquin flexed and unflexed his fists. I could practically see smoke coming from his ears. "Good day, gentlemen," he grunted.

I took Mom's cell phone from my pocket. It had betrayed us. It was the reason they'd found this place. And I was not going to be taken advantage of again.

I reared my arm back and threw the phone into the jungle.

"Let's get out of here before more of them come!" Aly said. "We have what we need."

"You're welcome," I said.

Aly smiled sheepishly. She threw her arms around me, nuzzling her head on my shoulder. "Jack, you're the best."

"Mush," Torquin said.

I pulled the Loculus of Flight from its sack. We would use both Loculi to get to the beach quickly, airborne and unseen.

But all I could think about was the phone. And its owner.

I don't even remember the flight back to the beach.

* * *

I do remember seeing the shining hull of Slippy from high in the air. And Fiddle's relieved smile as I let go of the others' hands, making them visible as we touched down on the sand. "Where's Jack?" he shouted, running to greet us.

Aly nudged me in the side. As I put my Loculus down in the sand, Fiddle jumped back. "Aaaghh! Don't scare me like that!"

"Sorry, it's the Invisibility Loculus," I said. "It makes you invisible. Which is useful when you're flying over enemy territory."

He nodded. "You got them both—awesome! Cass, Bhegad, and Dr. Bradley are on board. We're ready to book."

I slipped the Invisibility Loculus into its sack, grabbed them both by the canvas tops, and ran after the others toward the jet. "How's the professor?" Aly shouted.

"Dr. Bradley's doing the best she can. They're in the back of the plane. We managed to get a lot of equipment from the hospital—for him and for you." Fiddle slowed. "Dr. Bradley can continue your treatments for a while. If you guys die, our dream is over. The KI really goes down in flames."

"Sorry to spoil things for you," Aly remarked.

Fiddle blushed. "Plus I care about you guys. Seriously. We all do. Now come on. They're going to find us. While you were gone, more Massa flew into the compound. Top brass, I think. Huge plane."

As we raced the final few yards to the jet, Cass appeared at the jet's hatch, at the top of the ladder. "Sgniteerg!" he said. "Hope you're impressed I could say that."

Aly bounded up the ladder. "Just glad you're feeling . . . terbet?"

Cass winced. "I think you mean retteb."

Fiddle put his arm on my shoulders. "Good luck, tiger. Thanks for saving my sorry butt. You're in the hands of the Jolly Red Giant now."

"Aren't you coming with us?" I asked.

"I found some more of our people in the jungle," he replied. "A small group, mostly injured and scared. I don't know how they made it out. But along with the prisoners from the dorm—it's a core, and who knows how many more we'll find. I want to stay here with them. Build a force, if we can."

"The Massa will wipe you out," I said.

Fiddle gave me a wry grin. "Best brains. Biggest muscle power. Which would you bet on?"

"Good point," I said. "I feel sorry for the Massa."

I gave Fiddle a bear hug and scampered up the ladder.

As I took a seat near Aly and Cass, Torquin squeezed his frame into the cockpit. From the back of the plane, Professor Bhegad's voice called out feebly: "Children . . . Aly . . . Jack . . . Cass . . . Marco . . ."

He was lying on a set of cushions against the rear bulkhead. Dr. Bradley had managed to strap him down and was adjusting the drip on his IV.

"All here," I said gently. "All three of us. Marco is . . . gone, Professor. Remember?"

Professor Bhegad looked confused for a moment. "Yes," he finally said. "Of course . . ."

The engine started with a roar. "Belts!" Torquin said.

I strapped myself in. Over the engine noise I heard a high-pitched cry. I figured it was a seagull.

Until my eyes caught a motion at the edge of the jungle. People.

I shone my flashlight through the window. Two figures were running across the sand toward us, waving their arms. One of them was much faster—someone broad-shouldered, with a slightly bowlegged gait and flowing brown hair.

"Marco?" Aly said.

But my eyes were fixed on the other person—older, female, her head covered by a bandanna.

"Stop the plane!" Cass shouted. "Let's find out."

"Too late!" Torquin replied.

The jet began to turn. I grabbed binoculars from the

floor and peered through. The woman and Marco stood shoulder to shoulder now, looking up at us. Shaking her head, she removed the bandanna and flung it to the ground.

The breath caught in my throat. As the jet turned its pontoons toward the water, the coast grew smaller. Smoke passed across the moon's surface like lost ghosts.

"Jack?" Aly said. "What did you just see?"

I let the binocs drop from my fingers. "My mom."

CHAPTER TWELVE

MONGOLIA

"HOW CAN YOU be sure?" Aly picked up the binoculars and tried to scan the shore, but it was too dark to see anything.

I was shaking. "The walk. The way she moved her head when she took off that bandanna. Her eyes . . ."

"You could see all that?" Aly asked.

"I could see enough," I said.

Aly let out a deep breath. "So it's true. The photo was real."

"Which is a good thing, Jack," Cass said. "Even if you don't think so now. You have to have faith that you'll meet her. That things will work out."

"A mom who faked her own death." I whirled around at him, angrier than I ever thought I'd be. "Who didn't care

75

enough to be in touch for six years. Who's part of a team of killers and liars. How will that work out?"

"A mom who's alive, when you thought she wasn't," Cass said softly.

I backed off, taking a deep breath. I'd seen Cass's parents in a newspaper photo that Cass had kept in his backpack. The headline read "Mattipack Crime-Spree Couple Caught!" The mug shots showed two scowling people with bloated, angry faces.

"How do you have faith?" I asked. "Have you . . . have you ever tried to get in touch with your mom and dad?"

Cass nodded. "I called the prison a couple of years ago. It was weird. Mom couldn't believe it was me. I talked a lot, but she didn't say much. Just listened. When our time was up, I could hear that she was crying. She said 'Love you, Cassius'—and then, click."

"Cassius?" Aly said.

"From Shakespeare. The play *Julius Caesar*. Cassius is the guy who has a 'lean and hungry look.' They named me after him, I guess. How bad can they really be if they read Shakespeare?"

"*Romeo and Juliet*," Torquin growled. "Very sad."

Cass leaned forward. "I'm not giving up on them, whether they're innocent or not—which, by the way, I think they are. You can't give up on getting your mom back either, Jack. You have to believe that. Maybe she was brainwashed.

Maybe she's trying to escape. Or she's secretly a spy for the government. Maybe she's stealing information to save our lives and sabotage the Massa."

"Have you ever thought of being a writer?" Aly asked. "You have a good imagination."

Cass shrugged. "Ask me again when we're on the other side of fourteen."

For a pessimist, Cass was sounding pretty optimistic. Staring out the window, I let his words sink in. I wanted to be optimistic, too. But as I watched the island disappear behind the clouds, I felt like it was pulling my heart with it.

"I need to tell my dad," I murmured. "He needs to know about Mom. He thinks she's dead."

"Jack, you know we can't contact the outside world," Aly said. "We've talked about this a million times. Your dad will send people to get us. It's too risky."

"It was risky," I said, "back when we didn't want anyone to discover the island. But it's too late for that. The KI is destroyed."

"Not destroyed," Torquin said. "Fiddle still there. With others."

"A rebel band," Aly said.

"A bunch of injured geeks in a cave," I said.

"Hey, they know the territory," Cass said. "The Massa don't. It's a big, confusing place to newcomers. And the

Massa also don't have a Cass to help them expertly etagivan."

I sat back. Cass had a point. The Massa may have taken the compound, but they didn't have the whole area yet. There was a chance we could return with the Loculi. If Professor Bhegad and Dr. Bradley could keep us alive that long.

"Look, the rebels may be hidden for now, but what about us?" I said. "We have no place to hide. No support on the ground. We need that. I can swear my dad to secrecy. He helps run companies. He knows lots of people, and he's crazy smart. Besides . . ."

I stopped myself. I wasn't going to say I miss him. Even though I felt it.

"Jack has a point," Cass said. "Where else could we possibly go?"

"Maybe Disney World?" Torquin mumbled.

"What if your dad tries to blow the whistle?" Aly said. "If my parents find out, they will stop at nothing to get me back. They don't know I have a death sentence. They won't believe it."

"Not sure . . . trust . . ." Bhegad spoke up, his voice heavy and labored. "Your father . . . me . . ."

"Dad will keep this a secret from the other parents," I said. "Is that what you're worried about, Professor? I promise. It'll be just us and him. No one else. Until we finish the quest. I know this."

Cass and Aly exchanged a look. After a long minute, they both nodded. Professor Bhegad was shaking his head, eyes wide. I couldn't be sure if he was offering an opinion or just trembling.

"Use this," Torquin said, handing his phone over his shoulder. "Low enough altitude for signal. But not for long. Hurry."

"I'll text him," I said.

"Call him," Aly said. "He won't recognize the number. He might think it's a fake. He's got to hear your voice."

I took the phone. My fingers shook. The last time I spoke to Dad, I was home in Indiana and he was in Singapore. I'd made a total mess in the house. Then I went to school and never saw him again.

I tapped out the number, held the phone to my ear, and waited.

Beep.

At the sound, I nearly dropped the phone. After the fourth ring, a familiar voice chirped: "This is Martin McKinley of McKinley Enterprises. Sorry I can't take your call. So . . . you know what to do!"

My mouth was dry. I swallowed hard. "Hey, Dad? It's me. Um . . . I just wanted to . . ."

Click.

I took the phone from my ear. "It hung up!"

"You weren't loud enough," Aly said. "It didn't pick up

any sound. Try again—and speak up!"

As I held my thumb over the phone, it beeped. I nearly dropped it again. On the screen were the words MCKINLEY, M.

Shaking, I held it to my ear. "H-hello?"

"Jack?" I could hear Dad breathing on the other end. "Jack, is that really you?"

I nodded. I thought I was going to pass out.

"He can't see you nod!" Aly whispered. "Say something."

About a billion words were stuck in my throat, all trying to elbow each other aside. "Yes," was all I could manage.

He didn't answer, and I thought he'd hung up.

"Keep going," Aly urged.

"Sorry about the living room!" I blurted out. "And the bedroom. And the fact that Vanessa quit."

Dad's voice was choked. "Dear lord . . . it is you. Where are you, Jack?"

"I—I don't know," I said. "I mean, I'm on a plane. With friends. But we need to get away from some people. Some-where remote."

"Not too remote!" Torquin barked. "Need lots of fuel. Won't be enough."

"Why?" Dad replied. "Who are you getting away from? Who was that speaking?"

"Our pilot, Torquin," I said. "Dad, please. I'll explain everything later. You have to help us. Where are you?"

"Mongolia," he replied. "I can meet you here."

"Mongolia?" I took the phone from my ear and put it on speaker.

"Far," Torquin replied. "Very very very far."

"It's a small, private airport!" Dad's voice called out. "North of Ulaanbaatar."

"Can we make it?" I asked Torquin.

He shrugged. "No choice."

"Okay, Dad," I said into the phone. "Can you give Torquin directions?"

"Turkin?" Dad said. "Hello? Can you hear me?"

Red Beard was accessing the route settings on a console world map. "Name Torquin," he said.

* * *

Seven hours later, Slippy was above the clouds, but they were a blur. Everyone but Torquin and me had fallen asleep, but now Cass's face was plastered to the window.

"Can you tell where we are?" I asked.

Cass shrugged. "We're traveling about Mach 2, twice the speed of sound. Which means if I told you where we were, by the end of the sentence we'd be somewhere else. But I saw some desert. Maybe the Gobi. Which means we're close. Ask Torquin."

As I rubbed my eyes, I noticed Torquin's brow was beaded with sweat, his knuckles white on the controls. "Close," he said.

I glanced at the fuel gauge, which was nearly on empty.

I looked at Aly and Cass. She was awake now, and her eyes were fixed on the gauge.

"Um, Torquin?" I said. "About that fuel indicator? When my dad's car hits E, there's, like, thirty miles before the gas runs out. So, we're going to be all right. Right?"

"No," Torquin said. Sweat was dripping from his arm.

"What do you mean, no?" Aly snapped.

"Opposite of yes," Torquin said. "Cutting engine. Now. Will save fuel."

"Will kill lives!" Aly said. "You can't just glide!"

"Will turn it on when closer," Torquin replied.

From behind us, Dr. Bradley spoke up. "Oh, dear heavens, why didn't we just land in Russia?"

"Next time," Torquin said.

The plane went silent. We took an abrupt downward dip, hurtling through the clouds. Torquin began calling flight instructions into his headset.

Professor Bhegad let out a moan of pain. I felt Aly's hand clutching my arm. Below us stretched a green plain surrounded by mountains. A stampeding herd of horses sent up dust clouds, their shadows long in the morning sun, their manes flowing behind them. If we weren't about to die, they would have been beautiful. In the distance, covered by a ceiling of gray, was a sprawling city surrounded by plumes of smoke.

Torquin's phone, which was now resting in a cup holder,

began to buzz. He reached over to grab it but his hand was shaking. It clattered to the floor and I scooped it up myself.

My dad's name showed on caller ID. I put it to my ear. "Dad!" I shouted. "Do you see us?"

"You're coming in too low!" he shouted. "What is your pilot doing?"

Torquin took the phone from my hand. "Mayday!" he bellowed. "Low fuel. Mayday!"

He flicked a switch, turning the engine back on. The plane juddered hard, as if we'd flown into a solid fist. From the rear, Professor Bhegad cried out loudly.

I could feel us nosing upward. In the distance was a compound of low glass buildings.

"The runway is clear!" Dad's voice was shouting. "You're coming in short!"

"Do it, Slippy . . ." Torquin said. "Do it!"

The roaring engine sputtered weakly, then died.

We hit hard. My knee jammed into my chest. Beneath us was a noise like a thousand cars, flattened, dragged, scraping across the ground. It was punctuated by panicked screams—Cass, Aly, Dr. Bradley, everyone except Torquin. We whipped abruptly right and left. Rocks slammed into the windshield.

I heard the deep ripping of metal and felt a sharp jolt. Looking out the window I saw the wing break off like ice from a roof.

The plane tipped sharply upward. We were going to roll over. I struggled to turn toward Aly and Cass, to see them one last time. But my head slammed forward into the back of the pilot's seat and everything went black.

CHAPTER THIRTEEN

DEATH IS COLD

THE MANGLED STEEL *vanishes. The field is blackness. I
hear nothing but a distant whoosh.*

If I am dead, then death is cold.

*The darkness gives way to an emerging dream light, and I
am on a rocky cliff over a vast sea. The wind lashes my face and I
struggle to walk. My chest is bloody, my arms and legs weak, my
face chapped and burned. I shiver, huddling into myself.*

Is this the Dream again?

*I don't think so. Gone is the smoke-dark green of ancient
Atlantis, the bitter lushness of the air, the raging fire, steep can-
yon slopes—the recurring scene that has been with me for years.*

*Now I feel salt water in the air, and my arm aches from the
weight of . . . what?*

I look down, forcing myself to see. My arms are tightly clutching an orb. But not like the two I know: not warm and golden like the Loculus of Invisibility, nor luminous and white like the Loculus of Flight.

It is dense and deeply blue, almost black. It will not hide me from an enemy or save me from a fall.

What good is it?

As I breathe I gain strength. I move faster. Someone is chasing me and gaining ground.

In the distance is a majestic building, shadowed by the setting sun. I am filled with joy. I have not seen it complete. A man is waiting there for me. He looks relieved to see me but fearful of whatever is behind me.

But as he steps forward, the earth shakes.

I stop.

He is running now, yelling to me. His arms are outstretched. But I do not let go. Despite the acrid smell arising from the earth, twining into my nostrils.

The stench of death.

CHAPTER FOURTEEN

DAD

"JACK?"

Cass's voice piped up through the waning dream. "Tell me you're evila."

I peeled my face from the back of the seat. "Tell me you're not speaking Backwardish in heaven."

We were tilted sideways. Through the window I could see an airstrip about a hundred yards ahead of us, with a jet marked MGL parked at a hangar. Beyond it, a scrubby plain stretched out for miles to distant mountains. Cass was still belted into his seat, but it had ripped out of the floor and slid against the wall. "Heaven is really uncomfortable," he said.

I felt as if I'd been punched in the chest. I loosened my

seat belt to relieve the pain. Torquin was struggling to get out of his seat. I spun around to see Aly slumped forward, her hair limp over her forehead.

"Aly!" I staggered toward her, hanging on to the plane's wall for support.

Dr. Bradley beat me to her. She was feeling Aly's pulse and looking at her face with a flashlight.

Aly flinched and turned away. "Owww . . . turn that thing off. I have a headache."

I exhaled with relief, crumpling to the floor of the plane. "You have quite a lump," Dr. Bradley said. "We'll have to examine you more closely."

"Jack . . ." she murmured. "How is Jack?"

"Fine," Cass said. "I am, too. And Torquin. In case you were wondering."

I felt my face turning red. "How's the professor?"

"Shaken up but okay," Dr. Bradley said. "Ironically, lying down in that protected area, he was the least vulnerable of us all."

"Landing gear gone," Torquin announced, digging a rope ladder from under his seat. "Use this."

He unlatched the door and it swung open sharply. As he fastened the end of the ladder and dropped the rest of it out the door, my eyes were fixed on an old Toyota speeding toward us across the rocky soil. As it skidded to a stop, the driver-side door flew open.

I knew it was my dad without even seeing his face. I could tell by the angle of his feet, pointing outward as if they'd been screwed on slightly wrong. "Jack!" he shouted, running hard toward the tilted plane. "Jack, where are you?"

The ladder was only about eight feet. But I stood frozen in the doorway. Dad was smiling so hard I thought his face would crack. His hair was less brown than gray now, his face lined a bit more than I remembered. Which seemed impossible, because I'd seen him only a few weeks ago.

He stood at the bottom of the ladder, holding out his arms, and even though I'm way too heavy I jumped. He caught me and held tight, turning around and around, swinging me like I was a little kid. He was crying, repeating "Oh thank god" over and over, and even though I was crying, too, I kept silent because I just wanted to hear his voice.

"I'm okay, Dad," I said as he set me down and we began walking away from the jet. "Really. What is this place? Why are you in Mongolia?"

"Where have you been?" he said. "I want to know everything!"

As Cass and Aly scrambled down the ladder, a medical van with the logo MGL skidded to a stop.

"Look, Dad," I said, "there's someone on the plane who needs to go directly to a hospital. He's pretty old and in bad shape."

"Okay . . . right . . . roger that." As Dad's eyes moved

toward the plane, his whole face seemed to stiffen. I glanced back to see Dr. Bradley and Torquin carefully lowering the professor out of the plane. Emergency workers were already racing toward them with a stretcher.

"That's just Torquin," I explained. "He's a little strange looking, but he grows on you. These are Cass Williams and Aly Black."

But Dad wasn't paying attention. "Radamanthus Bhegad . . ." he murmured. "What is that man doing here?"

"You've heard of him?" I said. "He was a famous professor at Princeton or something."

"Yale," Cass called out.

Bhegad moaned painfully as the team of white-coated Mongolian workers set him on the stretcher. Dad stood over them, his hands on his hips. "Just a second," he said. "I have a few questions before anyone moves this man."

Professor Bhegad's eyes were hollow and scared. "M-Martin . . ." he sputtered.

How did Professor Bhegad know my dad's name?

"I'm Dr. Theresa Bradley," Dr. Bradley said. "We have to take the professor to a medical facility immediately or he may die."

"I am a fair and kind man," Dad said, his face turning redder. "I believe in charity and forgiveness and liberty, and I don't believe in hate. But this is the one man I can safely say the world would be a better place without. This man is . . . is a monster!"

"Dad!" I'd never seen him like this. I glanced helplessly at Dr. Bradley, who was speechless. "Okay, Dad, I know what you're thinking: This guy kidnapped my son. But as crazy as it sounds, he wants to save our lives. My friends and I—we have a condition. It's going to kill us—"

"By the age of fourteen," Dad said. "Like Randall Cromarty. Like all those kids your mother and I researched."

Cromarty. I remembered one of the last things he'd said to me over the phone on the day I was taken: *Did you see the article I sent you about that poor kid, Cromarty? Died in the bowling alley near Chicago . . .* He was always talking about these not-so-random tragedies, kids who were dying for no apparent reason.

"Researched?" I said. "You knew about G7W all along . . . and you didn't tell me?"

"It would have scared you," Dad said. "You were a kid. Instead, your mom and I tried to do something. We dedicated our lives to finding a cure. That's why I'm here. That's why I have been financing McKinley Genetics Labs all these years."

"You never told me—all those plans and *you never told me!*" I said. "Dad, please. Let them take care of Professor Bhegad. You have to talk to him. We've been at a secret institute devoted to the study of G7W. He did find the cure!"

91

Dad barked a sad, bitter laugh. "He told your mother that lie, too. Which was why she ended up in the bottom of a crevasse in Antarctica."

"He knew Mom?" I said.

Professor Bhegad's eyes flared with urgency, but he was too weak to speak.

"He killed her, Jack," Dad said. "The man is a murderer."

"No!" I said. "It's not true! She—"

"She went to meet him at a secret lab in McMurdo Sound and never came back." Dad barreled on. His entire body shook as he stood over Professor Bhegad, blocking the EMTs' path and ignoring their pleas in Mongolian. "Then, years later, he came for you. First my wife, then my son. When I got home from Singapore, you were gone. They said there was a man at the hospital, posing as a priest. An obese man with a red beard." He turned, peering at Torquin.

"Not obese," Torquin muttered. "Large bones."

"Dad, please, listen to me!" I tried to pull Dad away from Professor Bhegad, but he held on to my arm. "She's not dead."

Dad's eyes were filling with tears. "You always believed that, Jack. I never had the heart to contradict a little boy's optimism. But she fell hundreds of feet—"

"Into a crevasse," I said. "No one found the body, remember? Because there was no body. Because the whole story is wrong. It was faked, Dad. I don't know how or why. But I've seen her. We've spoken. Trust me on this. She's alive."

Dad's body went slack. He looked at me through hollow, uncomprehending eyes. "That's impossible."

"Anne . . ." Professor Bhegad murmured, struggling to get the words out, "was . . . my trusted associate. Lovely, smart . . . but impatient for the cure. Afraid for Jack's life. Our research was too slow for her . . ." He took a deep breath. "She thought . . . the Karai and Massa should join forces, to go faster. I told her . . . impossible to heal a rift centuries old. But she was young . . . persistent. She confided to me that she had contacted the Massa. This was a breach. I had to bring it up . . . to my superior."

"There's someone higher than you at the KI?" Aly asked.

The professor nodded. "The Omphalos. A code name. I do not even know if it is a man or a woman. We speak through a go-between. I relayed everything Anne had told me. The response was swift . . . angry. Speaking to a Massa agent . . . the highest-level breach of security. Punishable by death. I became afraid for your mother's life. I blamed myself for revealing too much. And then . . . the news came . . . her accident in Antarctica. I don't know what she was seeking there. The KI has no base in McMurdo Sound. Her death devastated us all. I never suspected she was staging a fake disappearance. That she was—defecting to . . ."

The professor began to cough, his face turning bright red. As he fell back onto the stretcher, his eyes rolled up into his head. "Please," Dr. Bradley said. "He is very weak."

Nodding numbly, Dad stepped aside. The medics lifted Bhegad and carried him away.

As they loaded him onto the van along with Dr. Bradley, Dad's face was the color of snow.

CHAPTER FIFTEEN

GENGHIS AND RADAMANTHUS

"SO...YOUR MOTHER looked okay?" Dad said. "Healthy?"

We were all packed into his small Toyota, bouncing up a rutted road—Torquin and Dad in the front; Aly, Cass, and me in the back. The EMT van was disappearing around a long, sleek, glass-and-steel building that looked all wrong in the rugged landscape. Out the other direction, a railroad train snaked across the flat Mongolian plain, and a flock of sheep moved away like softly blowing snowdrifts. My body still ached from the crash landing, but I barely noticed that. Half of me was thrilled to see Dad. The other half was angry at what he'd been keeping from me.

"Healthy, but working for the enemy," I said. "Why didn't you ever tell me you knew about the KI, Dad? Why were you keeping secrets?"

Aly put her hand on top of mine. That was the only way I knew it was shaking.

"You were a little kid, Jack," Dad replied. "We didn't want to alarm you."

"I'm not a little kid now," I said.

Dad pulled into a space in the glass building's parking lot and stopped the car. "You're right. I owe you an explanation. All of you." He rubbed his forehead. "You see, years ago, your mom had begun noticing strange deaths of young people—all fourteen, all amazing prodigies. They all had a similar mark on the backs of their heads, white hair in the shape of a Greek letter lambda. I thought it was just an odd news piece, but Mom believed it was something more. She had two cousins, both prodigies—one a musician, the other a mathematical genius. Both dead at fourteen. Both with a lambda pattern in their hair. And so she began obsessively looking for this pattern on you. And she found it."

"How old was Jack?" Aly asked.

"Five, six, maybe." Dad stroked his chin as he thought back. "The hair wasn't white yet, but it was a different texture. Nothing anyone would notice unless they were looking for it. Of course, we panicked. Mom tracked down thousands of obscure hints and finally learned about Bhegad's work, his theory of the Selects and their genetic abnormality. She contacted him and they began corresponding. He was always very secretive—I didn't trust him, but Mom was convinced he was onto something. He took more and more of her time and then one day she announced she had to go to Antarctica—to meet him, she said. I didn't want her to go, but I was so busy setting up biotech research companies, raising money, hiring geneticists, investigating theories. One day I got the call. Your mom was . . ."

He turned away. I felt a lump in my throat. I still remembered the day, the way it smothered everything in my life.

Aly pressed my hand harder, closing her fingers around mine.

"I never heard from Bhegad again," Dad went on, his voice barely audible. "I was devastated. Furious. I thought about tracking him. But that wouldn't have brought her back. So instead I doubled down—I became obsessed with finding a way to save you."

"Which is why you were out of town so much," I said. "You were setting up this place. In secret. But why here?"

"This country is paradise for geneticists," Dad said. "Mongolians share more common genes than any other human beings on the planet. Statistically, almost all descend from one ancestor dating to about 1200. We believe this to be Genghis Khan, one of the greatest conquerors in history. His achievements were superhuman. If anyone in history was a Select, he would be it. And he lived way past the age of fourteen. Which means there must be others like him, still alive."

"So you came here on a guess?" Cass said.

"I came here after a lock of the Genghis's hair was discovered," Dad said, stepping out of the car, "and genetic analysis suggested some abnormalities in the G7W area. An incredible finding! The problem was, the DNA was degraded. When I visited, I discovered a country with great natural resources, isolated from the rest of the world. It appealed to me as a location for a secret project. It wasn't easy, but we were able to collect more hair and bone samples. We have just completed a thorough mapping of the great khan's genetic code and are waiting for the findings. If we find the mechanism that kept Genghis Khan alive, maybe we have the cure for you."

As we all piled out, Aly said, "I'd like to see the genome."

"It's bewildering to a layperson," Dad said, walking toward the building. "A human genome has billions of lines of code. I'll show you when we get inside. But I have a few questions myself." He pulled a cell phone from his pocket. "What are your phone numbers? While we're waiting to hear about Bhegad, I'll call your parents."

"No!" Cass and Aly shouted at the same time.

"They can't know," I said. "If Aly's parents find out about the Karai Institute, they'll come after her."

"Jack, I'm a parent, and you mean everything to me," he replied. "I can't not call these other parents, knowing what they're going through."

"But she'll miss her treatments," I said, "and—"

"Treatments?" Dad stopped and turned toward us. "What exactly was Bhegad doing to you?"

Before I could answer, Dad's phone beeped. "McKinley," he said. "He what? Be right there."

He shoved the phone back in his pocket. "There's been a complication," he said. "Professor Bhegad has had a heart attack."

* * *

I'd seen Torquin fuss, fight, joke, and operate machinery, but I'd never seen him fret.

He had taken Cass's worry beads and was flipping them, one by one, down their string. I was feeling pretty worried myself. Bhegad was in the operating room and we were helpless in a small office down a glass-walled corridor. I sipped from a cup of warm liquid Dad called milk tea, but I could barely taste anything. My head ached, my stomach burned, and my legs felt weak. Dad had told me the tea would make me feel better, but it wasn't true.

"Bhegad strong . . ." Torquin was muttering to no one in particular. "Very strong . . ."

Cass and Aly were hunched over a desktop monitor, where Dad was showing a section of Genghis Khan's genome. The letters and numbers looked blurry to me and I had to blink a few times. "All these tiny combinations of As, Ts, Gs, and Cs?" Dad said. "They're amino acids—adenine, thymine, guanine, cytosine. The building blocks of life." He pointed to a spot on the screen. "Here's where the G7W gene resides. If our scientists are correct—"

"They're not," Aly said.

"Beg pardon?" Dad said.

"Your scientists are wrong." Aly was scrolling down the screen. "It is the general area of the G7W group, but you're off a few million places on the chain. It's . . . here. And right off the bat, I'm seeing a guanine where a cytosine is supposed to be, and a whole lot of discrepancies in this area at the top of the screen. I could go on. Khan may have been king of conquerors, but sorry, he has nothing to do with G7W."

Dad's jaw dropped open. "But—how would you—?"

"Because Aly is a Select," I said. "She can hack into any computer system, analyze data, break any firewall. Marco's an amazing athlete—"

"I nac kaeps drawkcab," Cass piped up. "Osla I have a photographic memory. I can tell you how to get anywhere from anywhere else. Try me."

"What on earth—?" Dad sputtered.

"Seriously," Cass said. "Anywhere."

"Okay . . ." Dad thought a moment. "New York City. Fifty-Third and Fifth. To, um, parking lot three at Jones

100

Beach. I used to work there as a lifeguard."

Cass thought a moment. "Uptown on Fifth. Right on Fifty-Ninth to the Queensboro Bridge. Queens Boulevard to either the Grand Central or the Long Island Expressway to the Meadowbrook Parkway to the end, where you veer left onto Ocean Parkway and find the parking lot. You may have to go around a rotary. But I think in New York they call it a traffic circle . . ."

Dad nearly dropped his milk tea. "That's right. That's absolutely right." He glanced at the screen and immediately took out his cell phone. "I need to have my team check your work, Aly. If you're correct . . ." His face suddenly looked years older.

As he called the genetics team and told them what Aly had said, I sat in a chair. My head throbbed. "Jack?" Aly said. "Are you okay?"

I nodded. "Guess the crash kinda shook me up."

"You kinda might have a concussion," Cass said.

"After they're done working on Professor Bhegad, I'll mention something to Dr. Bradley," I said.

"What? Are you sure?" Dad blurted out, his voice suddenly loud and animated. He hung up the phone and set it down on the table. "The head surgeon just cut into my other call with an update on Bhegad. He pulled through."

"Yyyahhhh!" Torquin bellowed, leaping up from his chair.

I felt a jolt of relief. Cass shot me a smile and said, "Emosewa!"

As Aly gave me a tight hug, Dad headed for the doorway. "And he wants to see you four. Immediately. Follow me to the recovery room."

We raced out of the room, down the hallway, and through a set of doors. Professor Bhegad was lying on a slanted bed, dressed in a white hospital gown that looked like a tent on his skinny frame. His face was papery white, his hands spotted and even more wrinkly than usual. "Hello . . ." he said, his voice hoarse and whispery, barely audible above the beeping and whirring of the machines.

Aly took his hand. "You look great, Professor!"

He managed a pained half smile as his head rolled to the side and his eyes fluttered shut. "He's still fragile," Dr. Bradley said. "Asleep more than awake. We found a lot of internal trauma. Bleeding. We'll monitor him and do what we can. But there's only so much we can do." She sighed. "He's an old man."

"Not exactly cause for great yoj," Cass said.

Dr. Bradley lowered her voice, casting a quick eye toward Dad. "The professor told me he's concerned you move as swiftly as possible in your quest."

That seemed to rouse Bhegad. "Go . . . g . . . go . . ." he said, crooking a gnarled finger to us, gesturing us to come closer. We sank to our knees in order to hear his soft voice.

102

"Neck . . . lock . . ." the professor rasped.

"Next Loculus?" I said. "Is that what you want, Professor?"

"Yes . . ." he said, staring at me with an expression of urgency. "H . . . h . . . he . . ."

"Jack?" Aly said. "*H*e meaning Jack? What about him?"

"L . . . l . . ." Bhegad swallowed and tried again.

I leaned closer. "What are you trying to tell us? Go slowly."

"Ling," he finally said.

"Ling?" Cass said. "Is there someone here named Ling? Dr. Ling?"

Bhegad's eyes fluttered and his body gave a sudden jerk. The room resounded with piercing beeps. "What's happening?" Aly exclaimed.

"Heart arrhythmia," Dr. Bradley said. "Get the pads, stat!"

We backed away fast. Medical workers swarmed into the room. Dr. Bradley lifted a pair of pads like small catcher's mitts and applied them to the sides of Professor Bhegad's chest.

The old man's body lurched upward like he'd been poked with a dagger.

CHAPTER SIXTEEN

NEWTON SPEAKS

ALY TURNED AWAY. "I can't watch this."

The surgical team was closing around Professor Bhegad, along with Dad and Torquin. With each electrical jolt, I could hear a deep, unearthly-sounding cry. My head, which was already hurting, began to throb.

I felt Aly's head settling into my chest, her arms wrapping around my waist. *Hug her back*, a voice screamed inside my head. But that was ridiculous. We had to move. The doctors needed room. So I backed away with Aly hugging me, and me not hugging back, which was awkward beyond belief. I tried to wrap my arms around her but they collided in midair trying to find a place to settle, until my back plowed into the side of an open door.

"Are you two all right?" Cass said. "Or is this Zombie Dance Night at the hospital?"

Aly and I let go of each other. I could feel my face burning. We stepped into the hallway, leaving Torquin, Dr. Bradley, and Dad inside with the medical team.

Cass began pacing up and down. He had the worry beads now and was flicking beads down the necklace-like cord. "He can't die."

Click . . . click . . .

I glanced back into the room. "We have to contact this Mr. Ling," I said.

"Maybe it's not a Mr.," Aly said. "It could be a Ms. Or a first name."

"Or linguini?" Cass shrugged. "Maybe he was hungry."

Click . . .

"Is there a 'Ling' in any of the names of the Seven Wonders we haven't been to?" Aly said.

"The Great Pyramid of Giza . . ." I said. "Lighthouse at Pharos . . . Mausoleum at Halicarnassus . . . Temple of Artemis at Ephesus . . . Statue of Zeus at Olympia."

"All Ling-less," Cass said.

Click . . . click . . .

"Will you please stop that?" Aly cried out.

"They're worry beads!" Cass protested. "I'm worried."

Click . . . click . . . click . . .

"Give me that!" Aly grabbed for the string, but Cass

105

yanked it back. With a soft snap, the clasp pulled open. The beads smacked downward against the lower part of the clasp. Cass held up the other half.

Jutting out of it was the end of a flash drive.

Aly's face brightened. "Cass, you are my hero."

"I am?" Cass said.

"Let's see what's on this thing." Aly took the beads and ran them down the hall to the room where Dad had shown her the genome. Its image still glowed on the screen.

Aly inserted the USB into the port at the side of the monitor. The screen went black, then showed a login screen. "Okay, let's hack this thing. Accessing a password generator from my VPN . . ."

The screen was going crazy with scrolling numbers and letters, error messages flashing at blinding speeds.

"Is this going to take a long time?" Cass asked.

The craziness on the screen abruptly stopped, revealing a folder. "Got it. Eight seconds. Owner of this drive is . . . him."

She showed us the screen.

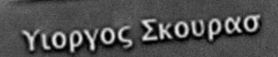

Υιοργος Σκουρασ

"Yiopyos?" Cass said.

I thought back to Rhodes. The Greeks called it Rhodos, and you saw it written everywhere as ΡΟΔΟΣ.

"I think that *p* is actually an *r* sound in Greek," I said. "This says Yiorgos Skouras."

Cass made a face. "Yiorgos knows how to use a flash drive?"

"He's like the nasty cousin of André the Giant," Aly said.

"Who?" Cass asked.

"You know . . . 'Anybody want a peanut?' From *The Princess Bride*?" Aly said. "Don't you two know anything about American cinema?"

"If I watched as many old movies as you, I'd be fat and bald and using dial-up," Cass said.

Aly ignored him, scrolling through a folder of documents. "Seven folders," she said. "All the labels are in Greek but I'm guessing each folder is dedicated to one of the Seven Wonders. Let's start with this one . . . it looks like it says pyramid."

She clicked on a folder marked ΠΥΡΑΜΙΣ. As she clicked through a trove of documents—architectural reports, images, Wikipedia entries, Cass exhaled. "This isn't helping. It's just research. Bhegad will be dead in the ground by the time we read all this!"

Dead in the ground.

I caught a blast of decay, a memory of the awful smell in my dream. "Let's think positively, okay?"

"Okay, I'm collecting everything that's in English," Aly said. "The rest we can show Torquin later. He knows Greek."

I watched documents fly by, and some images. One of them was a stately building overlooking a cliff. "What's that?" I asked.

"The Mausoleum at Halicarnassus," Aly said.

I leaned closer. Something about it seemed familiar. "Creepy looking," I said.

"Should be. Dead people are buried there. Some ruler named Mausolus. And his wife, Artemisia." Aly clicked on the folder titled ΜΑΥΣΩΛΕΙΟΝ.

Like the Pyramid folder, it contained tons of files. She opened all of them at once. We looked at a cascade of Greek words, every document complete gibberish.

Except for one.

"Whoa, go back," I said. "I think I saw something in English."

Aly toggled through the documents, pausing at one and then printing it out.

Charles Newton
Halicarnassus, 1846
The 7th, to the end

To my new friend Harold Beamish,

Great greetings! It was perhaps the easiest labor
I have yet imagined Efi and I would do at this place.
The knights told of the scariest moans, shriekings,
and cries, making every man quiver. This, as I'll readily
attest to, has caused a dread, even a terrorization, to
dampen all hopes I had of ever my seeing the formation
of a core of able men, but voilà! The team is ready.

CN

"Who's Charles Newton?" Aly asked.

"Turkey is pretty famous for figs," Cass said. "Maybe he named a cookie after himself."

She clacked away on the keys again, running a search on CHARLES NEWTON. First hit was a Wikipedia entry. Cass and I leaned over to read it. "Here we go," Aly said. "Newton is the guy who discovered the Mausoleum at Halicarnassus. Well, the remains of it."

My heart started to race. "Okay, I'm looking for the word *ling*. It would be great to find a connection . . ."

"Well, not here, anyway," Aly said. "Badly written letter. What person would write 'all hopes I had of ever my seeing'? Wouldn't you say 'my ever seeing'?"

"Maybe English wasn't his first language," Cass suggested.

"With a name like Charles Newton?" Aly said.

"He could have changed it," Cass said, "from Charles Ling."

I stared at the words "The 7th, to the end."

"Do you see what I see?" I said.

Aly nodded. "Sevenths. The Atlanteans loved that ratio of sevenths. We used it on the island and in Babylon."

One-seventh: 0.142857.

Two-sevenths: 0.285714

Three-sevenths: 0.428571.

The same digits, in the same order, only starting in different places. They were part of the codes we'd used in the

Mount Onyx labyrinth and in the Hanging Gardens of Babylon.

Cass took a sheet of paper and a pen from the desk and began writing. "So let's take the first, fourth, second, eighth, fifth, and seventh letter of the message . . ."

"Helpful," Aly drawled.

"Maybe it's an anagram?" Cass said.

Aly scratched her head. "FWONTY? As in, 'Don't go in the backy, go in the fwonty?'"

I took a deep breath. "There's another name there— Harold Beamish. Anything on him?"

Aly did a quick search. "Nothing."

"Okay," I said, rubbing my temples, which were starting to ache. "Okay. Maybe we're overthinking this."

"Maybe it's not one-seventh," Cass said.

"What if we just take every seventh letter of the message?" I suggested.

I took Cass's pen and carefully circled the letters of the message:

...harles Newton
...alicarnassus, 1846
...he 7th, to the end

To my new friend Harold Hamish,

Great greetings! It was perhaps the easiest labor I have yet imagined Fri and I would do at this place. The knights told of the scariest moans, shriekings, and cries, making every man quiver. This as I'll readily attest to, has caused a dread, even a terrorization, to dampen all hopes I had of ever my seeing the formation of a core of able men, but voilà! The team is ready.

CV

I wrote out the letters one by one:

WHERETHELAMEWALKTH
ESICKRISETHEDEADL
IVEFOREVER

"'Where the lame walk, the sick rise, the dead live forever,'" Cass read.

"It makes no sense," I said. "A mausoleum is where you
bury the dead."

I leaned back in the chair, my thoughts in total chaos.
"Did Professor Bhegad say anything else?"

"He called you over to his bed," Cass said. Flipping into
a croaky Professor Bhegad imitation, he said, "Jaaack!"

I shook my head. "No. He didn't say 'Jack.' He said 'He.'
Bhegad looked at me and said 'He.' That's why we thought
this Ling character must be a guy."

"Right," Cass said. "And when you leaned closer he said
that name. Ling."

"He . . ." I said. ". . . Ling."

The answer hit me like a wooden plank. "Oh. Oh,
wow . . ."

Cass and Aly looked at me blankly.

"He wasn't giving us a name," I said. "He was telling us
about the next Loculus!"

CHAPTER SEVENTEEN

DAD TAKES MORE WEIRD

HE. LING.

Healing.

I hoped I wasn't wrong.

"Jack, you can't just barge in here like that!" Dr. Bradley said. "He just had a highly painful procedure!"

"Sorry, Dr. Bradley, it's important." I darted around her toward Professor Bhegad's hospital bed. In the time it took to run from the office, my tiny headache had grown. Now it pounded. The old man was flat on his back, his eyes open but glassy and red. Dad, Cass, and Aly were huddled in the doorway, watching. Torquin was sitting in a chair in a corner holding a ukulele.

I stopped short. "What are you doing?" I asked.

"Playing." Torquin's eyes were moist. The little instrument looked even smaller in his huge hands. "'Oh! Susanna.' Professor's favorite."

I knelt by the professor, leaning close to his ear. "Professor, it's Jack. How are you?"

He didn't turn his eyes. But I sensed he could hear me.

"Jack, he's unconscious," Dr. Bradley said.

"A little while ago, Professor," I pressed on, "you looked at me and said something. I didn't understand you then, but were you telling us to look for a Loculus of Healing?"

I stared into his face for what felt like an hour, looking for the tiniest flicker of recognition. All I could see was a white ring in the pupils of his eyes, reflecting the fluorescent lights above. Cold and unmoving. With a deep sigh, I stood up to leave.

The white ring moved.

"Jack . . . ?" Aly whispered.

Bhegad's eyes were turning toward me. His mouth shuddered slightly but no sound came out. I leaned again, so that my ear was close to him. I felt a soft breath of air. A vowel followed by a kind of hiss. "Is that a yes, Professor?"

Professor Bhegad's face moved up and down in the weakest nod I have ever seen.

"We found a coded letter from Charles Newton," I said. "The guy who discovered the remains of the Mausoleum at Halicarnassus. The code said something about the lame walking and the sick rising. Is that the place we need to go? Is that where we'll find the Loculus of Healing?"

"Newton . . ." Bhegad said. ". . . Massa . . ."

"Charles Newton was with the Massa?" I said. "Is that what you're trying to say?"

But Bhegad's energy was spent. His lids slowly closed, his breaths deepening into a snore.

As Dr. Bradley stepped in, I backed away toward the door. If I had two spitballs, I could have launched them into Aly's and Cass's mouths, which were hanging open. "You were right about the Loculus . . ." Aly murmured.

"Which means we might be able to save him," Cass said.

"Dad," I blurted out, "we have an emergency. A big one. That aircraft on the runway with an MGL logo—can we use it? Can you get a pilot to take us to Turkey?"

"What?" Dad looked flabbergasted. "Would you mind telling me what the heck is going on?"

This was not going to be easy.

"Follow me." I barged past Dad, Cass, and Aly, jogging back to the office. Now my whole body felt weird, like I'd caught a cold. When we were all in the office, I shut the door behind us and gestured toward the black padded desk chair. "Sit, Dad, and listen. Promise you'll hear us out until the end. This is going to sound weird."

"I don't know if I can take more weird," Dad said.

"Inside that pack," I said, pointing to Torquin's bulky

backpack against the wall, "are two Loculi. Spheres. Orbs. One of them can make you fly, the other can make you invisible. They were made by Queen Qalani, wife of King Uhla'ar, mother of Prince Karai and Prince Massarym."

Dad's tense expression softened. "Karai . . . Massarym . . . of Atlantis. I know those names. Your mother was fascinated by the legend."

"It's not a legend, Dad," I said. "It's real. Atlantis was this unbelievably peaceful place, amazingly advanced. All due to this magical energy from a breach in the ground. Qalani was a scientist. She wanted to analyze the energy, thinking she could transport it if she needed to. So she managed to isolate it into seven components, which she put into the Loculi. They had to remain in a place called the Heptakiklos, passing their energy in a kind of circuit, so it would all be in balance. But Massarym liked to sneak off with the Loculi and play with them. When the continent was hit by earthquakes, wars, and disease, Karai thought his mom was to blame for disturbing the sacred energy source. So he figured destroying the Loculi would end the problem. Massarym freaked, and secretly hid them away where Karai would never find them. One went into the Great Pyramid. He commissioned six other structures, like storage lockers, but, well, magical and powerful. They became known as the Seven Wonders of the Ancient World."

"The continent sank," Aly went on. "Totaled. But

centuries later the explorer Herman Wenders discovered the remains, a small volcanic island. His son, Burt, was a Select like Jack and Cass and me. Wenders and his crew stayed there and founded the Scholars of Karai. They couldn't save Burt, but now there's an awesome high-tech laboratory where they've been working on many of the secrets of Atlantis—including finding a treatment for people like us. The problem is, the breach is widening, weakening. It could blast open a rift in time and destroy the world. Already some Atlantean beasts have slipped through."

"So we need to return the Loculi and close the breach," Cass said. "But here's the bonus—if the Loculi are put back into the Heptakiklos, and their energy is in balance, moob! We're cured. We have long, happy lives as superbeings and awesome people."

Our words hung in the air. Dad looked at each of us for what felt like a long time. "And you believe all this?"

"We've seen the evidence," I said. "Cass has talon marks from the griffin. We made the Colossus of Rhodes rise from rocks. We traveled to Ancient Babylon in a parallel world progressing at one ninetieth the speed of our own."

Cass had pulled open his shirt to show the griffin scars, but Dad was shaking his head. Both of his heads, actually—my eyes were starting to see double. I shook it off, but my head felt weird.

"Where are these things—the griffin, the Colossus, the

ancient civilization?" he asked. "If all this happened, why wasn't it in the news?"

"All destroyed," I explained.

Dad took a deep breath. "Look, I am so grateful that you're alive. I know you've been through a lot. But I'm a man of science. I don't doubt that these things happened, in some form. Many miraculous things happen. But all of them are explainable by physics, biology, brain studies, perception."

"So you think we're seeing things?" Aly said.

Outside the room, I saw people in white lab coats racing to the operating room. We were running out of time, fast. And I was starting to feel queasy.

I scooped up Torquin's backpack, then took Dad's hand. "Come with me, okay?"

Bewildered, Dad followed me out of the office, down the corridor, and outside. Aly and Cass ran behind. From the end of the hallway, I could hear the strains of a ukulele playing "Oh! Susanna" accompanied by a voice that was a cross between a foghorn and a complicated belch.

We left the building into the silence of the Mongolian steppe. The sun was beginning to set, and the early-evening chill soothed my aching head. I set the pack down against the glass building and took out the canvas bags holding the Loculi.

"Can you see what's in here?" I said, opening the bag

that contained the Loculus of Invisibility.

"No," Dad said. "There's nothing."

I reached down into the bag until I felt the surface, keeping a careful eye on my dad's reaction.

As I disappeared from sight, he jumped backward. Cass and Aly each took one of his arms. "Jack?" he murmured. "What the—?"

"I'm still here, Dad," I said. "I am going to reach out and take your hand now. When I do, the power will transfer. You will see me and the Loculus, but you and I will be invisible to everyone else."

I touched his hand, and he gasped again. "Aly?" I said. "The other Loculus, please?"

Aly took the Loculus of Flight from the other bag and approached Dad and me, hand outstretched. "Hang tight," I said, clasping my hand around his wrist. "To Aly and to me. Really tight."

Dad grasped Aly's hand. She began to rise, pulling him off the ground. He was heavy, and she went slowly, maybe about six vertical feet.

"Yeeeaagghh!" Dad cried out. His legs were dangling beneath him, his eyes wide as satellite dishes. "Set me down! Set me down!"

Cass was cracking up. "Oh . . . oh . . ." he said, nearly choking on laughter. "Sorry . . . this is the funniest thing I've ever not seen."

Aly brought us down gently. When we were sure Dad was stable on his feet, we returned the Loculi to their bags. He was breathing shallow and hard. "What . . . just happened?"

"Those," I said, "are the first two Loculi. The third, we're pretty sure, is a Loculus of Healing. We need to find it now. For Professor Bhegad and for us. The Mausoleum at Halicarnassus is in Turkey, which isn't that far from here, really."

"I can navigate," Cass said.

Dad closed his eyes for a long time, as if hoping this whole thing would go away. "My wife faked her own death," he said. "My son is doomed. I've built a genetic company based on a false premise. I just flew off the ground but no one saw it happen. As a father, husband, scientist, and businessman, I have failed. Tell me I'm dreaming."

"You're awake, Dad," I said, "and you're not a failure. You're the best dad ever."

Dad opened his eyes. Tears were forming at their corners.

"I think I'm going to cry," Aly said.

Dad put an arm around my shoulder. "You realize," he said, "this is totally flipping crazy."

"Crazy," I said, "is the new normal . . ."

"But I can't do this," he said. "Not without further study. I'm sorry, son."

I pulled away. My knees felt like they'd been swapped out with saltwater taffy. Dad was standing before me in duplicate, then triplicate. His eyes were floating before me, wide and intense.

"Jack . . . ?" he said.

"Jack, what's happening to you?" Cass demanded.

I fell to my knees. "Just . . . a headache . . ."

The last thing I saw before hitting the dirt were six pairs of arms reaching out to catch me.

CHAPTER EIGHTEEN

WORK TO BE DONE

THE STORM RAGES. *Though the building is not yet com-plete, it is a fine shelter, the construction solid. For my plans, it will be enough.*

I hear a thunderclap and look up. The door is open to the grim night. My would-be assailant lies unconscious over the threshold, at the feet of the guard. In silhouette the guard looks small and frightened, as though the worst is yet to come.

He has no idea how much worse.

At the foot of the stairs is a statue, not yet mounted onto the structure's roof — a ruler who has died, and his wife who is still alive. For a moment I think about my own father and mother, a king and queen in a place long gone. My throat closes and I choke back a sob. I will never have the opportunity to do for them what

I am about to do now for this ruler who calls herself queen.

The ocean crashes at the bottom of the cliff. The building is cold and forbidding. But this will soon change. Beyond the building is an unspeakable place that will make this darkness seem bright, this bleakness seem like great cheer.

The queen is about to rule again.

I reach into my bag and remove the smooth cobalt sphere. The earth shakes but I am no longer afraid. It is all as it should be.

I am Massarym. And there is work to be done.

CHAPTER NINETEEN

THE TAILOR WAKES

"HE'S AWAKE . . ."

"No, he's not . . ."

"His eyes are moving."

"Jack? Jack, do you hear me?"

Jack. My name is Jack.

The dream was breaking up into flinty shards, images that shimmered and vanished. I could hear voices. Real, not dream voices. Cass and Aly. I tried to move my eyes but they weren't working. I tried to talk but I couldn't.

"He needs at least a half hour recovery, maybe more."

"He can recuperate while we're moving him."

Dr. Bradley. Aly.

What was happening?

A warm hand clasped my arm. I was moving. Rolling. "He wasn't due for one of these for another week, you say?"

"Early. Like Cass."

"Then we can't waste time. What about Bhegad?"

Dad. Torquin. Dad again.

"I appreciate the concern . . . but I will feel better . . . if someone destroys that banjo . . ." Professor Bhegad.

"Is ukulele." *Torquin.*

Where am I going? What are you doing to me?

WHY CAN'T I—

"Taalk!"

The rolling stopped. My eyes popped open and I blinked. We were in the hallway, outside the recovery room.

"Did you say something, Jack?" Dad was staring down at me, his eyes creased with concern.

I blinked. "I said talk. I think."

"I knew it!" Aly blurted out, clinging happily to my dad's arm. "He's okay." She leaned close to me. "JACK, ARE YOU FULLY AWAKE? CAN YOU HEAR ME? YOU HAD A TREATMENT. YOU ARE BACK TO NORMAL NOW."

"Why are you yelling at me?" I asked.

Cass appeared on the other side of the bed. "Bhegad's awake. We asked him about the Loculus of Healing. And about the Mausoleum at Halicarnassus. Just to be sure. And guess what? You were right—about both!"

"Good work, Tailor," Aly said.

"Tailor?" Dad asked.

Bhegad's soft, breathy voice called out. He was on a gurney next to mine. "Tinker . . . tailor . . . soldier . . . sailor . . ."

"I'm the Sailor, because of my emosewa lanoitagivan ability," Cass explained. "The Soldier is Marco—you never met him, Mr. McKinley, but he's cool—because he's mad athletic. And Aly is the Tinker because of her tech amazingness."

Dad smiled. "So what's the Tailor's special ability?"

I smiled weakly. "I was hoping you'd tell me."

The one who puts it all together, Bhegad had once said. But that seemed like an excuse. Like the trophy you get even if your team finishes last.

Unfortunately, Bhegad had fallen silent.

"Whatever it is, I'm sure it's awesome," Dad said. He gave a signal, and I felt myself being wheeled again. We were heading away from the recovery room toward the exit.

"What's happening?" I asked. "Where are we going?"

"I had some time to think about what you told me before you passed out," Dad said. "Since then, I've chatted with Dr. Bradley, Torquin, and your friends. I have decided it's important to start planning for your fourteenth birthday. And fifteenth. So we've reserved Brunhilda to help us."

"What the heck are you talking about?" I said.

We stopped by a small, empty room. Two McKinley

Genetics Lab people stood just inside, holding some folded-up clothing.

"Brunhilda is the name of our corporate jet," Dad replied. "Change quickly. I'm going to get you a cell phone in case we get separated at any point. Wheels up in ten minutes. With Bhegad. Torquin's flying."

CHAPTER TWENTY

BRUNHILDA

"PAH!" TORQUIN YANKED the steering mechanism to the left. "Slippy is like Lamborghini, Brunhilda like mini-van!"

"Her ride feels smooth to me," Dad said from the copilot's seat.

The jet banked gently left. "Smooth, yes," Torquin shot back. "Fun, no."

Cass, Aly, and I sat quietly in three padded seats behind the two men. Cass was fiddling with his flash drive/worry beads again, staring at the Charles Newton letter. "There's something funky about this," he said. "Did you notice some of the letters are lighter than the others?"

Aly peered over his shoulder. "Bad photocopy," she said.

"Or bad typewriter," Dad added. "On those old machines, the keys responded to pressure. If you didn't type hard enough, the letters were lighter."

"But the light letters actually spell something," Cass said. "'The destroyer shall rule.' Look."

To my new friend Harold Hamish,

Great greetings! It was perhaps the easiest labor I have yet imagined. Ori and I would do at this place. The knights told of the scariest moans, shriekings, and cries, making every man quiver. This, as I'll readily attest to, has caused a dread, even a terrorization, to dampen all hopes I had of ever my seeing the formation of a core of able men, but voilà! The team is ready.

"Are you sure?" Aly said. "Because a lot of those letters look light."

Cass shrugged. "Doesn't seem like that could be a coincidence. Maybe it has something to do with King Mausolus."

"He wasn't a king," Aly said. "He was a satrap. Kind of like a governor."

"Maaa . . ." groaned Professor Bhegad from the back of the plane.

We all turned. Bhegad lay on a reclined seat, a wheelchair folded up and strapped to the wall behind him. "How's he doing?" I asked.

"The commotion drained him," Dr. Bradley said. "He hasn't been awake this whole flight. For a human being in his condition, travel is very nearly the worst possible thing."

"He'll make it as far as Turkey, right?" Cass asked.

Dr. Bradley cocked her head but said nothing.

Unbuckling her seat belt, Aly knelt by Bhegad and took his hand. "I don't know if you can hear me, Professor, but if there's a way to heal you, we will find it."

"Slippy," Torquin grumbled, "would already be in Holly—Holla—Turkey."

"Halicarnassus," Dad said. "And it's not called that anymore. The Knights of Saint Peter changed the name to Petronium. Which, over time, became Bodrum. That's where we're headed. Bodrum, Turkey."

Torquin nodded, then glanced at his GPS. "Ninety-seven miles from Boredom."

I turned away, focusing on the monitor that swung out

from the armrest of my seat. Since leaving home for the KI, we hadn't had internet. Now I was making up for lost time, collecting research on the Mausoleum at Halicarnassus. If I had time, I wanted to look into the other Wonders, too.

I zoomed in on some drawings. The place wasn't sprawling or gaudy. It wasn't a phenomenal feat of engineering like the Hanging Gardens of Babylon. But there was something unbelievably beautiful about it, almost modern—tall, columned, nearly square all around, like the top of a skyscraper. It was ornamented with massive statues and covered with carvings. At the top, like a hat, was a pyramid that rose in steps up to a statue of a chariot holding two people.

"'More than one hundred thirty feet,'" I read aloud. "Taller than the Statue of Liberty, not including the base. It lasted sixteen centuries. The whole thing is surrounded by columns, thirty-six of them. Mausolus and his wife, Artemisia, sat at the top in a chariot—well, they didn't, but a statue of them did. The place was called Caria back then, not Halicarnassus. It was part of Persia. The structure was considered crazy modern, even shocking. In those days fancy buildings were decorated with classical scenes, historical battles. But they used statues of animals, portraits of real people."

"Imagine," said Cass. "Must have been fainting in the streets."

"What happened to it?" Dad asked.

132

"Earthquake," I replied. "Totaled in the early thirteen hundreds. A century afterward, the Crusaders conquer the area. Near the old Mausoleum site they figure, hey, nice place to build a castle. Soon they need to reinforce it, so they use stones from the ruins of the Mausoleum. You can still see the actual stones—only now that old castle is a museum."

"Museum of the Mausoleum," Cass said. "MuMa."

"How do we find a Wonder that's been cemented into a museum wall?" Aly said with a groan. "Think about it. The parts of the Colossus were in a pile. The Hanging Gardens were tucked away in a parallel world. We could get to them. They weren't attached to anything else!"

Cass's face sank. "Good point."

"Well, just some of the stones were used," I said. "There's a collection at the actual site of the Mausoleum."

"I don't know how we'll get in," Dad said. "The site is closed for the day. I just checked."

"We'll figure something out," Aly said.

Dad sighed, glancing back at Professor Bhegad. "I hope I don't regret doing this."

Cass was peering out the window at a moonlit mountain peak of pure white that jutted up through the cloud cover. "Whoa . . . that's Mount Ararat. Eastern edge of Turkey. Where Noah's Ark washed up."

"Must have been some huge flood," I said.

"That must have been some huge ark," Aly added.

"Brunhilda is like ark," Torquin complained. "Without flood. Or animals. Hang on."

With a grunt, he yanked on some control so hard he nearly took off the lever.

Slowly, gently, we began to descend.

* * *

The rented van sped down the Bodrum highway along the coast of the Mediterranean. I sat in the back with Professor Bhegad, who was awake again but not saying much. His wheelchair lay folded in the van's wayback. Out the window, a carpet of moonlight led to the distant lights of the island Kos.

Those lights blurred as Torquin took an exit hard and gunned up a hill.

Professor Bhegad gasped. "Massa treachery . . . Torquin's driving . . . not sure which is worse."

Torquin pulled to a stop outside a gated yard, fishtailing to both sides as he slammed on the brakes. "We're here," he announced gruffly. "GPS says."

"Hallelujah," Cass said.

Torquin frowned at him. "Halicarnassus," he pronounced carefully.

As I unbuckled my seat belt, Dad handed me a cell phone. "Take this, in case we get separated."

I took it, and we piled out of the van. To one side was a guardhouse, but otherwise a flat yard stretched out before us. In its center was a big hole surrounded by a few piles of stone. "That's it?" Cass said.

"There's not enough material here for a decent-sized patio," Aly said.

I pressed myself close to the iron bars, staying still. Trying to sense the presence of the Loculus. Trying to feel the Song of the Heptakiklos.

Each time we'd come close—to the Loculi, to the Heptakiklos itself at the center of the island—I'd felt it. It wasn't music, exactly, although I did hear beautiful sounds. It was something that I felt deeper than that, as if something were playing the sinews and nerves of my body like an instrument.

I waited to feel it. I concentrated hard.

Finally I shook my head. "It's not here. I'm not feeling it."

"You can just . . . feel it?" Dad said. "Like some ESP thing?"

"Let's get closer," Cass suggested. "Just to be sure."

"We can try to disable the security," Aly said. "Or cut through the wire."

"I have a better idea." Cass ran to the van and returned in midair, holding the Loculus of Flight. As he touched down in front of me, I reached for the orb.

Together we rose over a field of stones and broken columns. There were far fewer than I imagined would be here. "Anything?" Cass asked. "Violins? Trumpets?"

I shook my head. All I felt was the wetness of sea air

and the slight tang of salt.

We landed outside the gate, where Dad, Aly, and Torquin were waiting expectantly. "What now?" Dad asked. "We go home?"

I glanced up the coastal road. In the distance, half-hidden by trees, was a massive structure that loomed over a bluff. "Is that the knights' castle?"

"Yup," Cass said. "Want to try it?"

"But . . . it's not the Mausoleum," Dad said. "So you won't find anything, right?"

"If the knights used pieces of the Mausoleum in their castle walls," I said, "what if they also used pieces of the Loculus?"

Aly nodded. "Stranger things have happened."

Dad sighed. "Seems far-fetched, but you guys have been at this longer than I have . . ."

We jumped in the van again. I felt bad for Dad. He looked more confused than I'd ever seen him.

Torquin gunned it up the road. The castle's small windows, like beady black eyes, seemed to follow us as we approached. Its towers were connected by a crenellated roof, and I imagined helmeted guards aiming crossbows at us.

"This place is mad creepy," Cass said.

"They were Crusaders, not luxury condo builders," Aly said.

I got out of the van and walked toward the museum. To

the side was a padlocked gate, thicker and more formidable than the Mausoleum site's, which led to a moonlit yard. Near the edge of the bluff I could see a roped-off area with a ragged pile of what looked like stones.

Relics.

My heart quickened. I grabbed the bars, concentrating hard for a few seconds. It has to be here . . .

After a few seconds, I noticed Aly and Cass were already beside me. Waiting. Not wanting to interrupt. I stared out past the museum. There, a bluff dropped to the sea. I could hear the rhythmic crashing of waves below. The breeze from the sea was bracing, almost cold.

The Dream.

It was coming back to me now: walking on a cliff . . . the sea raging and the wind biting into my skin. I was bleeding . . . shivering . . . holding . . . what?

"A Loculus . . ." I murmured.

"What?" Cass said.

"Did you say Loculus?" Aly said. "Do you feel it?"

"No, but I think I dreamed about this place," I replied.

"I think I did, too," Cass said, shivering. He looked up to the top of the barbed-wire fence. "I'll get the Loculus of Flight."

"No," Aly said. "This is a big place. There might be a night watchman, someone who'd see kids dangling from a flying beach ball." She took a couple of bobby pins from her pack and inserted them gently into the padlock. Pressing her ear against the mechanism, she began to fiddle with it.

A sudden hammering sound made us both fall silent. We crouched low as a steady *chink . . . chink . . . chink* rang out from inside the castle grounds. I looked toward the sound to see a glint of amber light.

"What's that?" Cass mouthed.

Aly shrugged. The lock fell open. Cass, Aly, Torquin, Dad, and I tiptoed inside the grounds. Dr. Bradley remained inside the van with Professor Bhegad. We slipped past the darkened museum entrance and followed the base of the wall. The crashing waves were loud, blotting out all other sound, but as we neared the cliff, I had to stop.

Chink . . . chink . . . chink . . .

I held a finger up, signaling everyone to stay put.

I inched my way along the wall. In back of the castle was a small, rectangular, gravel yard that extended from the castle to the edge of the cliff.

My eyes scanned the length of the wall to a tall pile of stones at the other side of the yard. The sound seemed to be coming from there. I crouched low, hiding in a dark castle door well. In the moonlight I could make out the silhouette of a severely hunched figure, not more than four and a half feet high. I couldn't tell if it was male or female. It rocked from side to side as it walked, its feet pointed outward and knees touching, as if its legs had been switched. I watched it silently walk to the edge of the cliff, leaving the pile unguarded. It stood looking over the sea.

I tiptoed closer to the abandoned stones. They seemed to glow. I felt strange, weightless. The wind boxed my ears, dulling all other sounds. Still I didn't feel the Song. I glanced back toward the cliff, but the strange figure was gone.

Maybe it was a thief, and we'd scared it away.

I drew closer. In the moonlight, the rocks were a pale amber. They were covered with relief carvings of some kind, but not with fancy designs, just straight lines. I reached toward the pile and touched one. It was warm to my fingers. It seemed somehow alive, pulsating.

"Psssst," came a warning from behind me. I turned to see Cass, Aly, and Torquin peeking around the corner of the castle.

Tucking the stone under my arm, I ran toward them.

"Watch out, Jack!" Aly cried.

Out of the corner of my eye, I spotted a movement by the cliff's edge. I turned to see something hurtling toward my head. I ducked, dropping the stone.

A baseball-sized rock whizzed above my head, smacking against the castle wall with a dull thwack and falling to the ground. A shadow came toward me, dark and low, moving like a bear cub.

Before I could scramble to my feet, it stood over me, one

foot planted on either side. It was human—male—his features all bunched into the center of his face. Hair sprouted in all directions like acupuncture needles, except the top of his head, which was bald but etched with lines like canals on a lost planet. One eye was focused outward, as if distracted. But the other stared at me directly, sharply.

Aly, Cass, and Torquin rushed toward us, but the man turned their way with superquick reflexes. His arm was cocked back, and he held a rock the size of a cantaloupe, ready to throw.

"W—we come in p-peace," Cass squeaked.

The man's mouth opened slightly. A line of spittle dribbled out and hung precariously. "And in peace thou shalt go," he said in a perfect English accent, his words clear and clipped.

"Who are you?" I asked.

The man eyed me with a strange expression that could have been disgust or amusement. "To those who address me, which are sadly few," he said, "I am Canavar."

CHAPTER TWENTY-ONE

GNOME? PIXIE? TROLL?

CANAVAR WAS SMALL, but his drool loomed closer and packed a world of disgust. "Could you please get off me?" I said.

"I know what thou thinkest." Canavar leaped off, his drool landing with a tiny splat about two inches from my ear. "Gnome! Pixie! Troll!"

"I wasn't thinking that at all!" I protested.

"Ha! My form may be crooked, but I am fast and strong," he crowed. "Thieves and cutpurses do well to fear such as I! But seeing as thou art young and inexperienced—well, a majority of thou—I will let thee go quietly."

"Please," I said. "If you have anything to do with this museum—"

"Anything to do?" He waddled over to the dropped stone, scooping it from the ground. "I am resident archaeologist, cryptologist, oceanologist, DJ!"

"DJ?" Cass asked.

"Doctor of jurisprudence!" Canavar replied. His face grew somber. "But, being of an appearance and temperament not suited for the general public, I prefer working after hours. Of which these are. Now go, or I shall trap thee overnight and cast thee tomorrow before the arbiters of civic judgment!"

"I think he means report us to the authorities," Cass said.

I thought quickly. "We need to look around a little," I said, standing up. "We brought a man here from very far away, a great archaeologist who is ailing badly. It's his . . . dying wish."

Canavar's eyes darted toward the van, where Dr. Bradley and Professor Bhegad were waiting. He waddled closer, peering into the window. "By the ghost of Mausolus," Canavar breathed, "is that . . . Raddy?"

"I beg your pardon?" Professor Bhegad said.

"Pardon granted!" Canavar said. "Raddy—thy nickname at Oxford amongst thy admirers. You are Radamanthus Bhegad, Sultan of Scholars, Archduke of Archaeologists, yes? What on earth has befallen thee? And what can I do? Canavar, thy acolyte, at thy service!"

Dr. Bradley and Professor Bhegad stared at the

misshapen man. For a moment neither knew what to say.

"Yes, yes, I am Bhegad," the professor said, his voice soft and weak. "And, um . . . yes, indeed, there is something you can do. For the sake of archaeology. These people . . . must have full access. To . . . er, everything you know about the Mausoleum at Halicarnassus."

Canavar stood to full height, which wasn't terribly impressive. "Oh, by the warts on Artemisia's delicate nose . . . I suppose I have a job to do now. I do, yes? Then come."

He sprang away from the van and skipped back the way we'd come, disappearing around the side of the castle. But we stood rooted to the ground, stunned.

"My mother told me not to believe in leprechauns," Aly murmured.

"But for this," I said, "we make an exception."

* * *

"By the blessing of Asclepius, what a tale!" Canavar exclaimed as he sat before a pile of rocks on the ground. "So thou seekest a sort of . . . sphere of salubrity? Is that what thou sayest?"

Cass gave me a look. "Did we sayest that?"

"I think he means a Loculus of Healing," I said. "Look, Canavar—"

"Dr. Canavar," Canavar said.

"Dr. Canavar. The organization I've been telling you about—Professor Bhegad's group, the Karai Institute—we

143

believe the relic was hidden within the Mausoleum."

"Oh, dear," Canavar replied, his brow furrowing, "then by now 'twould be presumably reduced to rubble. Cannibalized to construction. Stolen. Sunken undersea." He gestured toward the castle. "Behold, this is what is left of your Mausoleum! Stones ground into dust. Dust reformed into brick. A bas-relief here, a statuette there. All to build this . . . abomination! This monument to knightly ego! Oh, misfortune!"

He was starting to cry, his tears dripping on the collection of stones he was arranging. Cass and Aly looked at me helplessly.

I stood and began walking around the yard. Where was the Song of the Heptakiklos? I had felt it outside the labyrinth of Mount Onyx, the Massarene monastery in Rhodes, the Hanging Gardens of Babylon. I should have been feeling it now.

But all I felt was a vague warmth from the rocks. Was that a hint of a lost Loculus? Was this one hopelessly spread out in the mortar and stones of the castle?

"Canavar," I said.

"Dr. Canavar."

"Right. So, some of the Mausoleum stones were all ground up. But is it possible others were taken away? Are there parts of the Mausoleum in other places besides here?"

144

"This site was paradise for thieves," Canavar said. "Some escaped—well, mostly those that came by land. Some sold their stolen stones and jewels on the open market. But the largest thefts, my boy, came by sea. These were men of equal parts stupidity and fearlessness. And thou hast little chance of finding their booty."

"Their booty?" Cass said.

"Pirate booty," Aly explained. "Stolen treasures."

Canavar gestured toward the sea. "The sea bottom is littered with shipwrecks containing pieces of the Mausoleum still within their holds. The sand and coral are nourished with the bodies of those who scoffed at Artemisia's Curse."

"Artemisia," Aly said. "That was the wife of the ruler, Mausolus."

Canavar nodded. "Also his sister."

"Isn't that illegal?" Cass said. "Or at least incredibly gross?"

"The world was a different place." Canavar bowed his head. "I present to you the most important recent Mausoleum find. The rocks before thee were salvaged by the hands of a heroic, prodigiously skilled sea diver. Namely, me. This is my life's work—to find all there is. To bring them back. If they came from the Mausoleum, they must be returned. It is where they belong. It is where they have their life. Their meaning."

I knelt by the stones. They were small, none more than

four or five inches long, all of them in sharply cut geometric shapes. Some seemed new, others worn and ancient, and some were etched with straight lines.

Canavar's tiny features expanded with pride. "You see the etched lines on the stones? I believe they formed a kind of symbol, or logo. The Greek letter *mu*, equivalent to our *M*, for Mausolus."

"But this place was Persian back then," I said, trying to dredge up my research. "Not Greek."

Canavar nodded. "The Persian kingdom of Caria. But as a port, Caria was home to many nationalities. Mausolus was allowed to be an independent and flexible ruler. He hired Greek architects and Greek sculptors. Hence the Greek *M*. Wouldst thou like to see how the stones fit together?"

He quickly organized the stones with his spindly fingers.

"Ergo, an *M*!" Canavar said.

I nodded. "Some of these are lighter in color than the others."

"Yes. Those were the ones I salvaged from the ship. I studied these stones for years, wondering what they meant. I positioned and repositioned them until I saw, in my mind's eye, the possibility of this *M*, even though the other stones were missing. So I carved new ones, to represent them. To fill in the blanks, as it were. Those are the darker stones. It was the material I had."

"Wait, you made it up?" Cass asked. "You had a bunch of lines and just assumed it was an *M*? What if it was something else?"

Canavar glared at him. "Thinkest thou perhaps *Q* would be appropriate for Mausolus?"

He turned in a huff and stomped away toward Torquin and Dad.

Cass, Aly, and I squatted by the stones. I touched them one by one. "They're warm," I said. "Just the old ones. Not the new."

"They all feel the same to me," Cass said.

"Don't they seem kind of small?" Aly held one up, turning it around in her hand. "I mean, think about the carved letters over the columns of the House of Wenders—they're huge. Imagine this thing at the top of the Mausoleum. No one would see it."

147

I pressed my hand to one of the stones and kept it there. I could feel my palm tingling. Now Aly and Cass were both looking at me.

"These stones are different." I carefully separated the rocks, older on the left, newer on the right.

"I'm feeling something," I said. "From the lighter-colored ones, the older stones. It's not like the Song. But it's something."

"Walk one of them around," Aly said. "Maybe it's like a Geiger counter. It'll start singing to you when you're near a Loculus."

I picked up a stone and began pacing through the yard, circling closer to the gate and then back toward the cliff.

"Young fellow, seekest thou a men's room?" Canavar's voice called out.

"No, I'm good." I stared out over the coastline to the west. I pictured the ships of the Knights of St. Peter with sails unfurled. Over the bounding main. Whatever that meant. I imagined the holds filled with great statues and polished stones . . .

If they came from the Mausoleum, they must be returned. It is where they belong. It is where they have their life. Their meaning.

I turned and walked toward Canavar. He was deep in conversation with Dad and Torquin now. "Canavar—" I said.

"Dr. Canavar," he corrected me again.

"Dr. Canavar. I have a big, big favor to ask you. Can we take your stones to the location of the Mausoleum?"

"But we were already there," Cass whispered. "You said you didn't feel anything at all!"

"I want to try again," I said. "With these stones."

Canavar looked from Dad to Torquin and chuckled. "Ah, children do love rocks, don't they? And children, no matter how many times they are told, do not comprehend the value of antiquities. Mr. McKinley, thou wilt, of course, properly discipline thy offspring and restrain him from acts of cultural disrespect."

"Excuse me?" Dad said.

Canavar turned away and sidled back toward the rocks. "Thou art most cordially excused. Good night."

Dad looked at Torquin. With an understanding nod, Torquin lumbered past Canavar and scooped up the pile of rocks with two swipes of his massive paws.

"I—I beg thy pardon—" Canavar stammered. "Is this some sort of jest?"

Torquin shoved the rocks into his pack, then grabbed Canavar's collar and lifted him off the ground. "Torquin love rocks, too."

CHAPTER TWENTY-TWO

SECRET IN THE STONES

"THIS IS IT?" Dad said. "The whole thing?"

The pit was about thirty feet long and wide. It was surrounded by piles of rocks and stones, lit by soft lamps that rose from the ground. I knelt by a section of a column that lay on its side, like an uprooted tree trunk.

Dad was right. It wasn't much.

"Good rocks," Torquin said, dropping his backpack onto the ground with a thud. "Make nice patio."

"For this, thou humiliatest me," Canavar grumbled. "Thou forcest me to let thee inside with a magnetic card, and then thou belittlest a hallowed site."

"Can it, Munchkin," Torquin said.

"At least with the Colossus, we had the stones we

needed," Cass said. "How can you re-create a Wonder if its parts don't exist?"

Aly crouched by a sculpture of an animal's head. "This one looks like a *mushushu*."

"I think it's a lion," Cass remarked. "We're not in Babylon anymore, Toto."

Dr. Bradley pushed Professor Bhegad toward me in a wheelchair. "This will be difficult, Jack," Bhegad said. "But archaeology is a bit like finding a speck of diamond in a pile of sludge. Do not ignore one pebble, my son."

"Right," I said. "Thanks."

Where to begin? I knelt by a small, flat stone that looked a bit like one of the stones Canavar had been working on. I ran my hand over it.

Aly put hers on top of mine. "I feel it."

I flinched, yanking my hand back.

"What happened?" Aly said.

"Nothing," I said. "You startled me."

Aly narrowed her eyes at me. "You're turning red."

"No, I'm not." I turned away. "You . . . said you felt something. What did you feel?"

"Warmth," she said.

I swallowed. "Warmth?"

"Back up at the castle, you said that the rocks were warm. I was trying to feel that warmth through your hand." Aly smiled. "What did you think I meant?"

152

My face was burning. "I wasn't thinking."

She was staring at me. I stood there, dorking out. I couldn't help it.

I felt the slab again. Actually, it was warm. I ran my fingers along the top until I felt a diagonal ridge, a raised area like a vein in a clenched hand.

"Ah, thou discoverest my favorite relief," Canavar's voice piped up. He sidled close, running his gnarled fingers along the carved ridge. "Razor straight. Remarkable."

"Looks like it might have been carved by the same Greek dudes who made your *M*," Cass said.

"A trained eye will discern the difference in technique," Canavar said with cocked eyebrows. "These are raised upward, not carved into the stone. An entirely different process."

I noticed another flat stone, and another. Reaching into my pack, I pulled out a flashlight and shone it around, expanding the illumination from the glow of the weak lamps. "There's a bunch of these, scattered all over this place," I said, pointing the light at some of the other pieces I'd noticed. "There. And there. And there. I think they may all be parts of a bigger sculpture."

"Do you?" Canavar said with a mocking grin. "And perhaps with thy uncanny visual powers thou shalt conjure up a statue of Artemisia herself?"

"He's good at this," Dad said with a grin. "Won the state

middle school jigsaw puzzle championship, Division One. We had DQ Blizzards to celebrate."

"Competitive jigsaw puzzling?" Aly said. "With divisions?"

"And Blizzards?" Cass piped up.

"Sweeeeet," Torquin said.

My face was heating up again.

Focus. Ignore.

Retaliate later.

I stared at the pieces, letting my brain assemble them. Then I began to fetch them, putting them close to one another until I could find no more.

Carefully, I slid them into place.

"It's some kind of panel," Aly said. "With a backward seven, in relief."

"Maybe the Persians read from right to left?" Cass said.

Dad cocked his head curiously. "Any guesses what it means?"

I wasn't sure. But my brain was trying to recall the exact pattern of Canavar's *M*. There was something about it that didn't quite make sense. "Torquin," I said. "Can you give me Canavar's stones—all of them?"

"I believe it is proper to address that question to the stone collector himself," Canavar said, "who risked his life to assemble them."

"May I, Dr. Canavar?" I said.

Canavar lifted his head high with a triumphant grin. "Permission granted."

Torquin handed me the stones from the pack. I assembled them, one by one, sorting out the old and the new on the ground. Then, setting the new ones aside, I began shifting around only the old stones.

"Ah, may I remind thee," Canavar said, "to include the most important of these stones. To wit, the stones personally carved by me out of necessity to complete the historic *M*—"

Sliding the last piece into place, I smiled. "Your stones do not form an *M*."

"It's a seven!" Cass exclaimed. "I was right—this thing couldn't have been an *M*. Yesss!"

I could hear Professor Bhegad's feeble voice call out, "That's my boy!"

Canavar's small eyes seemed to double in size. "Well, I—I suppose it's a valid possibility—"

"A seven chiseled into stone . . ." Dad said, his eyes moving toward the flat raised relief I had just put together on the ground. "A bas-relief backward seven of the same size. Are you thinking what I'm thinking?"

"I think so." One by one, I placed the stones from Canavar's collection upside down on the jigsaw arrangement so that the chiseled lines locked into place.

When I put the ninth and last stone in place, I felt my body shake.

Dad gripped my arm. "What's that? The Heptococcus song?"

"Heptakiklos," I said. "Yes. Totally." Vibrations were coursing from my skull to my toenails.

Aly was shaking her head. "That's not the Song, Jack . . ."

I could hear rocks sliding down the cliff now, splashing into the sea. Aly's face was blurry, and my legs felt jellylike, as if I were on a train or a surfboard.

She was right. This was bigger than finding a Loculus.

It was an earthquake.

CHAPTER TWENTY-THREE

THIS IS NOT SCIENCE

THE PLATE—THE INTERLOCKING stone shape we'd formed—was jumping on the ground with a life of its own. The earth was cracking in jagged lines, radiating outward from the plate like rays from the sun.

"That . . . thing is causing this!" I shouted. "Pull it apart—the seven!"

Torquin was already there, digging his stubby fingers into the stone. Cass, Aly, and I jumped in beside him.

"What are you doing?" Dad called out.

"Trying to stop it!" I said.

"Stop an earthquake?" Dad said.

It was no use. The stones were stuck together as if glued. Torquin panted and grunted, sending flecks of spittle onto the stone. Soon I felt the plate rising off the ground. I figured Torquin was lifting it, so I stood, stubbornly trying to pry the arrangement apart.

"Set it down!" Aly said. "This isn't helping!"

"Won't go down!" Torquin replied.

Now the plate was changing. The chipped edges were filling themselves in, straightening, forming a perfect rectangle. The stone itself was smooth to the touch, growing hotter.

I pulled my fingers away. The cliff and the sea grew blurry, as if a stone-colored curtain had been drawn across them. As I fell back, a network of countless arteries and veins shot outward in all directions from the plate, filling the space all around, exploding into sprays of stone-colored plasma.

"Get away from that!" I called out.

Cass and Aly jumped backward. Torquin held on a moment longer, but finally he sprang away with a howl of pain.

A wall was forming before us, not gas, liquid, or solid, but somewhere in between. Its depths and shadows roiled and slowly hardened, taking on the shape of columns, statues, reliefs. In the center of it all was the plate, the connected seven. Now it was suspended at chest level, embedded into an arched marble door carved with snakes, horses, and oxen. On either side, massive marble columns lined up, spreading outward like sentinels snapping to attention.

The walls themselves thundered, sending deep echoes into the soaring space they now surrounded. Above the columns, facing us, rose a triangular section that featured a relief of a four-horse chariot. I craned my neck to see a tapered roof taking form, topped by two humanlike figures bubbling and flowing until they took the solid shapes of a man and woman.

As the earth heaved I fell back into my dad. "What in heaven's name—?" he said.

Now the entire columned structure was rising upward, pushed toward the sky by a thick stone base the width of a city block. A wider, thicker base formed beneath that, and another, until the graceful marble building was sitting atop a layer cake of stone. At each setback, statues glared down at us—stern figures in robes, grand horses and woodland animals. Finally, right in front of us, a tremendous stone archway opened within the wall, and a wide set of stairs rippled toward us, kicking up a thick cloud of dust.

Cass, Aly, Torquin, Dad, and I turned away, coughing.

"Hee-hee-hee!" came a trumpeting laugh from the dust.

"This is not . . . a trick of light . . ." Dad said between coughing jags. "This is not explainable by science."

"No, it's not," I said.

Cass swallowed hard. "I was kind of hoping it would be."

"Haaaa!" As the dust began to settle, I could see the tiny, wizened figure of Canavar dancing in the cloud, coughing and laughing. "It was a seven . . ." Canavar wobbled on unsure feet, lurching toward the door. "By the chariot of Mausolus, it wast not an *M* but a seven! Hee! Hee-hee-hee! We have unlocked the Mausoleum at Halicarnassus from the earth itself! I shall be world famous! Book me a flight to Sweden to pick up my Nobel Prize! Oh, teedle-de-dee! I float with joy! I float!"

He was dancing, flailing his arms, jumping onto the stairs. The Mausoleum towered above him, dwarfing the small man.

"Someone . . . pull him back . . ." Professor Bhegad called out, but his voice was barely audible.

From the archway came a blast of bluish-white light. Canavar rose off his feet. His legs dangled for a moment as if shaking out the last moves of his dance. Then his body stiffened.

As if pulled by an invisible arm, he whooshed toward the open door.

"Floating was an expression!" he shouted. "Wilt someone help me!"

I jumped to my feet, but Dad pulled me back. "No, Jack, stay here."

Torquin, with a speed I didn't know he had, leaped forward and grabbed Canavar's ankle.

"Yeeeow, that hurteth!" Canavar screamed. He was parallel to the ground now, his head pointed toward the door, his leg firmly in Torquin's beefy hand.

"Will not let go of leg," Torquin said.

"Yes, but leg will rip from torso, head, and arms!" Canavar screamed.

The archway itself shuddered. From the depth of its blackness a jolt of lightning spat toward the sky, with a blast of sound that hit my ears like a punch. I tumbled backward. Torquin fell, unhanding Canavar.

The air in front of the archway began to lighten and swirl wildly, like a cloud of fiercely battling mosquitoes. It swelled and settled into a human shape. A woman.

She raised her arm and Canavar lifted upward until the two of them were face-to-face. She bellowed something in a language I didn't recognize, and Canavar replied, "Please, spare me! I am so sorry. This was an accident, you see!"

The woman's eyes flashed orange red. Canavar shot into the air, toward the roof of the building.

Aly and Cass drew close to my dad and me. Torquin jumped backward, shielding us with his body.

The woman stepped down the stairs. Her face was sunken and gray, and the skin seemed to be peeling off. Her hair, white, lifeless, and nearly as long as she was tall. She raised a finger toward us, more like a bone covered with papery skin. Her nail was black and curved like a ram's horn.

As her jaw began to work, she let out a voice that was like a scraping of pins against my eardrum.

"Is that," she said, thrusting her arm upward, "the best you could do?"

CHAPTER TWENTY-FOUR

FLYING ZOMBIE SKIN

GETTING HIT IN the eye with a piece of flying zombie arm skin is not super fun. The sting is as bad as the stink.

I tried to blink the tiny shard from my eye, which was watering like crazy. "Are you all right?" Dad asked.

"Answer my question—is that the best you can do?" the woman demanded. Through my one good eye I could see her descending the stairs in lurching steps, leaving tiny fragments of herself all around her. I couldn't decide if they were pieces of bone, sections of her raggedy toga, or very bad eczema.

"It is!" Aly blurted out. "Or it isn't. I don't know. Could you rephrase the question?"

As the creature moved forward, leaving a trail of

withered debris, her arm remained pointing upward. My eye was clearing now, awash in tears. I followed the angle of her skeletal finger to the top of the Mausoleum, where Canavar sat uncomfortably on one of the horses of the marble chariot.

"For a soul, you half-wit!" the woman replied. "Is that the best you could do for a soul? That shriveled prune of a human being?"

"I have hidden qualities, O Lady of the House," Canavar shouted, peering down from the marble horse like a gargoyle. "Which I shall be delighted to enumerate, preferably face-to-face. Or . . . face to what remains of thine. Thou wouldst not happen to have a ladder?"

The woman twirled her finger in a circle, muttering under her breath.

With a screech, Canavar shot up into the air like a torpedo. He fell toward us, arms and legs flailing. Torquin stood, rocking from side to side as he positioned himself underneath. Canavar landed in his grip silently, as if Torquin had caught a giant marshmallow.

"Touchdown," Torquin murmured.

"We mean no harm," Aly said, her voice shaky. "My name is Aly, these are Jack, Cass, Torquin, and Mr. Martin McKinley. Those people behind us are Dr. Theresa Bradley and Professor Radamanthus Bhegad. And you?"

As the woman lowered her hand, the skin peeled off her

165

pinkie, dropping to the stairs. I had to turn away in disgust. "I am Skilaki," she said.

"A beautiful name indeed," Canavar blurted out. "Lovely. Lyrical. My name is Canavar—Dr. Canavar, to be precise—and I owe you a great deal of grati—"

"My name means 'little dog,' and I despise it!" Skilaki shot back. "I was called Sibyl Seventy-three, which was fine with me, but our ruler wouldn't have it. Too many sibyls, she said. And what the Great Queen Artemisia wants, she gets. Now, if it is entry you seek, let us trade and be done with it. Artemisia does not like to be disturbed! But perhaps I can bring her a better specimen than this . . . homunculus. Caviar."

"Canavar," the shrunken man said. "And thou art so right. I am not worthy. My soul is parched and wrinkled—"

"Silence, dwarfling, or you return to the chariot!" Skilaki shouted.

I swallowed. Facing Skilaki was not easy. Her eyes seemed to float in their sockets, as if they might fall out at any second. I tried to control my trembling as I spoke. "We're seeking the Mausoleum at Halicarnassus," I said. "We just want to walk in, find something we need, and leave."

"And what is it you need, child?" Skilaki asked.

Cass and Aly looked at me in panic.

Did she know about the powers of the Loculi? I had no idea. I couldn't tip our hand. If she knew what we were

166

really after, and why, it could make our job harder.

"A . . . stone ball," I said. "Nothing of much importance. But we humans prize its beauty. We understand it was given to Artemisia many years ago. Maybe you can help us."

Skilaki looked at me blankly for a long second, then stomped her feet angrily. I turned away, not wanting to see any more peelings. "Do not talk to me of silly rocks! The queen. Requires. A soul. For entry."

"I have a feeling you don't mean *sole*, like a shoe," Cass said. "Or a fish. Because those we could do—"

Skilaki narrowed her eyes, releasing a few eyelashes to the ground. "You try my patience!"

Cass backed away. "Just checking."

"Okay, you take a soul from us, just say," Aly said. "What happens to that person after the soul is gone?"

"The soul enters a glorious state," Skilaki said. "Floating free of physical constraints. Absorbing knowledge and wisdom. Eventually, perhaps, finding a home in another body. The original body is freed also—freed of emotions and thought, able to function at the level of pure action, as would the most industrious of insects."

"So you're asking us for a volunteer to become a zombie?" I said.

"I do not know this word. I am merely a gatekeeper for Artemisia," Skilaki said. "Does this request cause a problem?"

"Of course it does!" Aly shot back.

"Then fare thee well," Skilaki said, turning her back to us.

As she ascended the steps, the entire Mausoleum structure vibrated. The ground shook again, and the walls began to fade.

"Oh, great, it's all going to disappear," Cass said.

I broke away from Dad and ran after her. "Wait!" I shouted.

"Jack, get back here!" Dad called out.

I could hear him running after me. I raced past Skilaki and turned, blocking her way to the door. "I want to see Artemisia," I said. "Tell her I'm . . . I'm a descendant of Massarym."

Skilaki nearly lost her balance. "You dare ask for—" She cut herself off, leaning forward. "Massarym, you say? Actually, there is a resemblance."

"Tell your queen we will consider giving her a soul, but only if she gives us the stone ball and safe passage back," I demanded.

From the baring of what were left of her teeth, I knew that yes was not in the ballpark. Skilaki took a step back and began raising her hand. "You have no power to bargain."

I could feel my feet leaving the ground. I turned, trying to wrap my arm around a column to keep from being flung into the air.

"Keep away from him!" Dad grabbed her arm. He tried to pull her back but only came up with handfuls of shredded skin and toga. I was lurching upward as if my body were being pulled by a curtain cord.

"Stop!" a voice called out. "I volunteer!"

Skilaki turned. Dad froze. I felt my legs jamming back onto the ground.

Far behind us, Professor Bhegad stood up from his wheelchair. With a strength I didn't know he had, he held his head high. "I will do it. I give my soul to the Lady Artemisia freely."

CHAPTER TWENTY-FIVE

A GAME MOST DANGEROUS

WE RUSHED TO Professor Bhegad so quickly he fell back into his wheelchair. "You can't do this, Professor," I said.

Professor Bhegad shook his head defiantly. "My children," he said in a hoarse whisper, "look at me. I don't have long to live. You cannot conceive the pain I have been through. Once I'm gone, I'm useless to you. Please . . . let my death help in the quest for the Loculi."

Dad looked at the old man in bewilderment. "You're willing to die for them?"

Professor Bhegad nodded. "I am willing to do what's right."

"We can't let you," Aly said.

"You wouldn't like the life of a zombie, Professor," Cass said.

"Skilaki," I said. "Please. Let us have a minute or so."

She rolled her eyes, and one of them slipped out of the socket. As it fell toward the ground, she caught it in her right hand and popped it back in. "I have all the time in the world," she said. "Literally."

"I did not see her do that," Cass said.

I raced down the stairs, gesturing for the others to follow. Torquin stepped behind Professor Bhegad's chair and fastened a seat belt around him. He bent his knees, gripped the handrests, and lifted the chair chest high. As Torquin walked carefully down the stairs, Bhegad placed his hand on the big guy's. "I will miss you, old friend," he said.

Torquin coughed. His face was extra red. As he set the old man down, he wouldn't look at us.

What would Professor Bhegad's death do to him?

What would it do to us?

I glanced at Bhegad. Behind his watery, bloodshot eyes was a strength as solid as the marble columns above us.

"Jack . . . ?" Aly's voice brought me back to the present.

"Here's the plan," I said. "We let her take him. But we act superfast. We get Artemisia to give us the Loculus before they actually do anything to him."

"This is crazy, Jack," Cass said. "What if they zombify him first?"

"Remember Charles Newton's message—'Where the lame walk, the sick rise, the dead live forever,'" I recited.

"Doesn't that mean the Loculus can restore life? We bring Bhegad back with us and use the powers on him."

Dad blanched. "Jack, this is playing with life and death."

"'Tis a game most dangerous for mortals," Canavar warned.

"I have everything to offer and nothing to lose," Professor Bhegad spoke up. "If I die here, the quest ends. I will have lived for nothing. If my sacrifice brings forth a Loculus, at least my life will have had some worth. Please. Let us take the chance."

He looked at each us deliberately, deeply. No one said a word. Torquin let out an uncharacteristic squeak that sounded like a gulp or a sneeze. He stared fiercely at the distance, blinking.

Bhegad took Torquin's hand. "My trusty helpmeet, despite our myriad differences, I believe I will miss you most of all. Shall we?"

The big guy nodded, his features dark and hollow behind the bristling beard. Silently he gripped the wheelchair and started up the stairs again.

"Dear lady," Bhegad called upward as strongly as his voice allowed, "I will give you my soul on two conditions. That you allow my friends to accompany me there. And that you promise them safe return."

"Entry is possible for all," Skilaki said. "Returning is not, unless . . ."

"Unless what?" Cass said.

The ex-sibyl's arm whipped forward, grabbing Cass by the chin. With a sharp twist of her wrist, she forced him to turn around and she gazed at the back of his head.

Her jaw dropped to the ground. Literally.

After picking it up and reattaching it, she said, "I have heard of the mark, yet this is the first time I have seen it. You, my boy, shall be allowed free passage."

"Because of the lambda?" Cass said.

"Skilaki, all three of us have it," I announced.

"Then by your marking shall you return," Skilaki said. "But no one else."

Dad stepped forward, gripping my arm. "You're crazy if you think I'll let you go in there alone. I'm his father!"

Professor Bhegad reached out and took Dad's hand. "He has to, Martin. You know this. You want your son to live. Choose my death, not his."

Dad opened his mouth to reply, then clamped it shut. Time seemed to stop for a long moment, as we all stared at him. Even Skilaki.

I felt his fingers waver. And then, slowly he loosened his grip. His eyes were desperate, filling with tears.

"Jack will come back," Torquin said softly. "Good training. Good genes."

Dad didn't say a word. Instead he wrapped me in a tight hug and told me he loved me.

173

I felt Aly's arm around one shoulder, Cass's around the other. As Dad let go, Skilaki turned to climb the steps to the black archway. "Delighted this ordeal is over. Now come. Leave your bags," she added, pointing at the backpack in which I'd hidden the Loculi.

"But . . . my bag has stuff I need," I protested. I was not keen on entering one of the Seven Wonders without any magical help at all.

Skilaki shook her head. "You need nothing inside. You bring nothing. And leave the rolling chair here. You will not need it, either."

Cass, Aly, and I shed our backpacks. I handed mine to my father as Torquin helped Professor Bhegad up from the wheelchair. I took his arm. It seemed bony and fragile inside his tweed coat. "'Once more into the breach,'" the old man murmured.

As we stepped toward the portal, a blast of white light hit me in the face. For a brief moment, before I closed my eyes, I could see Bhegad's face lit up like a screen.

He was smiling.

CHAPTER TWENTY-SIX

THAT'S GNIŻAMA

"WHOA, WHO TURNED on the black-and-white filter?" Cass asked in a low voice.

I turned, forcing my eyes open. I was too dumbstruck to answer. We were only three steps into the Mausoleum, but there was no Mausoleum. No marble ceiling, no grand tiled floor, no fancy walls.

I spun around. Our door—the one we'd come through with Skilaki—was gone. We were outdoors, in a dry, rubble-strewn field that stretched into a dense fog in all directions. It wasn't nighttime anymore, but twilight, and everything seemed drained of color, like a charcoal landscape.

"I was expecting a palace," Aly said. "Not the anti-Narnia."

Skilaki was walking ahead of us, on a path of gray soil flecked with patches of gray grass. I was supporting Professor Bhegad, who leaned on my arm as he took tentative steps forward. "Courage," he said.

"Skilaki, how far are we going?" I called out.

"As far as necessary," she replied.

Professor Bhegad loosened his hold. He was walking on his own. "Fascinating. It's some kind of underworld."

"Easy, Professor!" Aly cried, as she and Cass rushed to help.

"No, no, it's all right." He gave us a baffled look. "My chest feels significantly better."

"Really?" Cass said. "That's gnizama."

Aly glared at him. "No, it's not, Cass. It's weird. It's disturbing. This place gives me the creeps."

"Just trying to be"—Cass gulped as he looked around— "positive."

I felt my feet touching the ground, but all our footsteps were muffled, nearly silent. On either side of us were distant groves of leafless trees. Their gnarled black branches reached upward into a dull, dirty-white sky. I blinked my eyes, hoping to see it all clearer, but nothing changed.

Skilaki was slowing now. She stopped at a place where another path veered off toward the woods to our left. I couldn't help noticing there was no castle in sight, no trace of a building.

"Where's Artemisia?" I demanded.

"Impatience," Skilaki replied, "is meaningless in Bo'gloo."

"Is Bo'gloo another name for Hades?" Cass said. "Tartarus?"

"Hades and Tartarus, always Hades and Tartarus!" Skilaki shook her head, and I ducked to avoid a flying skin flake the size of a bookmark. "This obsession with mainland Greece! They are . . . related. But Bo'gloo has its own dreadful merits, as you will see."

"I haven't noticed any yet," Aly muttered.

Skilaki was studying Professor Bhegad. A strange smile twisted her withered lips. "You are called Radamanthus," she said. "You know, don't you, that Radamanthus was one of the three judges of souls who entered Hades?"

"Of course." Bhegad's eyes brightened. When he spoke, his voice sounded disturbingly eager. "Shall I meet my namesake today?"

Skilaki laughed. "Of course not! Radamanthus has no sway in Bo'gloo. Only Queen Artemisia."

"Wait," Cass said, "I thought she wasn't technically a queen— "

"She is queen here!" Skilaki shot back. "But let me explain all as I show you our home."

"You told us you would take Professor Bhegad to Artemisia," Aly said. "People are waiting for us. We don't have time to sightsee Bo'gloo."

"Time," Skilaki said, "will not be an issue."

I glanced at my watch. It was perfectly still, stuck at 3:17 A.M. I tapped it a couple of times. "It stopped."

Aly and Cass were staring at their watches, too.

"It is not the only thing that has stopped," Skilaki said. "I believe you were in great pain, Professor. And now?"

"Nothing," Professor Bhegad said. "This is remarkable."

Skilaki's papery lips drew upward like a tiny curtain, her smile revealing exactly four brownish-gray teeth. "Time, you see, is greatly overrated."

We continued to follow the old lady down the right-hand path, which veered off into a maze of twisted black trees. Ahead of us was a rushing sound, like the static from a car radio.

As I squinted into the distance, my foot wedged under a branch and I felt myself hurtling headlong into a tree. I put my arm out for protection—and I came face-to-face with a tiny, grinning skull.

I jumped away, screaming.

Skilaki slowly turned, her laugh a rhythmic *sss-sss-sss*. "Oh, dear boy, no need to be frightened," she said. "These are merely here to outline the path."

"You use skulls as markers?" I said.

"Paint works pretty well," Cass volunteered.

"Where would be the style in that?" Skilaki replied with a sigh. "But if you're offended . . ."

She snapped her fingers and the skull disappeared.

Aly grabbed my arm. "I hate this place, I hate this place, I hate this place."

As we followed Skilaki along the unmarked path, the distant noise grew louder, like a giant vacuum cleaner pressed into my ears. Soon I had to cover them with my hands.

"My dear sibyl, this noise is unbearable!" Professor Bhegad shouted.

Skilaki stopped at a clearing. She crouched, picking up a clot of soil flecked with pine needles, pebbles, and who knew what else. As she held it toward me, kneading it with her hands, it became rubbery and smooth, shrinking to the size of a vitamin pill. "Insert it into your ear," she said. "You'll be much happier."

"It's dirt!" Cass shouted.

"Give it to me!" Aly grabbed the little pellet and popped it into her ear. She dropped to her knees and dug out another clot of dirt. Quickly she repeated what Skilaki had done, massaging it with her fingers until the grains of soil and tiny twigs smoothed out. Then she inserted that one, too. "Whoa. It works. It feels like Styrofoam."

Cass, Professor Bhegad, and I wasted no time plugging our ears.

"Our natural materials," Skilaki explained, "are multi-purpose."

I couldn't believe it. The static noise was nearly gone, but Skilaki's voice was loud and clear. All of our voices were clear. Even our footsteps. Only the frequency of the river's sound seemed to be blocked.

Skilaki gestured into the clearing. "Proceed," she said.

As we cautiously stepped forward, the clouds thinned. I could make out the shape of what seemed to be an enormous river stretching into the thick grayness to our right and left. The opposite bank could have been a football field away or a mile—in this strange landscape, it was impossible to tell.

A silent current raged not two feet beneath us. It seemed weightless, a flow of silver streamers in midair, reflecting light and nearly transparent. It splashed against the steep banks and broke into a spray of droplets. I could feel them on my arms, tiny pokes with no sign of wetness at all.

I removed my plug—but only for about a nanosecond. The static noise was unbearable. "That's what's making the sound," I said. "The river water."

"I don't think that's water, Jack," Aly said, her voice unmuffled and clear.

I stepped closer and knelt by the edge of the bank. The river bottom was alive with movement. But not fish or seaweed. Bright images churned upward, bursting through the sand and mud—people, panoramas, views of villages and mountains in intricate, black-and-white detail. Some seemed harmless and dull, but others were impossible to look at. A gutted home, a screaming face, the twisted grille of a truck.

Aly let out a gasp. Or maybe it was me. I turned away, unable to watch any more.

"This is where you proceed on your own until we meet on the other side, which may be awhile," Skilaki announced. "I'd like to say it's been a pleasure, but I barely remember what pleasure feels like."

Cass's face was taut, his eyes wide. "You expect us to swim across that?"

"Unless you can walk on the top," Skilaki said.

"What is it?" Aly asked.

"The River Nostalgikos," Skilaki replied. "The Greeks have one like it, too, of course."

"I mean, what's the stuff at the bottom?" Aly said.

"Memories," Skilaki said. "The river feeds on them. Our guests arrive with sadness and broken dreams. Their thoughts eat at them for an entire lifetime. They may have an image of themselves they cannot live up to. Or hold a grudge. Or pine for a love that can never be. Nostalgikos makes you face your worst memories and realize how fleeting they are. And if you do face them, it takes those memories away, cleanses them completely."

"So . . . they stay at the bottom?" Cass said softly. "Like old Facebook posts?"

"Ah, but only if you give yourself to the river," Skilaki said. "Fight it, and the bad memories will consume you, like all diseases. I have seen it happen. So tragic. So useless."

"That's it?" I said. "You just wade through, drop the memory, and you're free?"

"Not free," Skilaki said. "All good things require a sacrifice."

Cass paled. "Sacrifice? Are we talking body parts?"

Skilaki gave a wet, rattling chuckle and drew forth a yellowing scroll from her pocket. "If we should become separated," she said, "this will help you reach Artemisia's palace."

Cass stared at it with intensity. I could tell he was memorizing it. I pointed to the river marked Photia, close to the center of the map. "Is this one a memory sucker, too?"

"The River Photia protects the palace," Skilaki said. "For those who have passed through Nostalgikos, who come to Artemisia with a true heart, it will allow safe passage. But if it senses intruders, it will destroy them. And you have no idea how difficult it will be for me to explain that to my queen."

"Wait, that's the sacrifice?" Aly said. "We have to approach with a true heart? Are we going to Artemisia or the Brothers Grimm? I mean, how can we be sure our hearts are true?"

"You cannot," Skilaki replied. "Photia will determine that."

"And if it makes a mistake, we're drowned in a flood?" Cass said.

"Photia is not a river of water," Skilaki said, turning to leave. "And neither is Nostalgikos. Remember, all of you must give in to Nostalgikos. Or the process shall not be complete. I shall meet you at the other side. I have a long path to the bridge. If, by some ludicrously unlikely chance, you should arrive first, wait for me."

"Why can't we take the bridge, too?" Cass pleaded.

Skilaki spun so fast a clump of her hair flew off. "If you

do not follow the rules, then you will not see Artemisia. You forfeit your promise. And there are consequences to that."

"Like what?" Aly said.

Skilaki turned away. "You will all share the fate of Radamanthus."

CHAPTER TWENTY-SEVEN

COLD FEET

CASS STOOD FROZEN at the side of the river, staring downward. "I can't."

"You were the one who wanted to do this," Aly reminded him. "Why the cold feet now?"

The face of a howling wolf rushed up from the sludgy bottom. Its teeth were sharp and bloody. "That's why!" Cass said.

"Those are just images, Cass," I said, putting my hand on his shoulder as if I weren't scared to my bones. Which I was.

"Hey," Aly said. "What would Marco do?"

Cass spun around. "He'd get us to the other side. He'd face down whatever is in there. And he'd do it with a smile."

"So let him be your inspiration," Aly said.

"I don't see either of you jumping in!" Cass shot back. "We can't do this without Marco. We fail without him. He's brave. Competitive. Fearless. All the things we're not."

Marco.

I'd been doing my best to forget about him. But Cass was right. It didn't feel the same. It hadn't, ever since he'd gone over to the Dark Side.

We needed him. Badly.

And for the first time, I was beginning to feel like we had a chance of getting him back.

"He is competitive," I said. "And right now, our side is winning. We have the Loculi. If there's any chance to get Marco to come back, this is it, guys. Make the Massa fail. Gain power. Continue with the mission of the KI. Marco wants to be with a winner."

Professor Bhegad nodded. "Wisely said."

"Okay, so who's going to lead us?" Cass said, looking at me. "You, Jack?"

"You must all lead," Professor Bhegad said. "Marco will follo-o-o-o-ow!"

His voice became a weak shout as he allowed himself to fall into the river. His body jittered like a scarecrow's, his hair waving like cobwebs in a wind and his glasses flying into the river.

I looked at Aly and Cass. There was no going back now.

I slid off the bank next. My legs made contact with the surface. Like water, it slowed my descent. Like water, it gave me a feeling of buoyancy.

But unlike water, the Nostalgikos felt tickly, like feathers. It flowed in bands of liquid silver, churning hundreds of moving images that boiled upward and sank. Some were minuscule and vague, others enormous and lifelike. I screamed and jumped away as a head the size of a medicine ball emerged directly below me. It rolled back, revealing thick eyebrows raised high into a sharply wrinkled forehead. A face emerged, oozing blood from one eye. Its nose was strangely twisted and its mouth wide open in a silent scream, framed by a matted silver-black beard.

I felt Professor Bhegad's hand on my shoulder. Cass and Aly were in the river now, too. Even though we were different heights, we were all chest deep in the not-water. I had no sensation of sinking, but I couldn't feel the bottom under my feet, either.

"I s-s-saw that face," Cass said. "I want to look for the bridge."

I took a deep breath. "These are images, that's all. Memories that belong to other people."

A severe-looking woman rose up from below, her hair tied back into a bun, a hairy mole on her left cheek. She wore a tight-necked tweed jacket and long skirt, and she tapped a yardstick in her hand.

You will not let this frighten you.

I reached out for the yardstick and felt nothing. My hand passed through the image, and the old woman plunged back downward and out of sight. "Harmless," I said. "Now, come on. Let's get to the other side. Swim. Wade. Whatever."

"Okay," Aly said, stepping toward the other side. "Okay . . ."

As I moved with her, I heard a phone ring. The river seemed to dissolve into whiteness before my eyes. Another image rose up, this one so big and encompassing that it blotted out everything else.

Our old cordless phone. Just the way it was, sitting by the desk in the kitchen. The ring jangles my whole body head to toe.

I'm eating mac and cheese and I nearly jump out of my chair. I hope it's Mom.

But Dad gets there first. He's excited, too. At first I'm mad, mad, mad. I wanted to talk. Then I step back and listen. When he says "Hello?" I get all excited again. My legs can't stay still. I'm dancing like a scratchy monkey. Like I have to pee.

And that's what I remember most. The dancing. The way Dad's face changes. The darkness. The words.

The news that tells me what has just happened in a place at the bottom of the world.

What does "crevasse" mean? I am shouting now. Screaming. WHAT DOES "CREVASSE" MEAN?

I wanted it to go away.

Every part of me, every nerve in my brain, was trying to dull the image, to shove it away, make it disappear.

"Stay with it . . ." Professor Bhegad was holding on to me.

Remember, all of you must give in to Nostalgikos. Or the process shall not be complete.

I had to do it. But the memory was killing me.

NO!

I had to take a break. Just a moment.

I would do it. I would try again and succeed. Just not now. I needed to gather strength.

Somehow I managed to turn my head, somehow I made myself stop seeing the phone, the kitchen, Dad's eyes.

Amazingly, the professor had found his glasses, but they were slipping down his nose. His face was twisted into a pained grimace. Next to him, Aly breathed hard, talking to herself, her eyes buggy and white. Cass was far ahead. I couldn't tell if he was crying or laughing. But I could only pay attention briefly. My own pain tore at my insides like wild horses.

Ahead of us, Cass let out a shriek that shocked me out of my own nightmare.

"Cass . . . Cass, my son, let it go!" Bhegad was releasing me, trying to wade toward Cass.

He was twisting side to side, chest high in the tinselly stream, his arms raised above the surface. "Let go, let go, let go, go, go!"

"It's an image!" Aly cried out. "Release it! Do not fight it, Cass!"

"I can't!" he said. "Get it away! Get it away!"

His teeth were bared now, his eyes enormous. Below him, a blotch of red slithered slowly toward him, taking shape along the river bottom.

I grabbed Cass by one arm and Aly took the other, but his eyes were fixed on the river's surface. "No . . ." he said. "Not you . . ."

"Jack, look!" Aly cried out.

A pair of yellow eyes burst through the surface, followed by a snout filled with knifelike teeth, and a pair of leathery wings that seemed to suck the stagnant air from around us.

A blast of putrid breath nearly knocked me off my feet.

The griffin was back.

CHAPTER TWENTY-EIGHT

LOST

MY EARPLUGS COULDN'T dim one decibel of Cass's scream. I could smell the griffin, hear its ugly cry, feel its heat. It sprang upward, lifting its talons like just-sharpened daggers above our heads. A spray of toxic spittle flew off to both sides as it opened its jaws.

Aly was yelling something. Cass's arms windmilled as he tried to backstroke away. I knew in that moment we were toast.

Fight it, and the bad memories will consume you, like all diseases. I have seen it happen . . .

Skilaki's words echoed in my head. This river was going to kill us if we let it. I took a deep breath, gulping down a blast of hot, rotten-meat air. I stared the griffin in the eye despite the fact that every twitching muscle in my body was telling me to jump away.

Instead, I opened my mouth and shouted the first thing that came to mind:

"I AM NOT AFRAID TO THINK ABOUT YOU!"

The second thing that came to mind was that I was an idiot. The talons were inches from my eyes.

I ducked. I felt the talons dig into my shoulder. Pain shot through me to my toes. I was rising upward, out of the river.

"It . . . didn't . . . work," I said through clenched teeth.

Cass grabbed my arm. "Let go of him, griffin!"

"The bird is your memory, Cass!" Aly shouted. "Not Jack's. Face it. Say something!"

Cass was shaking. "Uh. Uh. I will not forget and—"

"Mean it, boy!" Professor Bhegad croaked.

"I am not afraid to think about you!" Cass shouted.

The griffin faltered. Its talons loosened and I felt myself plunging downward. Cass was still shaking. Overhead the griffin seemed to bounce away as if it had hit a Plexiglas wall. It glared at Cass, growling and spitting, but it was fading from sight, losing color.

Professor Bhegad was shaking, staring at the bird creature. "Please no, please no, please no . . ." he murmured.

The griffin seemed to take strength from this. It did a roll in midair and came down on Professor Bhegad. The old man let out a scream as the beast dug its talons into his tweed jacket, lifting him clear out of the water. His lips were shaking, his eyes wide and bloodshot.

"It's his worst fear, too!" Aly said. "He was the first person the griffin attacked. It nearly killed him. He's not strong enough to do what Cass did."

"Tell it, Professor!" I said. "Find it in yourself!"

The old man was flailing miserably. The beast shrieked in triumph, carrying Bhegad toward the other shore like a hawk carrying a rat.

Aly and I began to run as fast as we could, our legs churning through the dense but transparent river. Cass was right behind us. In a moment the beast was nearly to the land. But its wings were faltering, its body losing altitude. Professor Bhegad's body lurched downward, and then fell back into the river.

We could see him struggling to stand, throwing his shoulders back, looking straight at the beast. From this distance we couldn't hear him, but the griffin was reacting, lurching backward.

It came across toward us again, barely keeping itself above the surface of the river. Its talons, legs, and body faded to black-and-white, a pencil cartoon of a beast. I held my arms wide and our bodies merged, the griffin and me. I could feel the beast passing through me like a wave of summer heat. It shimmered down my body, through the molecules of my legs, and into the sand below.

The obnoxious scraping of the river's static was delightful in comparison to the griffin's noise.

"I've got you, Professor . . ." Aly said as she lifted Bhegad off a boulder just below the river's surface.

We were just a few yards from the opposite bank now. Cass was just to our right, staggering along. "His glasses," he said. "They're missing . . ."

"Never mind that," Professor Bhegad replied. "They won't be much use to me where I'm going."

I helped Aly lift the professor out of the river and onto the land. The effort exhausted me, yet the minute I waded out onto the bank, it was as if nothing had happened. My body felt fine, even where the griffin had grabbed me. And my clothes were totally dry.

Professor Bhegad looked dazed. "Wh-what just happened?"

"Last I remember," Cass said, "Jack was shouting something about a crevasse."

I laughed. "A necktie?"

"It's a big crack in the earth," Aly said. "Wait. You don't remember that?"

"You know . . . your mom?" Cass said.

Mom . . .

Yes, it was all coming back. The ringing phone. The awful news. Dad's eyes . . .

Aly squinted at me, then turned toward Cass and Professor Bhegad. "Do you two guys have any recollection of . . . a griffin?"

"Like the mythological beast?" Cass said.

"At the Karai Institute, we believe it may not have been so mythological," Professor Bhegad said.

Aly stared at them in disbelief. "You called it up, Cass," she said, "out of the river. And both of you defeated it."

Cass's eyes widened. "Do I get a medal?"

"Okay, okay," Aly said, looking back over the river. "Let's figure this out. We know this river makes you forget bad memories, but you have to stand up to them first. For you, Cass, it was a griffin. It came. We saw it. We had an adventure with it in Greece. But that's been totally wiped out from your memory. And you, Jack . . . you don't remember the image of the phone call. You don't know that your mom . . ."

She looked at me and clammed up.

I knew in that moment she didn't want to tell me news I had forgotten. She didn't want me to know that my mom had died.

But I knew. I remembered.

I had not "lost" the bad memory at all.

"What about Aly?" Cass asked.

"I don't know. I remember everything, still." She grinned. "Guess it's because I'm not afraid of anything. Now where's Skilaki? She was going to meet us here."

I looked up to the shore and called the old woman's name. "Guess we'll have to climb up there," I said.

But Aly was leaning over the bank, gazing into the river. A pair of glasses bobbed on the glittery surface. "Hey, Professor, you'll be able to see again!" she said. "One second . . ."

She lowered herself back into the river and grabbed the glasses. As she tossed them up, Cass and I both reached out, but they plopped down onto the soil.

"Be glad Marco wasn't here to see that," Cass murmured. "Be very glad."

"Thank you, my dear . . ." As Bhegad scooped his glasses off the ground, his voice trailed off. He was staring at Aly, who remained in the river, standing motionless. Her mouth dropped open in an expression of unspeakable fear. "Jack . . . ?" she said.

I moved toward her, but a churning blur of red and white surged up from the river, inches from her.

Spinning like a basketball, a hideous clown face thrust through the surface.

I jumped back in shock. *A clown?*

As it bounced toward her, laughing, she let out a scream that made my hair stand on end.

* * *

"The figure of the clown has long been used to represent both horror and childlike joy," Professor Bhegad said as we walked along a wooded path, looking for Skilaki.

"Clowns scare me, too," Cass said. "Those painted smiles. Creepy. I don't blame you, Aly. I hated the circus."

Aly looked at him as if he had just spoken Mongolian. "What are you talking about?"

"Never mind," Cass said.

We had been walking at least fifteen minutes. Or what would have been fifteen minutes if time still worked. Aly had faced down the memory of the clown and promptly forgotten it. Cass had confronted the griffin. And so had Professor Bhegad.

But I could not shake the memory of that phone call. And the realization that I hadn't forgotten it.

What had I done? Did I totally screw up? Did I need to go back into the river?

It was the last thing I wanted to do. I was hardly consumed by the bad memory, which Skilaki had predicted. Maybe three out of four memory confronters were enough. We were here, after all. Alive and in one piece.

I looked around for the ex-sibyl. She had asked us to wait, but I couldn't bear the idea of staying near that horrible river. There was only one path away from it anyway. We couldn't help but meet Skilaki if we stuck to it.

Cass was leading us, but his pace had slowed. The trees had grown thicker, and the path was narrowing and overgrown. "Is it possible . . ." Professor Bhegad said, leaning against a tree, "that this is the wrong way?"

We stopped. Aly looked back the way we'd come. "Cass? Where are we headed?"

Cass glanced around. "Actually . . . I'm not sure. I lost the map in the river."

"Don't play games," Aly snapped. "You don't need it. You know the route."

"I did," Cass said. "But . . . it's not there, Aly. In my brain. I can't call it up."

"What do you mean, not there?" Aly said. "If you're being insecure again, like you were in Babylon, now's the time to stop."

Cass's eyes were hollow and scared. "I don't feel insecure. This is so strange . . ."

I looked at him closely. "Cass, can you say 'River Nostalgikos' backward?"

"Nostalgikos . . . River?" Cass said.

"Oh, dear," Professor Bhegad muttered.

"Cass, you had the ability to say anything backward, letter for letter," Aly said. "You called it Backwardish."

Cass swallowed hard. "Dishwardback?"

"The river . . ." Professor Bhegad said. "It took the ability from him."

"Skilaki warned us," Aly said softly. "She said the river required a sacrifice . . ."

"I thought she was talking about maybe giving up a

finger or a toe," Cass replied. "I didn't think I would lose the thing . . ." He trailed off, but I knew what he was going to say. The thing that made him Cass.

"Let's go back," Aly said. "We should have waited for her anyway. She said she'd take a while. Maybe she took some other route."

I took Bhegad's arm. "I'll help you if you're tired."

"I'm not," he said.

We began walking back the way we'd come, but after about fifty yards we came to a three-way fork. "I didn't notice this coming in," Aly said.

"The tines of the fork are slanted in the direction we came," Professor Bhegad said. "Easy to miss when you're going the other way."

"Let's split up," I said. "Aly takes the left, Cass the center, me the right, Professor Bhegad remains here. Count a thousand paces and then come back. And let's hope one of us sees the river."

As my two friends went off, I jogged onto the right-hand path. Almost immediately I could no longer hear their footsteps. The dull grayness of the woods made it hard to avoid roots and brambles, which lashed into my legs as I passed. They made pinpricks of blood that never turned into trickles. Even the blood was gray in the odd light.

The path meandered in many directions, and soon it became noticeably warmer. Overhead I heard a soft chittering sound and looked up to see a cloud of bats explode from a tree, swooping downward.

As I fell to the ground, covering my head, I heard a different sound, farther into the woods—a scuffling, a murmur that sounded nearly human. I stood. Through the twisted trees was a shifting of blackness, a movement of shadows. The air was brightening now into a dull silver, as if a gray sun were rising. "Hello?" I called out.

"Uhhh . . ."

The sound made me leap to my feet. My forehead was now bathed in sweat. Smaller shadows skittered through the woods, ragged-looking squirrels, moles, mice, all going the opposite direction from me, as if they were running from the day's first light.

I trudged onward carefully, until I reached the edge of a vast, dry field. It too swarmed with fleeing animals—and along the edges, in the surrounding trees, larger forms. Human.

But my eyes were focused on the forest beyond the clearing. There, a raging fire was licking up the trees like matchsticks. Its flames were ash gray, and it gave off a gray light that was frighteningly intense.

And it was headed my way.

I turned and ran. I didn't stop until I reached Professor Bhegad. He stood, dumbfounded, his eyes focused on the woods behind me. "By the Great Qalani . . ."

"The place is going up in flames," I said. "We have to get out of here. Where are Cass and Aly?"

"She warned us," Professor Bhegad said. "Skilaki. I should have known . . ."

The River Photia protects the palace. For those who have passed through Nostalgikos, who come to Artemisia with a true heart, it will allow safe passage. But if it senses intruders, it will destroy them. Skilaki's words clanged in my head.

"But she told us about a river," I said. "Not this."

"She also told us it wasn't a river of water," Bhegad said. "*Photia* is Greek. It means fire."

CHAPTER TWENTY-NINE

THE DOOR

BEFORE I COULD turn to run after my friends, Aly came racing out of the woods. "Guys," she said, "this path circles back to Nostalgikos. But we won't make it. The flames are moving fast. Where's Cass?"

I started up his pathway, but he was already coming into view, running toward us. "I think I found a way out!" he cried. "Hurry."

We followed Cass down the center pathway. I stayed with Professor Bhegad, helping him along. In about a hundred yards we reached an iron gate, which hung open on a rusted, broken hinge. Beyond it, a steep hill led upward to a windowless stone blockhouse. "What's that?" I called out.

Cass was already far ahead of us, jogging quickly toward

a distant clearing. We caught up with him at the edge. I looked out into a field of dirt, pebbles, dead vegetation. "Look closely," he said, his voice a little shaky. "Nothing, right? Now watch this."

He took five strong paces forward. Before him, a wooden door materialized out of thin air. Its brass doorknob was clearly golden colored, the wood a deep, polished brown.

"What the—?" I said.

"You should see what's on the other side," Cass said.

"A door in the middle of the air," Aly said. "Um, I think I'll stay here with Professor Bhegad."

"I'll go," I said, with a confidence I didn't truly have.

Cass took my arm. With his other hand he turned the knob to open the door. We both stepped through.

The air was like a blast of cold water. I was coughing, gulping oxygen, as if my lungs had gone into spasm. For a moment all I could see was a circular metal railing directly in front of us, and a cement floor at our feet. Nothing else. No fire, no trees, not a sign of the underworld.

"Take your time, Jack," Cass said. "You are not going to believe this."

From below I heard a loud mechanical farting noise.

Holding tight to the railing, I squinted outward. The austere gray of Bo'gloo was gone.

Totally gone.

In its place were the bright lights and narrow streets of

203

a city at nighttime. I looked across a panorama of roof-tops—brick buildings and water towers, radio spires and streetlights. A horn honked and music blared from an open window across the street. In the distance, between buildings, I could see a giant clock face that read 11:17, exactly four hours earlier than the time we'd entered Bo'gloo, back in Turkey.

The mechanical fart came again. Peering down, I saw a bright red double-decker bus pull away from the curb.

"Where the heck are we?" I asked.

"How should I know?" Cass said.

"You have to know—you're Cass!" I replied. "Oh, wait. Sorry, I forgot . . ."

"Hey!" a voice shouted from below. "What do you two hooligans think you're doing?"

It was an English accent. I forced myself to look closely at the surroundings now. At the clock face, which was immediately familiar.

"Cass," I said. "I think that clock is Big Ben. Which means we're in London."

"That's ridiculous!" Cass turned full circle, looking around desperately. "And, um . . . true." He froze as he faced the structure behind us. "Jack . . . look."

I turned, too. The door we'd come through was part of a massive wall decorated with columns. "It's a fake mauso-leum," I said.

Cass peered through the open door. "Bo'gloo is gone," he said in an awed voice. "There's just a stairway. It must go down into the main part of the church."

"Up there, mates!" the voice below was shouting now. "Two lads, in the spire of St. George's Church!"

The two-toned squeal of a British police siren echoed up the street. "They think we're vandals," Cass said.

He pushed me back through the door but I resisted. "Where are we going to go? If the stairs go down into the church, we'll walk right into them!"

"I don't know—we'll figure something out. Just go!" Cass said.

As we rushed through, Cass slammed the door shut. I felt around for a handrail, shifting my feet slowly so I wouldn't fall down any stairs.

But the cement floor had become soil. And the darkness was lifting.

Instantly the underworld formed around us in all its stifling dullness. Aly and Professor Bhegad were standing where we'd left them, and they stumbled backward, their eyes wide with shock. "What happened to you?" Aly said. "You disappeared."

"Quick," Cass said, taking Professor Bhegad's arm. "Come with me. We have an escape route. Another portal. We may be arrested, but it's better than staying here."

"Arrested?" Aly said. "Are you nuts? We can't just leave!"

205

"We'll die if we stay here," Cass replied, pointing at the flames that now were leaping across the field toward us. He pushed Professor Bhegad forward, and the door emerged from the gloom again.

Cass swung it open and he pushed Professor Bhegad through. "Let's get him to safety first."

The old man's scream was louder than anything I'd ever heard from him. A blast of white light seemed to grab him by the shoulders, pulling him away from the door and back into Bo'gloo like a giant fist.

He flew past Aly and would have collided with a stout tree if he hadn't been caught by two withered, bony arms.

"We must stop meeting like this, Professor," Skilaki said.

CHAPTER THIRTY

THE BLAZING FIELDS

HIS EYES ROLLING upward, Professor Bhegad slid downward to Skilaki's ankles, taking a shower of powdery skin with him.

"No see long time?" the old lady said calmly. "Is that your expression?"

"No. I mean yes. I mean, we're sorry for going on without you, Skilaki, okay?" I said. "We blew it. We made a mistake. We thought we'd find it on our own, but we just found—"

"You banked on Cass's superior memory, yes? Oh, how Nostalgikos loves superior memories." Skilaki cackled.

"You told us it only removed bad memories!" Aly protested.

"The Nostalgikos is a river," Skilaki said with a shrug, "not a surgeon. Its precision is famously uneven. You, however, were left with very specific instructions, and you failed. Quite a mess this is. Perhaps you don't realize what a responsibility I have to Bo'gloo. To the queen. Who do you think Artemisia will blame?"

"Skilaki, that is a portal!" Cass screamed, gesturing toward the blazing field behind us. "To London! We can escape the fire."

Skilaki sighed heavily. "You can." She pointed a gnarled finger at Professor Bhegad. "But not possessing the mark, he is not allowed to leave the underworld."

Professor Bhegad was writhing at Skilaki's feet, trying to get up. "Now," the ex-sibyl said, "you have a choice. You can escape and leave him with me if you like. He, after all, is our prize. Artemisia, however, is not known for her compassion. She will most likely allow the fire to consume the professor and me. But what do you care? You will be home again."

"Or?" Aly said.

"Or, you may follow me," Skilaki said.

She began walking up the hill directly behind us, drawing Professor Bhegad along as if he were a floating dog on a leash.

I looked at Aly and Cass. The flames of the fire were drawing nearer, and smoke twined around our nostrils. But

Skilaki seemed to know where she was going, and we really had no choice.

A plan was a plan.

We followed, trudging up the hill. The air seemed to clear the higher we got. In hushed tones, Cass and I explained to Aly what had happened beyond the portal.

She listened skeptically. "You went into the real world . . . through a replica of the Mausoleum?" she said. "That's . . ."

"Bizarre?" Cass said. "Uh, yeah."

Aly turned away. I knew the rabid look in her eyes. She got that way when she was in front of a computer, figuring out some impossible problem. "So if this replica is a portal to Bo'gloo, what's to say it's the only one?"

"Not following you," Cass said.

"Think about it," Aly said. "Plenty of Seven Wonders replicas exist in the real world. We saw tons of Colossus statuettes in Rhodes, key chains, whatever. And we read about the Mausoleum, too. The replica of the Mausoleum in England isn't the only one . . ."

"The municipal courthouse building in St. Louis!" Cass blurted.

"I can't believe you remembered that," Aly said.

"Maybe your memory talent is coming back," I said eagerly.

Cass shook his head. "No. That was just an ordinary bizarre factoid. I couldn't, like, tell you how to get there by car. I can still feel this sort of hole in my brain."

Aly put a hand on his shoulder in wordless sympathy.

"So there are other replicas, big deal," I said. "But there's no guarantee they're all portals to this place. And even if they are, how are we supposed to find them? And what do we do about the Loculus, and Professor Bhegad?"

Ahead of us, Skilaki had stopped. A blockhouse stood at the summit of the hill, grimy and windowless. It was a stone bunker, a nearly perfect cube. A wooden door lay rotted and splintered on the ground, leaving the entrance wide open.

Skilaki stepped inside, guiding Professor Bhegad to sit in an old, lopsided wooden chair. He looked dazed. Behind them was a long table full of glass tubes and accordion bellows and mammoth old-timey computer screens.

Aly's eyes widened. "Is this your control center?"

"Atop the highest hill, remote from the advancing fire," Skilaki said.

Aly sat a table, staring into the old monitor and sliding a thick coating of dust off the keyboard.

"Ha! It kind of reminds me of an Apple IIe," I said. "My dad took me to see one at a museum. It's like the most basic computational system around."

"Really quite an impressive arrangement, no?" Skilaki said. "Alas, the poor soul who controlled it has been taken from us. But cheery news! Here, my children, is where the ravages of Photia may be stopped."

"That thing controls the River Photia?" Cass said.

"Thank you, Skilaki," I said with a sigh of relief. "We'll take the blame for the fire. We'll tell Artemisia it was our fault."

"I should think so," Skilaki retorted.

Then, folding her hands in front of her, she stood there placidly—or at least, as placidly as possible for someone who was losing bits of flesh and hair right and left.

"Um . . ." I said after a moment. "So . . . how do you work this thing?"

She exhaled, sending a blast of putrid air across the room. "Dear boy, do you really suppose I can operate this object of bewildering complexity?"

Aly was moving the mouse around, fiddling with the keyboard. She stared at the black screen, where a glowing orange C:\> blinked steadily. "Um . . ."

"Oh, great," Cass said. "Too primitive for your super brain?"

"Just look at the file structure," I suggested. "The list of programs and data."

Aly turned to me. Her face was pale. "Yes," she said. "Of course. But I've forgotten how."

"Not funny, Aly," Cass said. "Look at my face. Do you see me laughing anymore? Don't freak us out."

"No, I mean it." Aly's lips trembled, as if she were about

to cry. "My mind is blank."

Cass groaned. "No . . . no . . . no . . . this cannot be happening . . ."

Professor Bhegad's face drooped. "Cass's directional ability, Aly's hacking skills . . ." he muttered. "The very meat of their G7W talents. Gone."

"Their worst fears are gone, too, no?" Skilaki pointed out. "You have to give to get."

"Then why is Photia coming after us?" Aly demanded. "We did everything right! We sacrificed the memories of what is most important to us." A tear slid down her cheek.

I swallowed hard. *Everyone's fears except mine.*

Before I could say a word, Cass spun around. "How can we get our memories back, Skilaki?" he said. "I want whatever I was afraid of. I want my whole brain. I'll figure a way out of here. Just show me the thing I was afraid of."

"It's a griffin," I told Skilaki. "He has no memory of it anymore."

"I do not know such a thing either," she said.

"A big red monster?" Aly said. "Half eagle, half lion, disgusting breath?"

"Greef?" Skilaki said. "You mean, the greef? You're saying it oddly."

"Wait, you have one?" I asked.

"The queen keeps one, of course," she said simply, turning her back to us, "to guard her possessions."

Aly shot me a glance. Griffins guarded Loculi. That was their whole reason for being. And it seemed Skilaki didn't know a thing about the Loculus's true function.

If we could find the griffin somehow—and get past it without being devoured—we would get what we needed. And Cass might get his ability back.

"We want to see it," Aly said. "Maybe the queen can show us—"

"As you wish." Skilaki stepped outside the bunker, reared her head back, and let out a cry so loud and shrill that the hair stood up at the back of my head.

"Wait, not right now!" Aly called out.

"Children . . ." Professor Bhegad said, his face taut with fear, "I feel it. The fire."

I could feel it, too. The room was becoming hotter. From the baseboards, smoke began rising in black wisps.

"Out of here!" I shouted. "This place is about to go up in flames!"

Cass ushered Professor Bhegad toward the bunker entrance. I pulled Aly out of her seat by her shirt collar. We bolted outside and collided with Skilaki, who was still looking up at the sky. The acrid smell of burning wood seared my nostrils and I put my hand over my mouth, trying to edge down the hill. Aly was holding my arm and Professor Bhegad was coughing uncontrollably.

Above us I caught a flash of red. The griffin's

unmistakable screech pierced the night air, through the crackling sound of the advancing fire. I craned my neck to see the beast flying jerkily, its wings tinged with fire, its giant beak open wide.

I went to help Bhegad walk down the hill, but my hand never reached him.

With a bone-shattering boom the bunker exploded, blasting us off our feet.

CHAPTER THIRTY-ONE

VASILISSA

"WHAT IS THAT thing?" Cass screamed.

My eyes flickered open. I had hit the ground hard. Cass had landed a few yards to my left. The griffin was thrashing crazily in the scraggly bushes just beyond him. Its awful screeches felt like blows to the head. Above us, the building was a pile of stones and smoke. The fire surrounded the hill now, raging toward us. There wasn't anywhere to retreat but toward the griffin.

"It's a griffin, Cass," I shouted back. "One of these things took you from the KI to Rhodes. It nearly killed you!"

He stared at the beast in utter horror.

"By the great Qalani, just take me now," Bhegad groaned. "I can't endure this."

Skilaki stood wearily, her wispy hair drafting upward as the fire neared. "You asked to see the greef," she muttered, "and not so much as a simple thank-you."

The beast turned to face us, its yellow eyes and red body the only color in the gray forest. It had managed to smother the flames on its wings, which were now edged black with soot. As Cass stood and faced it, the griffin bellowed in anger.

"I left you," Cass said, staring at the red lion-bird. "I left you at the bottom of the river."

"He's remembering!" I said.

"This thing . . ." Cass said. "Yes. I do remember. I do. It nearly killed me. Twice. The second time . . . was the river. Took part of me with it. To the bottom. My memory. My ability. It wasn't fair!"

The griffin snorted, sitting back on his furred haunches. It cocked its head at Cass, baring its teeth.

Cass stared for another minute. Then, to my astonishment, he bared his teeth right back.

The griffin jerked its head away, looking startled.

"What is he doing?" Aly whispered.

"I don't know," I muttered, "but it looks dangerous." Aly and I ran to Cass, grabbed him from behind, and pulled him toward us.

"I remember it!" Cass shouted, stumbling along the path at our side. "And I'm not scared of it anymore!"

216

"Remind me to give you a medal," Aly said. "If we live."

We nearly collided with Skilaki, who was staring at Cass. "Very curious," she said. "This boy's memory is not quite human, I suspect." Then, turning toward the griffin, she trilled: "Greef, *metaphero aeroporikos eis vasilissa!*"

"What does that mean?" Cass cried out.

"How should I know?" I said.

Professor Bhegad was saying something, but I couldn't hear him. The griffin reared back and let out a scream. Beating its wings downward, it lifted itself on red-furred haunches, revealing legs as tautly muscled as a lion's. It was coming for us.

Quickly I draped one arm around Professor Bhegad's shoulder and dug the other under his legs. He felt bony and brittle, and by now he weighed little more than a child. "Run!" I called out. "Now!"

"No . . ." Professor Bhegad said. "We can't . . ."

"Yes, we can!" Aly replied. "Or that thing will eat us!"

With a thrust of its wings that sent a gust of hot wind our way, the griffin leaped.

We raced back down the hill, away from the fire. The griffin's shriek pierced the air. I felt its talons dig into my shoulders. Again. I tightened my grip on Professor Bhegad—partly not to lose him, partly to deflect the pain. "Help . . ." I shouted through gritted teeth.

The griffin yanked me upward so hard I thought it

would rip my shoulders off. As my feet left the ground, I clasped my fingers as tightly as I could under Professor Bhegad.

Aly and Cass raced toward me, grabbing at my leg, trying to pull me down to the ground. "Don't—I'm going to drop Bhegad!" I cried out. "Grab . . . Tweety's . . . leg!"

I could feel them both reaching upward, wrapping their fingers around the beast's ankles. The pain of the talons had taken over my body, pushing every nerve fiber beyond its limits, pushing me beyond thought and feeling. I could hear Cass and Aly yelling. I could sense the heat from below, washing upward in waves. But I felt nothing, sensed nothing, as if they were in a dream, shut away from reality.

I held tight. The professor was slipping. I concentrated every thought on my fingers, on locking them like magnets.

"*Vasilissa!*" Skilaki called, as if in another realm. She was floating beside us under her own power. And with considerably less pain.

"Is she telling the griffin to kill us?" Cass demanded.

"*Vasilissa*," Bhegad said, "means 'queen.' She is telling it to take us to Artemisia."

We were dropping now. With the downward motion, the professor felt lighter in my arms. A dry, stagnant coolness wafted up from below. I blinked, forcing my eyes open.

We plunged toward the central, open court of a sprawling stone castle. Its crenellated towers were cracked and broken, its battlements empty, its walls overgrown with scraggly vines that had sprouted between its bricks. Just outside its walls lay piles of bones and rotting carcasses, in a narrow ring of soil that served as a bank to the River Photia. The so-called river, I realized, was actually a wide moat of raging fire that ringed the castle.

In a moment the castle walls blotted out my view. My eyes quickly took in the center court's cracked, crumbling walls, festooned with flaming sconces. I felt my feet jam against the hard soil. The griffin loosened its grip and I tumbled away. I felt as if knives had been jammed into my shoulders, and I must have been screaming, because Aly was holding me tight. "You're going to be okay, Jack," she said. "We're here. Everything's working out."

Blinking my eyes, I looked upward into Skilaki's face. She was shouting commands at the griffin, which retreated on its coiled legs, chittering, until its flanks hit the castle's inner wall.

Professor Bhegad was facedown in the hard-packed dirt. I turned him over. His eyes were shut, his mouth open, his chest still. The flames from a wall sconce sent eerie dancing shadows across his face.

I tried to remember a junior CPR class I'd taken with my dad. Kneeling over the old man, I dug the heels of my hands into his chest. One-two-three-stop . . . one-two-three . . . Cass and Aly knelt beside me.

One-two-three . . .

"Pkachh!" Bhegad let out a violent cough, his eyes bugging open. "My boy, you are hurting me!"

I sat back as he struggled to sit up. Aly was hugging the old man, and I leaned toward Cass, who put his arm around my shoulder. "Good work, Jack," he said.

Our relief lasted only a few seconds, interrupted by a deep, echoing boom behind us.

We turned. A half-rotted wooden door had smacked open, crashing against the castle's inner wall. Splinters flew into the courtyard.

The open door revealed a portal of total blackness. Two pairs of eyes slowly emerged, white as golf balls, as if the irises themselves had been bleached away. As they came closer to the portal, moving steadily up and down, gaunt faces appeared around them.

I heard a sudden choking sound from Cass. I wanted to hurl, too. Two men trudged out of the darkness, dressed in rags and harnessed to a wooden yoke like oxen. Their skin was flaked and shredded, their scalps scraped down to the skull in spots. Hair sprouted in odd places like random loose wires, and neither of their mouths had lips. They grunted and drooled, pulling a pair of chains attached to a giant chariot that creaked on broken wheels.

"I don't like this at all . . ." Aly murmured.

"Zombies," Cass said. "I hate zombies."

The chariot was an ornately carved wood cabin on a frame of four rickety wheels. Draped around the cabin was a curtain of dingy gray fabric. From inside, a voice shouted something in an unintelligible language.

"Unngh," replied one of the two creatures of burden.

A hand reached out of the curtain and snapped a long, leather whip hard against the zombie's back.

I winced, but he didn't seem to notice.

Out of the cabin stepped a tremendous figure, a man so large that the entire vehicle seemed to lift off the ground as he stepped off. He didn't appear to be a zombie, but that's not to say he looked like a normal human, either. His skin had a strange rigidity, as if it was actually some weird kind of plastic. His chin had chins, and you could hide small kittens in the rolls under his eyes. He lumbered toward us, leaning on a jeweled bronze staff, whose handle was a small alabaster replica of the Mausoleum. His mouth was pushed into a kind of grin by the pressure of the flab underneath it, but his eyes were dull and cold as he looked at us.

"They speak English, Mappas," Skilaki said.

The man called Mappas didn't say a word, but held out his palm toward the cabin.

From out of the curtain came a slender hand that was dwarfed by the big man's. A woman emerged, with thick silver-white hair that spilled over the shoulder of a flowing golden gown. Its hem was ripped in places, but its

221

embroidered pattern was festooned with jewels. The woman's ankles were thin, and the skin on her face was dry, seamed and puckered like a walnut. She seemed withered and ancient, but compared to the zombies around her, she was the picture of health.

"Bow all to Queen Artemisia!" bellowed Mappas.

I looked at Cass and Aly, who shrugged. We were already on our knees so we bowed from the waist.

As her wrinkled lips curled upward, she sucked in a breath and clasped her hands together. "Which one of you," she said, "is mine?"

CHAPTER THIRTY-TWO
THE TRADE

I THOUGHT ZOMBIES weren't supposed to have emotions, but judging from the increase in drool, the two cabin pullers seemed pretty excited. "Miiiine," one of them echoed.

Or maybe it was "maaa" or "mooo." With zombies, it's hard to tell.

I stood to face Artemisia, which was no easy task. She was much better maintained than Skilaki, but her skin was as stiff and wrinkled as tree bark, and it creaked when she spoke. Eyelashes had been painted above and below her lidless eyes, giving her a look of permanent surprise. "Well?" she said, her voice like the cry of a dying seagull. "Speak or I shall take you all!"

I tried to say something, to explain our mission, but my lips were dry.

"I . . . am yours, my queen," Professor Bhegad said softly, struggling to his feet. "I offer my soul to you in return for a favor."

"These three have the mark of Qalani on the back of their heads," Skilaki interrupted. "They have the ability to leave, and they shall. But they require a certain . . . stone orb in exchange for this soul."

"The stone was left in your keeping," I said, "by our ancestor—"

"You were not asked to speak, wretched child!" The queen stepped forward. Her legs wobbled like matchsticks, but she held her chin high. "Am I to understand that you dare attempt a bargain with Queen Artemisia?"

"Boof! Boof-boof-boof!" bellowed Mappas, his body quaking with laughter. The force of his breath blew out the flame on the wall sconce nearest him.

"Silence, useless vizier!" Artemisia cried, and the man snapped to attention. She stepped closer to Bhegad, her eyes growing wide. "Do you imagine that I have any shortage of souls? That your meager corpus would satisfy me so that I would agree to a deal like this? Or are you cleverer than you seem, with some other offer for the ruler of Bo'gloo?"

One of the zombies began bowing and grunting. The

other looked at it in momentary confusion, then picked its nose.

"Trainees," Artemisia explained, shaking her head wearily.

"All three of them—Jack, Aly, and Cass," Professor Bhegad said, "are descendants of the great Massarym."

It rankled me to hear the name Massarym mentioned in the same breath as *great*, but I knew what Bhegad was getting at. And it seemed to have an effect on Artemisia. As hard as it was to see any expression on that leathery face, she seemed kind of impressed.

"Really?" she said, extending a bony finger toward my chin.

It took all my willpower not to jump away. She lifted my chin gently and pushed my head to the right, turning me around. "I see the mark. And, yes, the jawline is similar in this one. As for the others . . ."

"Show them," Professor Bhegad whispered.

Both Aly and Cass turned to reveal the backs of their heads. "Mine's covered with hair dye," Aly explained. "But if you look close at the roots, you can see it growing in."

Artemisia let her finger drop. She eyed Aly and Cass for a moment, and then slowly stepped backward, without turning from us. Mappas whispered something in her ear. He seemed to be giggling, but it was hard to tell because of the permanent uptwist of his mouth.

She nodded, waving him away. As she stepped forward again toward Professor Bhegad, he stood slowly. "Well," she said, "as my Skilaki, my dear pet, my lapdog, has no doubt told you, I do not believe in one-sided arrangements. As you are descendants of Massarym, I can accept an exchange that will be satisfactory to us both."

Artemisia came nearer. Even in her wrinkly state, she towered over Bhegad. Her thin lips pulled back, revealing sharp, gray teeth. I eyed the doorway to the palace. Was that where the Loculus was? Would she actually give it to us?

Her words hung in the air, odd and unreal, like a mirage in a desert. "Wait. Did you just say yes?" Cass said.

"The boy does not understand me," Artemisia snapped, "yet I speak English to him!"

"He expresses joyous disbelief, my queen," Skilaki replied.

Artemisia snapped her fingers "Mappas! Bring them what they asked for!"

The vizier waddled an about-face. Leaning on his bronze staff, he huffed and puffed into the doorway. "Thank you, merciful Artemisia," Professor Bhegad said softly.

As she eyed the professor, her gray cheeks gained color, first a pale amber and then a warm brick red. "Your speech is courtly. It excites me to gain a worthy soul. An educated man, are you?"

"Archaeologist," Bhegad said. "I taught at university.

Made many discoveries in the field."

Artemisia seemed to shiver with joy, and I felt my stomach churn.

To her, the thought of the professor's death was fun. "What will you do with him?" I asked.

"His soul will reside here for as long as it pleases me," Artemisia replied. "I will learn from it, take life from it. When I am through, I will release it to roam the Cavern of Souls, until the day when, or if, it is placed in another body. In exchange, the professor himself—that is to say, his body—shall live eternally. If he is lucky, I will give it fine labor in the palace. I am growing weary of Nine and Forty-one."

One of the two zombies, hearing his number, began braying and snorting. The other was digging a large glob of wax from his ear and hadn't heard the remark.

"You'll turn him into a zombie?" Cass blurted.

"I don't know that name," Artemisia snapped. "My Shadows do not have names."

"You call them Shadows?" I said. "They look pretty solid to me."

"Here, perhaps, but they take on a more . . . diaphanous appearance . . . when they wander the upper realms." Artemisia flicked her fingers impatiently. "But I am not here to explain the mysteries of Bo'gloo to you. I am hungry for a soul."

"A moment, dear queen," Bhegad said. He turned to us, lowering his voice: "Do not protest, dear Aly. Trust Jack's plan. Take the Loculus and return home, even if it must be without me. I am not long for this world. Urge your father to the Karai cause. Contact the rebels on the island. Three out of seven Loculi is tremendous progress—"

"But we can't just leave you," I protested.

"You have no choice!" Bhegad insisted.

"Enough!" Artemisia screamed. "Are you plotting to challenge my simple request?"

Bhegad spun around. "No, indeed. My apologies."

Leaning on his staff for support, Mappas emerged from behind Artemisia, holding a large, round canvas bag that was dwarfed by his torso. "Here, my queen," he snuffled. "As you wish. Ur, wished."

The Loculus . . .

I ran for it, but Artemisia raised a hand and I felt myself flying backward. I landed hard on my butt.

The griffin, still huddled against the wall, perked up its ears.

"First things first," Artemisia said. "Come forward, Professor Bhegad. Alone."

Professor Bhegad squeezed our hands. "I have faith in all three of you," he whispered. "I always will."

Aly was the last to let go. She was crying.

Holding his head high, Professor Bhegad strode on

wobbling legs to Artemisia.

She raised a hand to his shoulder and touched him. For a long moment nothing happened, and I held a small hope that Bhegad was battling her, resisting in some way. But when a bolt of bright white light exploded from his chest, we all screamed.

The blast shot upward and Bhegad cried in agony, crumpling to the ground.

I ran to the professor, knelt beside him, and turned him over. His eyes looked past me to the gray sky, his glasses shattered on the ground beside him. His chest was still. Aly began pounding it, CPR-style.

"No, Aly," I said, pulling her away.

Aly's eyes were desperate. "He's dead, Jack!"

Dead.

I knew it, but I couldn't believe it. I stared into his lifeless face, immobile. Unable to think.

"Remember the p-p-plan," Cass whispered. He looked toward Mappas, who was still holding the sack. "Let's get the Loculus now."

I heard a hawklike shriek. Artemisia had reared her head, her silver-white hair flashing gold and red. Her wrinkled skin smoothed and glowed with youth. Aly, Cass, and I sat back as if blown by a hot gale. Artemisia rose into the air, turning slowly. For a long moment she seemed to float like an angel, a smile of ecstasy on her regal, beautiful face.

She was young and golden, her skin radiant, her feet and hands delicate, her gown bejeweled.

"She's feeding on his soul . . ." Aly murmured.

Below her, Mappas swung the canvas bag like a shot put. With his piglike grin, he sent the Loculus soaring over our heads. It bounced off the inner castle wall and dropped to the ground.

Cass and Aly were too stunned to do anything, but I broke away to the bag and fetched it back. As I held it to them, I could see they were both in tears.

"Let's do it," I said, reaching into the bag. "Let's revive him now!"

The Loculus was rougher than I expected it to be. Heavier.

The bag dropped away and my knees buckled. In my hand was a round, polished globe. It looked like marble. As I stared at it, my ears rang with the silence.

No Song of the Heptakiklos.

The thing in my hands was not a Loculus.

CHAPTER THIRTY-THREE

IT IS GOOD TO BE BEAUTIFUL

MARCO WAS GONE, but a part of him must have been inside me, because I hurled that rock like a baseball. It flew toward Artemisia, bashing her in the right arm. Mappas was on top of me in a nanosecond, yelling into my ear and pushing me across the courtyard.

"She tricked us!" I yelled back into his slablike face.

Artemisia's arm circled lazily in the air where I'd hit it, as if she were underwater and it had brushed against a fish. Turning blissfully, she began to descend. If she noticed the hit, she showed no signs of it.

Cass retrieved the rock from where it had fallen. His face was streaked with tears. As he, Aly, and I closed in on the descending queen, Mappas plopped himself into our paths, ordering Nine and Forty-one to flank him on either side. The Shadows slobbered and grunted, shuffling into place.

"Thank you, my loyal and fearsome protectors, but I shall face the children myself," Artemisia said, "to personally offer my gratitude."

Mappas merely grunted, pushing the two Shadows aside with his staff and then waddling away.

Artemisia smiled at us through a face we'd never seen before, her skin silky, her cheekbones high, and her eyes dark and probing. Her once dry, silvery hair was lustrous and wild, and as she strode toward us, Mappas followed with a brush, fussily combing out the tangles. "You see, my darlings, what a service you have provided to me," she said, flashing a radiant smile. "The sight of my face no longer repulses you, yes? It is good to be beautiful. This will not last forever, of course. But for the fleeting enjoyment, I thank you."

"You're a murderer," Aly yelled, "not a queen!" She sprang toward Artemisia, but a flick of the queen's right index finger sent Aly flying backward.

Cass and I ran after her, picking her up off the ground. "You lied, Artemisia," I said. "You didn't live up to your end of the deal."

For a moment the queen's eyes flashed with amusement. "You asked me for a stone orb. I gave you a stone orb. One of the handsomest I have."

Cass and Aly looked at me, speechless.

"Artemisia, there's been a misunderstanding," I said quickly. "Our ancestor, Massarym, left something of much greater value than this. We call it a Loculus. That was the stone we wished to have. Not this one."

Artemisia let out a long, flutelike laugh. "Take this one, my dear, deluded child. For I cannot give you something I do not have."

"What do you mean?" Cass said. "This place was put here to protect the Loculus. It must be here!"

"But it isn't," Artemisia said with a shrug. "It was stolen ages ago."

"You're lying!" Aly cried out.

Artemisia glared at her. "I built this magnificent structure," she hissed. "All I wanted was a peaceful afterlife for myself and Mausolus. I did not plan to become mother to this vast wasteland. To these bloodless, brainless children. I did not expect to reign over fires, rogue memories, and vengeful souls. This was all thrust upon me by your uncle Massarym. Do you think I care about protecting his silly toy? Good riddance to it!"

Breathe. I could barely see straight. Professor Bhegad was lying dead on the ground. No. Mappas was dragging the body away into the blackened archway.

My plan had failed. Bhegad was gone for good. His death was on my shoulders.

Soldier, Sailor, Tinker, Tailor. That was what Professor Bhegad had called us. Marco the strongman. Cass the navigator. Aly the fixer. Me? I was the one who supposedly "put it all together."

He was wrong. I had managed to take everything apart. I was no Tailor. I was a Killer.

"We will find that Loculus," I said. "And I will not rest until I make you pay for what you did to Professor Bhegad, Artemisia."

"I acted exactly as our deal required me to," Artemisia said. "It appears you are the ones not living up to our agreement. So, yes, I agree, you will not rest. Because you will be quite busy here as part of the army of Shadows. In eternal service to me."

With an unearthly howl, she turned back toward the palace. Nine and Forty-one began jumping up and down, snorting and slavering. The queen nodded at her vizier, Mappas, who let out a piercing whistle into a dark archway that led into the castle.

In the blackness, more pairs of eyes appeared.

Aly, Cass, and I gripped each other's arms as Artemisia's army of the dead began crowding into the courtyard. They knocked one another down and stepped over the bodies, unable to coordinate their own movement as a group. They spat and bit and howled, scratching at each other, scratching themselves. They lurched toward us with open toothless mouths and silver-white eyes.

Artemisia stood to the side and laughed as if the whole thing were a comedy act, her hands clasped together. We backed away, too stunned to talk.

The griffin let out a fearful, high-pitched squeak I'd never heard before. It was unfolding its wings, preparing to fly.

Cass spun around. With a strength I'd never heard in his voice, he shouted, "Stay!"

The beast's wings drooped. It lowered its head toward Cass.

"Come on!" Cass shouted, running toward the beast. "Grab its legs!"

We followed close behind. "How did you do that, Cass?" Aly asked.

"This thing owes me," Cass said. "For what its cousin did to me in Greece."

Cass and I dived for the red beast. He grabbed on to its tail and began climbing its back, grabbing hunks of fur. I clutched its left leg just above its talons.

The griffin was twitching anxiously. Cass was settling himself up on its back. Aly reached for its right leg, but it kicked her away. She stumbled backward—toward the approaching mob of Shadows.

"Whoa, easy . . ." Cass patted the beast's flank until it seemed to calm down. Then, carefully, he held his hand down toward us.

Aly caught her balance and darted forward. But as she reached for Cass's hand, one of the Shadows seized her arm, yanking her back.

Wrapping one arm around the griffin's leg, I reached out and managed to grab Aly's hand. We locked fingers. "Hang on!" I said.

Aly was sliding backward. "I can't!"

The Shadow was pulling hard, shaking Aly from side to side, yelling in a garbled voice: "Orrrrrmm."

Above me, I could hear Cass talking to the griffin. "Steady," he said. "Those zombies are more afraid of you than you are of them . . . 'attabeast . . ."

The griffin snorted. My fingers were greasy and sweaty. I felt my grip slipping.

"Jack, pull her up—I don't know how long I can keep it calm!" Cass said.

Aly screamed. Another Shadow reached for her leg, colliding into the first Shadow with a confused groan.

Above us the griffin shrieked, pumping its legs, trying to kick us off. "Hold on, Aly!" I cried out.

"I'm trying!" she screamed.

I felt her fingers slide out of mine. A cry ripped up from my toes and torched through my throat.

Aly was disappearing into a throng of hooting, drooling dead. The last thing I saw was her outstretched right hand.

CHAPTER THIRTY-FOUR

SHADOWS ON FIRE

"GET HER!" CASS shouted. "I'll worry about the griffin!"

I didn't need the prompt.

Letting go of the griffin's scaly leg, I ran into the mass of Shadows, following the sound of Aly's cries. As they turned to attack, I gritted my teeth. The Shadows were strong, but not quick. One of them grabbed my shoulders, and I lowered my head, butting it sharply in the nose.

Its head dislodged from the neck, hanging at an odd angle. It staggered away from me, letting go. As it careened against two others, they all fell like dominoes in a spray of shattered flesh and bone.

I saw Aly in a circle of slavering, moaning undead. She leaped and spun, uncorking a kick into one of her attackers.

Its hip snapped in half. As she fell to her side and rolled in the dirt, two other Shadows smashed into each other above her head.

I leaped over them and took her arm. "Wow, what has gotten into you?"

She looked as surprised as I felt. "I don't know. G7W? I'm Marco-ing out."

The Shadows were pouring out of the archway now, outnumbering us. Aly slipped away from me, and I lost her in the crowd.

Above me, Cass screamed something I couldn't make out. I glanced up. He was holding tight to the griffin, gesturing desperately toward the wall, where a sconce blazed brightly.

I grabbed the chalicelike fixture, ripping it out of the cracked stones. "Aly!" I shouted, lunging into the crowd, swinging the fire left and right.

Out of the crowd, Forty-one slumped toward me. I thrust the flame toward it, thinking I'd scare it away. But the zombie's hand passed directly into the fire. Sizzling, the skin fell away in charred flakes. No flinch of surprise, no gasp. Instead, with a curious grunt, Forty-one stooped to pick one of the pieces of flesh off the ground and eat it.

Gross.

I whirled around, my eyes frantically scanning the mob of dead things until I spotted Aly. She was on the ground, thrashing and yelling. It took five Shadows to drag her toward the doorway. I screamed again, swinging the sconce wildly. It collided with Forty-one's head. A clump of hair went up in flames, spreading around the zombie's face and leaping onto its ragged clothes. Forty-one began shaking uncontrollably, consumed by the flames. Other Shadows took notice, turning to look. They followed Forty-one's shimmying body as it hopped around. A couple of them raised their palms as if warming them at a campfire. Soon another Shadow was on fire, and a third. They were all in a froth now, drawn to the commotion and the brightness.

"Stop him, you idiots!" came Artemisia's voice, piercing through the din.

Where was Aly? I'd lost sight of her. I backed away, trying to see. I held the sconce in front of me, both as a light and a weapon.

As I circled around the mob, I felt a blow to my neck. My air was instantly cut off, as if my windpipe had been surrounded by an inflating truck tire. I turned to my left to see Mappas. The huge vizier's staff lay on the ground, but his hands, each one the size of a plump Thanksgiving turkey, were clutched around my neck.

"You may outwit Shadows," he said through gritted yellow teeth, "but not Mappas!"

"Ghhh—hhhh—" I tried breathing but my eyes were beginning to see red dots and my knees began to buckle.

Mappas was so massive I was falling against his bulging torso.

His bulging torso clothed with fabric.

With my last remaining bit of strength, I shoved the sconce toward him. As my knuckles brushed against his tunic, I felt the pads of Mappas's thumb sink into my neck.

My eyes closed and I saw nothing.

CHAPTER THIRTY-FIVE

GATHERING THE CLOUDS

"KAAAAAH!"

The griffin's screech sliced through the courtyard's clangor. I sat up, coughing violently. I heard the grunting of zombies, the breaking of brittle bones, but all I could see were black and red dots.

Inhale.

As bodies flew above me, I forced the air in and out of my lungs.

I blinked hard. To my left was the body of Mappas, lying unmoving on his back. His bronze staff lay at his side, the miniature alabaster Mausoleum broken off the top. His tunic was charred black, and wisps of acrid smoke lifted from his body. Skilaki was kneeling over him, feeling for a pulse.

Had I done that?

Horrified, I scrambled away. My feet slipped on the ground. It was wet. I could feel droplets on my head now.

As I staggered toward the wall, I managed a look upward. Hovering over the courtyard was a perfect circle of darkness in the gray sky, a mushroom cap of clouds. By the wall, Artemisia was floating off the ground, her eyes shut, her arms raised high.

She was chanting. Gathering the clouds.

I scooped my sconce off the ground. Luckily, the rain wasn't falling hard enough to have put it out yet. With my other hand I lifted Mappas's staff, its fancy top now a jagged shard of alabaster. Shadows closed in on me from all sides.

As I backed away I swung the staff, warding off the flailing zombies. Out of the corner of my eye, I could see the griffin trying to take off but slipping on the wet, greasy stones. Cass was still on the red beast's back, hanging tight, patting its fur, talking intently into its ear. Two other Shadows were clutching the griffin's other leg, trying to get to Cass, weighing the beast down.

"Jaaaack!"

Aly's voice. From inside the zombie archway.

I scrambled toward the sound, swinging the staff to stave off Shadows. Inside the opening, the smell of death and rot hit me with the force of an open-palm punch. In the feeble light of my sconce I saw piles of bones along the walls, slithery movement that could have been snakes or rats, beady eyes floating in the distance.

As I passed into a small, dark room, my foot landed on something solid.

"Yeow!" Aly screamed. "That was my leg."

She was sitting on the dank ground, her arms shackled to the wall. "Sorry! Are you all right?"

"Watch out, Jack!" she shouted.

I spun around, dropping the sconce and jumping away from a running zombie. Before it could stumble onto Aly, I swung Mappas's staff and batted the creature away.

As it fell in aa heap against the wall, I caught my breath. It wouldn't be long before the rest of them wised up. Aly and I would be trapped. I had to think fast.

"Pull your hands away from the wall," I said.

"Wh-what?" Aly said.

"Just do it."

Aly backed away as far as the chain would let her. I lifted the bronze staff high over my head and brought it down hard.

The first hit did nothing. The second dislodged the shackle's mooring an inch or so from the wall.

I would need more strength, more speed.

Time to Marco out.

"Geeeeahhh!" I shouted, pounding with all my strength.

The mooring came loose, thumping to the ground. Aly stood, stunned, the shackles hanging from her wrists.

"Stand still and hold your arms wide," I said, preparing to knock the chain loose from her hands.

"Are you kidding?" Aly yanked back her arms. "Don't push your luck. I can pick these locks. Let's blow this clambake."

She picked up my sconce and darted back to the archway, the chain dangling.

We emerged into the courtyard, slipping and sliding on the muddy, churned ground. The entire place was carpeted with fallen Shadows, writhing and moaning, unable to stand. We headed toward the griffin. "Think of what must be in this dirt!" Aly called out. "The blood and guts of slaughtered animals and humans, all rising up as the rain seeps underneath it."

"There goes my appetite," I said.

Cass's voice shrieked through the din as we came near. "Hurry!"

The griffin was in a hysterical frenzy now, jumping up and down on its untrapped leg. One Shadow remained clinging, its jaws sunken into the beast's flank. With a sharp kick, the griffin jettisoned the zombie into the courtyard. Four teeth remained stuck in its leathery skin, like kernels of corn.

"I can't . . ." Cass shouted, ". . . keep it still . . ."

I dropped Mappas's staff. My fingers closed around the tip of the griffin's wing as it swooped to the bottom of a downswing.

The red lion-bird screamed in surprise. Unbalanced, its body tilted and its legs flew sideways. With a thump that shook the courtyard, it fell to the ground.

I scrambled up the wing, clutching the wet feathers. As I grabbed onto its body fur, the griffin screeched in protest, nearly throwing me off, but I managed to pull myself up to its spine and hoist myself over. As I sat up behind Cass, gripping hard with my legs, I felt Aly thumping into place behind me. "All on!" I yelled.

Aly wrapped her arms around my waist. Out of the corner of my eye, I saw Skilaki calling to Artemisia. The queen, still floating, spiraled downward to the ground. Her eyes were opening, her trance coming to an end. The rain immediately stopped falling, the clouds vanishing into the white-gray sky.

As the griffin leaped with a deafening caw, she cried, "Get them!"

I felt a hand close around my left ankle. I tried to shake off the attacker, but it held tight. The griffin faltered, smacking against the palace's stone rampart. The wall split, sending up a shower of dust and rock. "Kick it away!" Cass shouted. "We need altitude!"

"I'm trying!" I replied.

But the Shadow's grip was like a metal clamp. It hung beneath me, its feet dangling just off the ground. My eyes focused on the bronze staff, lying useless below me. I needed it. Now.

But before I could figure out how to get it, the Shadow reached down with its free hand and snatched Mappas's weapon. Without hesitating, it swung the staff at me. I kicked my leg away, and the broken alabaster tip stabbed the griffin's side. With an earsplitting shriek, the beast thrust hard and jerked sharply upward. The Shadow dropped its weapon.

We were rising. Cass and Aly both shrieked with triumph.

But my zombie attacker still held tight to my ankle, and there was nothing I could do about it. It took all my strength just to keep from slipping off the griffin's water-slicked back.

"Astrapobronto!" echoed Artemisia's voice.

"What does that mean?" Aly yelled.

A jolt of white light ignited the skies, with the electric crack of thunder.

"That!" Cass said.

The griffin let out a keening cry that sounded to me like fear. The lightning had been close. I could feel Aly digging her heels into the beast's flanks. "You can do it! Fly!"

Below us the entire courtyard sizzled as the lightning passed through the wet surface. I could hear Artemisia's

Shadows grunting with surprise. I could smell the searing of leathery flesh.

"You cannot escape!" Skilaki's voice echoed over the din.

"She's going to destroy the whole place!" Aly said.

The destroyer shall rule. That was what the Newton letter said. It was about Artemisia, not Mausolus. She was ruthless.

But Newton had never met a Select.

I felt the Shadow's fingers tighten around my ankle. I grabbed Cass, holding tight. The thing was deadweight, but I wasn't going to fall. I glanced down, past its dangling body, into a dull gray expanse of scrubby trees. We had cleared the palace grounds.

"We're over!" Cass cried out. "We're going to do it!"

"Where to now?" Aly shouted.

"The northeast quadrant!" Cass turned to us with a huge smile. "That was where we came in. It was on Skilaki's map. I remember it! I remember!"

He kicked the griffin hard with his right heel. The lion-bird immediately veered to the left. We were headed to a dense forest now with gargantuan trees, dead gray redwoods that thrust up like barbed spears.

But the griffin was losing altitude. My fingers loosened and I slipped to the left. Toward the clinging Shadow. Aly gripped tighter around my waist. "Jack, can't you shake it off?" she shouted.

"Does it look like I can?" I said.

247

I could hear Cass talking gently to the red beast. "You're not used to carrying so many people, are you? Too heavy, huh? Well, let's do something about that. Head straight for the tops of those trees, and in a minute we'll be fine. Ready?"

Cass pointed downward, and the griffin dropped. Now my ankle-grabber was on a direct course for the thick, pointed top of the tallest tree, jutting high above the rest. The body was swinging forward with the momentum.

I looked down. For the first time, I caught a glimpse of the monster's face. It stared at me with empty, wild-animal eyes, its grimace framed in a salt-and-pepper beard.

I nearly fell off the griffin. It was a face I knew very well.

"*Don't, Cass!*" I shouted. "*It's Professor Bhegad!*"

CHAPTER THIRTY-SIX

NADINE

"UP, GRIFFIN!" CASS commanded.

The beast faltered for a moment, confused.

"No . . ." Aly said, looking downward at Professor Bhegad in stunned disbelief.

"*Go up—now!*" Cass shouted.

The griffin veered in midflight. We rose so quickly I thought I'd lose my balance. Professor Bhegad's eyes met mine. Briefly. His irises were gray. His face showed no fear. No recognition. He opened his mouth to speak, but all that came out was an incoherent grunt.

I felt a sharp tug. Saw the blur of a barren gray branch. Heard a dull *whump*.

I closed my eyes and held tight to the griffin.

My leg was free. But I was crying.

* * *

With an exhausted caw, the griffin set down on a dry, dusty plain. My arms were nearly rigid around Cass's midsection, but I managed to pry them off and slide to the ground. I landed on my side and rolled to my back, staring upward into the unchanging sky. Aly and Cass flopped down beside me. Aly immediately went to work on her shackles, digging bobby pins into the lock.

With two sharp, metallic snaps, she was free. She lay back with a groan of relief, massaging her wrists.

The griffin folded its legs underneath itself, like a lion. It turned its beak toward a long gash on its flank and began licking it. "Great job, Big Bird," Cass said. "Hey, you're much nicer than your cousin in Rhodes."

"Careful, he looks hungry," Aly warned.

"It's not a he, it's a she," Cass said. "I'm calling her Nadine."

"How do you know it's female?" Aly asked.

Cass shrugged. As he scratched underneath the griffin's chin, she closed her eyes and let out a soft purring noise. "We shared."

I closed my eyes, but all I could see was the professor's face. His colorless eyes.

Aly turned onto her side and propped her head on her hand. "Thanks, Jack," she said.

"For what?" I murmured.

"Saving me in the castle," she replied. "Breaking the shackles."

I turned away. "I didn't save Bhegad."

"What you did just now—you couldn't have done anything else," Aly said.

"He dedicated his life to us," I said. "We were supposed to save him. We had a plan. And . . . I just let him go . . ."

Cass sat down next to me. "That wasn't Professor Bhegad hanging on to you, Jack. He was a number, like Nine and Forty-one. A shell of Bhegad. You didn't kill him. Artemisia did, when she took his soul."

"We knew the plan had risks," Aly reasoned. "Even if the Loculus was there, we don't know if it could have brought him back."

I nodded. I knew all this. I knew Professor Bhegad would have died even if we hadn't come to Bo'gloo.

But none of this changed the facts. Bhegad was gone. So was the Loculus of Healing. With them went our own chances of surviving.

And until the day I died, I would never forget those eyes.

Cass gave the griffin one last pat on the neck, then jumped to his feet. "Let's get out of here."

As he turned and began walking across the field, I stood. My ankle was sore from where Bhegad had been hanging. Aly took my arm. Together we followed Cass into the emptiness before us.

I trained my eyes on the edge of the woods, where the fog snaked like a river. Where was the portal?

Aly stopped. "Do you hear something?"

"No—" Before the word left my lips, I saw a rock flying over our heads.

I spun around. Now I could hear a low grumbling noise. I squinted and saw shifting forms in the trees. Behind us the griffin let out a loud screech.

"Shadows . . ." I said.

"How did they find us?" Aly screamed.

I heard Skilaki's voice in my head—*You cannot escape!*

They were everywhere, like insects—lurching toward us on all sides, out of the trees and bushes. There were teams of them, swinging slings, throwing rocks and branches. Snorting and braying like animals. "Cass, how far?" I called out.

He was running into their midst. "This way!" he shouted. "Hurry! We have to get there before they do!"

Two projectiles hurtled through the air toward my head. I dived to the ground and rolled.

Aly let out a scream. She was on the ground, blood oozing from her head.

KIIIIIAAAHHHHH! The griffin's cry blotted out all sound. She swooped above us, plunging into the zombies' midst like a cannonball.

I lifted Aly off the ground. "Can you run?"

She blinked her eyes erratically. "Yes. I think."

"Here!" Cass screamed. He was thirty yards ahead of us, his arm half vanished into thin air.

The portal.

Cass was reaching toward us. I pushed Aly ahead of me. "Take her, she's hurt!"

I saw Cass's hand close around Aly's. In a nanosecond, they both disappeared. I prepared to leap.

But my feet never left the ground. I felt a sharp set of fingers grabbing my arm. Pulling me back.

"*Graammpfff.*" Cold, musty breath blasted my face, and I gagged.

I swung my body around and faced a Shadow with a massive frame. I lowered my head and thrust it forward, hard. My forehead smashed into the zombie's head with a dull splat, like a baseball bat hitting a cantaloupe. The fingers loosened for a moment. I tried to pull away, but this one was bigger than Forty-one and not as fragile. It held tight.

My feet left the ground. I looked around desperately for the portal, but it was invisible. The Shadows were converging on me now. In the distance I could see a team of them pelting the griffin with rocks and sticks, overwhelming the screeching beast.

I was moving now. The Shadow had me by the arms and was swinging me around. The others backed off, waiting in a circle, grunting, clapping hands. It was a game to them. Dodgeball for the undead. I felt my feet lift upward, parallel to the ground, gaining speed.

I closed my eyes, preparing to be thrown. I thought about Cass and Aly. I thought about Dad. They would be on their own.

Now my ankles smacked against a palm. And another. Fingers closed tight. My hands wrenched away from the Shadow's grip and my top half fell.

My face and palms hit the ground at the same time. Pebbles dug into my cheek as I scraped along the parched soil.

Something popped in my ears. Around me was a flash of bright white.

I screamed.

CHAPTER THIRTY-SEVEN

BECAUSE OF THE EYES

ARTEMISIA IS YOUNGER. *I barely recognize her face. Her skin is smooth, her figure plump. Her robe shines with jewels.*

But I know who she is because of the eyes. They are sharp. They see everything, one step ahead.

She tells me she does not want any more responsibilities. Building the temple was difficult. She gestures behind her, to a pair of men eating and drinking at a thick oak table. One is younger than the other by a generation, yet both are tearing into goose shanks, devouring grapes, swigging from flagons that are replenished by slaves.

Mappas. And Mausolus.

He will not approve, Artemisia explains. He will not want anything in his realm that does not belong to him.

It cannot belong to him, I explain. But he must keep it safe. For the safety of the world.

Artemisia shrugs. These are not his concerns, she says. And she bids me farewell.

I snap my fingers and the sky darkens. Overhead the hovering griffin has begun its dive. Artemisia looks up and shrieks. The slaves are running into the castle. The satrap and his vassal jostle to follow them. Neither of them seems concerned with Artemisia.

The creature is hungry. Its mouth froths, sending flecks of spittle into the air.

I can call it off, I say. Or you can grant me this simple request.

The elegant woman's eyes are wide and desperate. She nods, holding out her palm as I hand her my sack.

CHAPTER THIRTY-EIGHT

WE TRIED

GRIFFIN SPIT RAN down my face like a warm shower.

I bolted upward with a scream.

"He waketh," came a voice above me. "O rapture unexampled."

The surrounding gray had darkened. I took in a gulp and nearly choked.

Humidity.

I could taste the salt in the air.

Above me loomed the face of Canavar, leering down at me as if I were some vaguely interesting ancient relic.

My father's joy was a lot less restrained. As he lifted me into a big hug, I closed my eyes. I couldn't believe I was here. Back with him. Back with them all. Cass and Aly were kneeling by my side, along with Dr. Bradley. Torquin was still at the entrance, pacing.

"Dude," Cass said, "I thought you were going to kick my hand off the wrist."

"Cass held on," Aly told me. "So did I. Together we were practically a whole Marco."

"Well, a fraction of a Marco," Cass added. "But enough to pull you through."

I was starting to understand. The hands I'd felt on my ankles had not been zombie claws after all. They'd been Cass and Aly, pulling me to safety.

Dad was grinning, his cheeks moist. "You went in. And then Cass and Aly bounced right back out. What happened?"

I glanced at my watch. The second hand was moving again, but the other hands were still on 3:17. To Dad and the others, no time had passed.

"No Loculus!" called Torquin from the Mausoleum entrance. "No professor. Go back."

Cass and Aly stared at me.

"Torquin . . . we tried," I said.

"Tried?" Torquin thundered. *"What means tried?"*

"He didn't make it," Aly said softly.

Torquin's body sagged. Even in the dark I could see the panic in his eyes and the deepening of his skin's natural redness. He took a step backward as if he'd been pushed, and his shoulders began to shake. Dr. Bradley rushed

258

toward him, but Canavar got there first. He put his arms around Torquin's knees in the best comforting gesture he could manage.

A sound welled up from the ground below us, deep and disturbing, like the bowing of a cracked cello. Dr. Bradley and Canavar jumped in surprise. They reached toward Torquin and coaxed him down the steps.

The ground began to vibrate. The wall was glowing now, its solid stone shimmering and blurring. We scrambled backward across the rubble-strewn field.

The Mausoleum seemed to flare with light. Then, just as it had arrived, it began to fade from existence. The chariot went first and then the roof, until the wall gave way to the darkness beyond.

In a moment, all that was left was a moonlit pile of rocks. On top of them lay the matching number seven plates.

Dad knelt beside us, his face drawn and pale. "Your shoulder, Jack," he said. "I hadn't noticed . . ."

I looked down. My shirt was torn, and blood had started to well from the gashes where the griffin had clawed me. "It's only a flesh wound," I said.

"I'll have to treat that," Dr. Bradley called out. "I want to examine all of you."

As the doctor dabbed at my shoulder, Dad put a warm, comforting hand on mine. "Start from the beginning, Jack. Please."

Taking a deep breath, I told him everything I could. From the waters of Nostalgikos to the river of fire, from Artemisia's palace and Bhegad's death to the flight back on the griffin. Aly and Cass chimed in with details.

Dad listened, quietly nodding, wincing at the painful parts. I knew we'd come a long way from Mongolia. His questioning, skepticism, stubbornness—all of it had peeled back for a moment.

He believed me now. I could tell. He believed everything.

As I finished, Dad let out a deep sigh. "Bhegad followed through. He gave his life for you. And I never had the chance to forgive him. To let him know I didn't blame him any longer for what happened to Mom."

Dr. Bradley brushed a tear from her eye. "I think he knew how you felt."

"Yes," came the muffled rumble of Torquin's voice. "He knew."

He was sitting on the ground, his back to us. Looking straight ahead into the darkness.

Into the space where he had last seen Professor Bhegad.

CHAPTER THIRTY-NINE

THE GRAND CARBUNCULUS WIZENDUM

I AWOKE FROM a dreamless sleep in an airless hotel. The heat had been jacked up and I was sweating through the sheets. Tinny music blared from a clock radio, and bodies were lying on every surface—Cass on another bed, Aly and Dr. Bradley sharing a fold-out sofa, and Dad on a cot. The closet door was open, and Canavar slept curled up on the floor. I could see Torquin's silhouette outside, pacing back and forth in the early-morning sunlight. We were all dressed in the same clothing as the day before.

"Rise and shine," I groaned. As I slipped out of bed and into the bathroom, I threw open a window. We were just off the highway, and a gust of gasoline-scented air blew in.

"This hotel has bad breath," Cass said.

"Sorry, it was the best we could find at four in the morning," Dad replied.

One by one we washed up. Dad was last. No one was saying much of anything. Cass busied himself with a pad of paper and a pencil he had taken from the hotel room desk. I watched as he wrote the heading GOING FORWARD? across the top.

He stared at it a moment, then quickly erased the question mark.

I sat on the sofa. My head ached and my shoulder felt swollen and sore. We had agreed on a planning meeting in the morning, to discuss the future in a post-Bhegad world.

A future that was looking very, very brief.

As Dad began pacing the room, the gnarled figure of Canavar emerged from the closet. He sat in a corner, picking something out of his hair and popping it quietly into his mouth.

"I didn't see that," Cass murmured.

"Artemisia," Dad said. "She told you the Loculus was stolen, yes? Did she give proof?"

"Never," Cass asserted.

"Maybe she was lying," Dad said.

I shook my head. "The whole time we were there—the forest, the control center, the palace—I never once felt the Song of the Heptakiklos."

"How big is Bo'gloo?" Dr. Bradley asked.

"We must have passed through maybe half of it, on foot or on the griffin," Cass said with a scared gulp. "Why? Are you going to suggest we go back?"

"I'm sure Artemisia wasn't lying," Aly declared. "She had no reason to hide it from us. She resented the Loculus."

Cass nodded. "Also, if the Loculus was in Bo'gloo, Nadine would have been all over it. Griffins are bred to protect Loculi."

"Okay, so who knew about the Loculus—and who'd have the motive to steal it?" Dad continued. "Seems to me there are only two possibilities."

"The Karai Institute didn't," Dr. Bradley said. "Professor Bhegad would have known about it."

"Which leaves the Massa," I said. "But we were at their headquarters. They were bragging on how great they were, on all the cool things they could do for us. One thing they didn't brag about was having a Loculus. If they did, don't you think they'd say something? Also, we found the safe where they were keeping Loculi—"

"And there were two of them," Cass said. "The ones they'd taken from us. No others."

We were back to square one. The room fell silent. Outside a car blew its horn at Torquin, who was wandering a little too close to the highway, muttering to himself.

"Would it be impertinent to speak up?" Canavar squeaked, raising a tentative hand.

We all stared at him, and he flinched.

"Erm, I take that as a yes," he continued. "Well, as I mentioned upon thy arrival, many of the Mausoleum's treasures were stolen long ago. Perhaps this Loculus of thine was among them."

"Impossible," I said. "Crossing into the Mausoleum requires the mark of the lambda."

"Indeed, yes." Canavar nodded. "Many tomb robbers were known to employ youths for their ability to enter small spaces. Is it inconceivable that among them may have been one marked with the lambda? Or have there never been such genetic prodigies in any of the generations before thee?"

His words hung in the stale hotel air.

Cass, Aly, and I shared a look. Of course there had been Selects through the years. Dad and Mom had been studying them. But the likelihood that one had lived in Turkey and managed to get into the Mausoleum?

"I guess it's possible," Aly said.

"Of course it is!" Canavar said. "I may be small of stature, but I bow to no one regarding powers of deduction—"

"Get to point!" Torquin was standing in the doorway now. His face was drawn, his eyes swollen.

"I am saying thou must . . . follow the money," Canavar replied, "as they say."

"Canavar, are there any records of the thefts in the

museum?" I asked. "Have there been projects to recover the stolen loot?"

"No," the small man replied. "Not at the museum. But in a grand ancient chamber convenes a regular meeting of scholars, the Homunculi, dedicated to the return of such purloined treasures."

"The Homunculi?" Aly said in an undertone. "You mean there's a whole group of creepy little humanoids like Canavar?"

Canavar gave her a severe look and raised his voice slightly. "A group to which, I must add, I have been elected Grand Carbunculus Wizendum for twelve years straight."

"Grand what?" Cass asked.

"Roughly equivalent to treasurer," Canavar said. He slipped off the sofa and moved toward the door. "Our rituals are sacred, our methods arcane. Thou shall be the first of the noninitiates to enter the inner sanctum." He smiled. "It is fitting, I suppose, for those named Select."

CHAPTER FORTY
THE FENCE

OUR VAN PUTTERED to a stop in an empty, weed-choked lot. Torquin parked right up next to the entrance of a warehouse building with corrugated metal walls. A cardboard sign hung lopsided over the front door. On it, in thick marker, were three lines of words in Greek, Turkish, and English. The bottom line read GRAND AND SECRET ORDER OF THE HOMUNCULI MAUSOLIENSIS.

"Behold!" Canavar said, his face pinched with pride.

"I quiver with awe," Cass drawled.

"Very secret," I whispered to Aly. She smothered a laugh.

As we poured out of the van, Canavar skittered to the front door and fiddled with the rusty combination lock. After a few unsuccessful tries, he gave the door a swift kick and it swung open.

He reached in and flicked on a light switch. A chain of bare lightbulbs illuminated a vast, musty room. It was lined with metal bookshelves, file cabinets, piles of papers, tables containing unfinished jigsaw puzzles, and a spilled container of congealed orange liquid labeled SEA BUCK-THORN JUICE. Black streaks wriggled along the baseboards as unidentified small creatures ran for shelter.

"Love the scent," Cass said. "Mold, mildew, or mouse?"

Canavar went straight to a desktop PC with a monitor the size of a small doghouse. He pressed a button on a giant CPU and waited as a logo lit up the screen: WINDOWS 98.

"Even the computer is an antiquity," Aly said.

Canavar let out a disturbed *fnirf-fnirf-fnirf* sound, which I realized was a laugh. "Ah youth, thou canst not envision a world without the flash and blaze of computerweb. I shall now use the mouse-clicker upon its pad, to activate the documents folder . . ."

Aly slipped by him and sat in a ragged office chair. "I'll do it."

She stared at the screen for a moment, motionless. I gulped, remembering our encounter with the river Nostalgikos. "Aly," I said. "It's okay if you can't do it. You'll be able to build your skills again . . ."

Aly raised an eyebrow in my direction. "Dude, that griffin scared the pants off all of us. Whatever it was

267

that I lost—it's back, big-time. She turned back, clicking confidently away at the keyboard. "Lots of data here. Ship-wrecks . . . sonar scans . . . correspondence . . . auction house records . . . periodical archives . . ."

"Yes. That one—the archives!" Canavar blurted. "Most are in Turkish, of course, but owing to my English educa-tion, I have endeavored to include many translated pieces from the international press. I would draw thy attention to a newspaper report dated March of 1962 . . ."

"Got it," Aly said, clicking on a pdf that instantly filled the screen:

THE INTERNATIONAL HERALD TRIBUNE, MONDAY, MARCH 26, 1962

EARTHQUAKE

An earthquake of 6.3 on the Richter scale erupted yesterday evening in Turkey, with an epicenter in the city of Bodrum. In the Kamal Market that afternoon, Turkish delight was literally flying off the shelves. "Sixteen boxes, directly onto my head," said the shop's impish owner, Turan Kamal. "Delicious!"

But to other merchants, and local sites of antiquity, the quake meant looting and lawlessness. According to Yiannaki Hagio-glou, archaeologist at the Mausoleum at Halicarnassus excavation, "The earthquake becomes an opportunity for looters to sneak in and steal. They have no concep-tion of the dangers, the instabilities caused to fragile structures."

Reports led to the arrest of a man, known only as Khalid, identified by locals as belonging to a band of petty thieves. Haggard and shaken, the man claimed two of his associates had been killed in the quake. At press time, no bodies have been found, and police say that one of the thieves, a man called Gencer, is still at large. Shortly after the quake, tavern owner Bartu Bartevyan claims to have seen a "ragged man with a slight limp" running down an alley holding a "glowing blue ball, solid like a giant jewel." Mr. Bartevyan, whose establishment is popular for its strong ale, is currently under questioning.

"'Glowing blue ball,'" Cass said. "That could be it."

"It could be the ale talking," Aly said. "Do you have anything on this guy Gencer?"

"Naturally," Canavar said, directing Aly to another folder marked RESEARCH: LOOTING, PERSONNEL.

Another pdf opened on the screen, and Aly read aloud from a blurry image of a typewritten list: "'Arrested for public misconduct, 1962 . . . arrested for impersonation of public official, 1961 . . . arrested for forging the name of the Beatle Ringo Starr on a check, 1963 . . . arrested for assaulting a prominent German art and antiquities dealer named Dieter Herbst, 1965 . . .' Nothing on Gencer after that . . ."

"Dieter Herbst?" Cass said. "I would kill for a name like that."

"Why would an art dealer consort with a small-timer like Gencer?" I asked.

"Fence," Torquin grumbled.

Cass scratched his head. "They had sword fights?"

"A fence is someone who sells stolen goods," Dad spoke up, "someone who has a side deal with a thief. Since the fence didn't actually steal the stuff, he or she can claim ignorance. Fences can be a sleazy lot, but sometimes they run outwardly respectable businesses."

"It sounds like the two men had a falling out," Dr. Bradley said, "maybe over a deal gone bad. Canavar, have you collected any info on Herbst?"

"No, but I believe he has a . . . what dost thou call it? Web screen page?" Canavar replied. "Thou canst make a connection with the internet."

Aly rolled her eyes. "Thanks for the tip."

In a moment, she was looking at a badly designed site that seemed like it hadn't been touched in years. "Not a lot about him," she said. "There's no date on the site and it looks like it was designed the day after they invented HTML. Opened shop in 1961, but I can't tell if he's still in business. I guess we could call or email him. He'd be really old, if he's still alive at all . . ." She quickly opened a new browser tab and typed "Dieter Herbst obituary" into the search bar. Her face fell. "Died in 2004. While conducting a transaction at an auction house called the Ausser . . . Ausserge . . ."

"Aussergewöhnliche Reliquien Geschäft," Torquin piped up.

Cass's mouth dropped open. "You can pronounce that?"

"Professor Bhegad . . ." Torquin began, but at the mention of the name, he let out a squelched sob and rubbed his eyes. "Sorry . . . *hrruphm*. Sometimes Professor sends Torquin to auctions. Collectors sell relics. Torquin buys. Mostly two auction houses. Smithfield and ARG."

Aly already had the ARG home page open. "Much slicker site . . ."

I leaned over her shoulder. "What are the chances you

270

can find records from back in the sixties?"

"I'm not hopeful," she said, as her fingers flitted on the keys, "unless they park the scans in some archive on the FTP site."

A window popped up, and digits began scrolling in a blur. In about twenty seconds, Aly had broken through the firewall and was rooting around in a company file structure.

Canavar gasped. "In form and movement how express and admirable! In action how like an angel! What alchemy hath possession of this callow child? What arcane wizardry in her soul, what access to worlds unknown—"

"What a gasbag," Torquin said. "Shut mouth."

"Woo-hoo!" Aly nearly leaped from her seat. "Check this out."

Dealer	Date	Artifact	Country of Origin	Offer($)	Settled	Purchaser
Heller, F.	3/4/64	Chalice,Bronze	Iran	$2,000	$1,950	PMFA
Heller, F.	10/23/64	Tapestry	Persia	$4,532	$4,850	SMI
Henson, R.	5/2/64	Statuary	Macedonia	$11,900	$15,000	MMA
Herbst, D.	9/17/64	Marble relic	Asia Minor	$1,200	$950	BM
Herbst, D.	9/17/64	Marble relic	Asia Minor	$900	$500	NAA
Herbst, D.	9/17/64	Statuary	Asia Minor	$2,600	$1,300	HU
Herbst, D.	9/17/64	Stone carving	Asia Minor	$5,200	$3,100	BM
Herbst, D.	9/17/64	Relic,spherical stone	Asia Minor	$6,900	$4,000	AMNH
Herbst, D.	9/17/64	Marble relic	Asia Minor	$1,000	$500	YU
Herbst, D.	9/17/64	Stone carving	Asia Minor	$4,500	$2,000	MMA

"Amazing," Dad said.

"Old Herbster was busy," Cass said. "And in Asia Minor—which is what Turkey used to be called."

"The guy had a big haul in September," Aly said. "He sold them off on the same day."

"And he wasn't very good at it," I added. "Look at the other sellers—Heller and Henson. They offered their relics at one price and totally got what they asked for. Sometimes more. But Herbst sells at a way lower price than he asks, every time. Like he's totally incompetent."

"Or," Aly said, "he's in a hurry. Which he would be, if he knew the goods were stolen."

"'Relic, spherical stone,'" I said. "That could be a Loculus, I guess. Sold for four thousand dollars to AMNH. Which is . . ." I took the mouse and scrolled down to the list of abbreviations. "The American Museum of Natural History, in New York City."

"Yyyesss!" Cass said. "Brunhilda to the Big Apple!"

As we headed for the door, Torquin shouted, "Wait!"

We turned. He had lifted Canavar by the back of his shirt collar, and he was holding him toward us as if he were a kitten. "Must say thank you to Canavar. He helped do the work of Professor Bhegad."

"'Twas nothing," Canavar said, his voice choked by the pressure of his shirt collar. "Wouldst thou kindly release me?"

As Torquin set the little guy down, we each shook his gnarled hand. "Peace out, Canavar," Cass said. "How could we ever repay you?"

Canavar gave us his odd, twisted smile. "When thou hast successfully reached the age of fourteen years, consider returning to Bodrum to give me the joyous news."

"Will do," Cass said.

"We promise," I added.

Dad was heading back toward the door of the warehouse. "Let's load in some good Turkish grub now," he said. "Food is expensive in New York City."

CHAPTER FORTY-ONE

CODE RED

ERROR.

Aly's monitor beeped at her for what seemed like the dozenth time on the flight to New York.

She pounded on the screen and sat back in her seat. "I need a nap . . ."

"Whoa, another new tower on Fifty-Seventh Street near Seventh Avenue," Cass said, his face plastered to the window. "Construction on the West Side Highway, too—and check out Williamsburg, on the horizon!"

"Will you stop that, Cass?" Aly said, rubbing her forehead. "They're buildings, that's all."

Cass spun around. He looked hurt. "Sorry, Aly. I geek out over this stuff."

"Apology accepted. Wake me when we're there." Aly's head lolled back in her seat. By the time it clonked against the window, she was fast asleep.

I glanced at Dr. Bradley. She had a newspaper unfolded in her lap, open to a crossword puzzle. But she was ignoring that now, staring intently at Aly.

As Brunhilda began her descent, Torquin yanked the steering mechanism this way and that in an attempt to do tricky moves. Dad was radioing the Marine Air Terminal for runway instructions. Cass was grinning out the window like a little kid.

Aly let out a sharp snoring sound. Her head began to slide downward. As she slipped off the seat, I realized she hadn't fastened her belt.

"Aly?" I said.

She thumped to the carpet, her legs twitching.

Dr. Bradley was already on the move. She lifted Aly, swung her around to the back of the plane, and deposited her on the reclined seat that had once held Professor Bhegad. "Someone take the phone from my purse!" she shouted.

Aly's chest lurched up and down. A *cccchhhh* sound came from her mouth, and her eyes rolled back into her head. I knelt by Dr. Bradley's purse and fished out the phone.

Cass's face was bone white. "She's . . . she's not due for an episode . . ."

"I have the phone!" I shouted.

"Do exactly as I say," Dr. Bradley said. "Send a text to one-four-two-eight-five-seven. Two words. Code red!"

Dr. Bradley was holding Aly's arms down. Trying to keep her from flailing. From hurting herself. My fingers shook as I tried to follow instructions.

CODE RESD.

Steady. Backspace . . .

CODE RED.

I jammed my thumb on send.

"No phone now!" Torquin bellowed. "Give treatment!"

"I would if I could!" Dr. Bradley shouted. "I don't have my equipment! I may be able to sedate her briefly, but that's it!"

Aly's face was turning blue. Dr. Bradley's hand was in Aly's mouth, trying to keep her from swallowing her tongue.

The phone vibrated. I nearly dropped it.

Its screen now glowed with a string of characters:

1W72PH4

"What the heck does this mean?" I said.

Cass was out of his seat, staring over my shoulder. "It's an address," he said. "Number One West Seventy-Second Street. Right off Central Park. Not sure about the last part—PH four . . ."

"Penthouse four!" Dad said. "The apartment on the top

floor, most likely. Is this where we're supposed to go?"

"Who are we seeing?" I asked.

"Never mind that!" Dr. Bradley said. "And don't even think of calling nine-one-one. We have no time. We need to land now."

"We're third in line for landing clearance!" Dad said.

Torquin yanked hard on the throttle. "Now we are first."

* * *

The taxi screeched to a stop in front of 1 West 72nd Street. Dad had pulled some sort of strings to get us through customs in no time. He also promised the cabdriver double pay if he got us to the address on Dr. Bradley's phone in twenty minutes. He made it in eighteen fifty-three.

Torquin, Dr. Bradley, and Aly were in another cab. It pulled to the curb directly in front of us.

The building loomed overhead, a brick urban castle surrounded by a black cast iron fence festooned with carved angry faces. In a dark, arched entranceway, two guards stood, hands folded. Cass gazed at them, a spooked look in his eyes. "This is exactly where John Lennon was shot and killed," he whispered.

"Will you stop it?" I said.

As Dad paid the fare, a man darted out of the archway toward the first cab. He wore a wool cap, dark sunglasses, jeans, and a black leather jacket, and he had something shiny and metallic in his hand.

277

"What the—?" Dad murmured.

The man leaned into the open back window of Aly's cab. I couldn't hear what he was saying, but when he backed out, his hands were empty.

Before we could do a thing, he was pulling open the back door of our cab. "To the river!" he shouted to the taxi driver, yanking open the rear door and squeezing into the backseat with Cass and me. "And step on it."

In front of us, Torquin was lifting Aly out of the other cab. I caught the flash of silver as her arm flopped limply down.

"Sir," the cabdriver said meekly, "I must discharge these passengers—"

"*I said go!*" the man barked.

As the taxi squealed away from the curb, Dad whirled around. "I beg your pardon!" he said. "We have urgent business in that building."

The man put a hand into his jacket pocket. "If you know what's good for you, you will do exactly as I say."

CHAPTER FORTY-TWO

HACKED?

IF YOU EVER wondered what it was like to ride down a New York City street in the backseat of a taxi whose driver is whimpering "We are going to die, we are going to die, we are going to die," I'll tell you: it's not fun.

He was careening from side to side. He sideswiped a parked minivan, then cut across two lanes and nearly collided head-on with a baby-supplies truck driver with a potty mouth.

The car screeched to a halt at a red light on Columbus Avenue. "I said go, not kill your passengers," said the man in the leather jacket. He was holding a leather wallet, which he had just pulled from his jacket pocket. "If you expect a tip, I recommend you drive in a sane manner and deposit us alive at Riverside Drive."

The driver looked warily over his shoulder. "This is not a stickup?"

"What? Of course it's not." The man sighed and sat back, removing his hat and then his sunglasses. His hair was silver and thick, swept straight back like a marble sculpture. His eyes were a cold blue-gray, set into a rocklike face that was tanned and deeply cragged.

"Who are you?" I demanded.

"Your dream come true," he said. "Dr. Bradley did well. By calling a Code Red, she was following KI protocol for emergencies."

"You're a part of the KI?" Cass said. "But the KI was destroyed!"

"Correction—the island was occupied," the man said, "but the Karai Institute still exists. For reasons of security, the leader of the KI is never on-island. All Code Red messages go directly to the central office. We have satellites in many places, one of them here."

Number One.

Omphalos.

Professor Bhegad had told us about a Karai leader, someone who he took orders from. But not much. Not even a name. "Is that who Aly is seeing?" I said. "Bhegad's boss?"

"Your friend is in very good hands." The man leaned forward. "Driver, let us off at the far corner, end of this block."

We climbed out on Riverside Drive, at the entrance to a park. Just beyond the jogging path flowed a wide, silver-blue river. "The Hudson," Cass said. "And that's New Jersey on the other side —"

"Quickly," the man said, ushering us past a low stone gate. He was shorter and older than my dad. Under his leather jacket was a white turtleneck shirt that revealed a little paunch. "You were followed to New York."

"We couldn't have been," Dad said. "We were in Turkey. And before that—"

"Mongolia, yes, we know this." Reaching into an inner pocket, he took out two thin, silvery bracelets. "Put these on. Iridium bracelets. Aly has one, too."

I took one and turned it over in my hand. *Iridium.* These bracelets were replicas of the ones given to us at Massa headquarters in Egypt.

"This is the only substance that blocks our trackers— the ones you implanted in our bodies on the island," I said.

"Why do we have to wear them now?" Cass asked.

The man looked at Cass stonily. "The Massa are on high alert. They have access to your trackers—which means we have just led them here, away from your friend Aly. Once you put yours on, the signal becomes a dead end."

I shook my head, remembering Aly's antics in Building D. "No. Aly disabled the KI's tracking machines. Fried them with an overload of electricity."

The man's rocklike expression twitched.

"You . . . have this much confidence in her ability?" he said.

"If you knew her, you would, too," I said.

The man nodded. "So if they're not tracking, how did they find you?"

Cass and I exchanged a look and shrugged.

The man took our arms. He pulled us toward Seventy-Second Street, back the way we'd come. "Tell me who exactly you met in Turkey."

* * *

"What do you mean they *hacked* you, Canavar?" I barked into the speakerphone.

We were back in the KI meeting room in the New York City headquarters, in a sprawling corner apartment in the castlelike building. Dad was glaring at the silver-haired man, still upset about the way he'd hijacked the taxi.

Canavar's reply squeaked through the tiny speaker. "Perhaps I have not used the proper terminology. It appears that early this morning thy dreaded nemesis the Massa made several phone calls. They reached out to each vicinity that is home to one of the Seven Wonders—including our museum at Bodrum. My employer. Naturally by that time, I had, well, mentioned our exploits to a discreet friend or two . . ."

The back of my head hit the seat's leather headrest. "That's not hacking, Canavar," I said. "That's a big mouth.

You weren't supposed to say anything!"

"But . . . an experience so momentous!" Canavar said, "of such singular archaeological interest!"

"Canavar, did you tell them where we were headed?" Cass demanded.

The phone stayed silent for a long moment. Then a tiny, "Mea culpa."

The gray-haired man pressed the off button. "That's Latin for 'my fault.' We have our answer."

He sat back in his thick leather seat, closing his eyes and pressing his fingers to his temples. The room fell into a tense silence. Cass gave me a kick under the table. His hands still in his lap, he pointed to our companion.

Omphalos, he mouthed.

I don't know if it was a question or a statement. But I felt a shiver up my spine.

Was it possible?

The man was no-nonsense. Steely. Smart. Cagey. Hadn't answered when we'd asked his name. He kept his cool, said exactly what he meant and no more, and understood Latin. He didn't draw attention, yet he could strike fear with a glance or a gesture. The perfect profile for a leader.

And this realization made my heart sink.

Because he was no longer the KI's best-kept secret. He was here with us, on the ground. Pulling antics in a cab.

Totally misunderstanding how we were tracked. Taking unnecessary risks. Revealing his weaknesses. To me, it was a sign. This centuries-old organization, the KI, was on its last legs.

The Massa were out there. Somewhere. Stronger than ever. About to win the game.

I gazed through the window. Below us, tourists wearing green-foam Statue of Liberty crowns were heading into Central Park. Some of them were tossing flowers onto a colorful mosaic that spelled out one word:

IMAGINE.

I turned away.

I didn't want to.

CHAPTER FORTY-THREE

LOSING IT

DR. BRADLEY'S LATEX gloves snapped as she pulled them off her fingers. Her face was lined and haggard. "Aly will be all right for now. Thanks to my New York colleagues. They are lifesavers."

Cass and I stood in the doorway of the makeshift operating room, watching the two other medical personnel carefully unhook electrodes from Aly. Her mouth moved slightly. I could hear a soft moan. As the KI doctors left with the silver-haired man—Number One, aka the Omphalos—we shook their hands. Torquin sat quietly on a stool, which barely contained him. "No ukulele . . ." he said sadly to no one in particular.

"This is amazing news, Dr. Bradley," I said, "because we

were just told we have to move Aly right now."

She shook her head. "She'll need some recovery time. I told that to Number One."

Cass gave me a quizzical look.

"When did you talk to him?" I asked, puzzled.

"I didn't. Not directly." She pointed to a monitor on the wall. "He texted us, on that."

"Sneaky guy," Cass said. "I didn't even see him take out his phone, did you, Jack?"

"Take out his—What are you talking about?" Dr. Bradley asked. "You've seen Number One?"

"We took a cab ride with him," I said.

Dr. Bradley dropped a length of IV tubing. "You *what?*"

Before we could answer, our taxi companion came running up the hallway. "They're onto us. The Massa. We were hacking into their text messages and they just went dead cold."

"Do you know where they are?" Dr. Bradley asked.

"Unclear whether they've landed in New York yet," he replied. "If the girl isn't ready, the other two must get to the museum now."

"Not two," Torquin grunted. "Three."

Behind us, the monitor on the wall beeped. A message instantly materialized:

NOT SO FAST.

Cass jumped back. "Who's that?"

The response crawled quickly across the screen:

GREETINGS, CASSIUS. YOU WILL EXCUSE ME FOR NOT SPEAKING. ANONYMITY IS KEY. YOU AND JACK LOOK WELL, FOR TWO WHO HAVE SURVIVED THE UNDERWORLD. AND THE INCOMPETENCE OF MR. KRAUS.

The silver-haired man's face lost its composure. "The iridium bands were an honest mistake."

"Wait—you're not the Omphalos?" Cass said, slowly looking from the silver-haired man to the screen. "And *that* is?"

SECURITY HAS BEEN COMPROMISED AT ALL LEVELS. THE KARAI INSTITUTE WILL BE OFF-LINE UNTIL FURTHER NOTICE WHILE WE RESTRUCTURE. MR. KRAUS WILL COMMENCE ERASING ALL EVIDENCE OF OUR EXISTENCE.

"I have a patient!" Dr. Bradley said. "She needs to recover. There will be more episodes. We will continue to need emergency protocols."

"I—I'm good," Aly said, rising groggily from the bed. "Maybe not ready for a marathon right this minute, but I'm good."

BRAVA. TAKE WHAT YOU NEED TO CONTINUE YOUR MISSION. PORTABILITY IS NECESSARY. I AM ASSEMBLING A HANDPICKED COMMITTEE OF OUR ABLEST REMAINING SPECIALISTS. WE WILL REPORT WHEN WE CAN.

"What does this mean for us?" Dr. Bradley blurted out. "What good is the KI if you disappear?"

A TRANSPORT WILL ARRIVE FOR TORQUIN IN EXACTLY 20 MINUTES AT THE TRUCK DOCK ON WEST 68TH BETWEEN BROADWAY AND COLUMBUS. FURTHER INSTRUCTIONS WILL AWAIT. TILL THEN, TAKE HEART.

Torquin stood abruptly, knocking over his stool. "Leave Select? Cannot. Will not!"

The screen glowed again as words formed.

I COUNT ON YOU TO BE THE CORNERSTONE OF OUR PHYSICAL REBUILDING. AND PLEASE BE AWARE, THERE ARE CONSEQUENCES FOR DISOBEDIENCE.

I saw Torquin's fists flex. I nudged him. In the hall outside was a man I hadn't seen before—a man almost as big as Torquin, with a serious-looking pistol hanging from his belt.

Torquin's fists uncurled.

Mr. Kraus wiped his forehead and gave old Red Beard a sympathetic look. "Brother, trust me, you don't have much of a choice."

* * *

Seven minutes later we pulled to a stop at a sprawling building with broad stone steps.

"Who's the dude on the horse?" Cass said, gazing out at a statue of a heroic-looking horseman with a Native American standing by his side.

"Theodore Roosevelt," Dad said as he stepped out of the taxi, clutching the bag with both Loculi. "He and his father

288

played huge roles founding this place."

We left the cab and began climbing the steps, passing a school group about my age. They were taking selfies near the Roosevelt statue, making faces and goofing off. One of the girls looked at me and turned away, giggling. She was annoying, but she was *normal.* For a moment I imagined Dad and me as normal people visiting the museum. The thought of it was . . . well, amazing.

Fat chance that would ever happen now.

I looked left and right. I didn't know what I was looking for. The Massa could be anybody.

"Buddy, dollar for a cup of coffee?"

I gasped and jumped away from a stringy-haired man in tattered clothing, who was standing at one of the top steps, holding out a cup to us. "Easy, Jack," Aly said, fishing coins out of her pocket and dropping them in his cup.

"Bless you," the man replied, then winked at me. "And take care of that anxiety, kid. It'll kill you."

Easy. Aly is right.

Dad led us into the front hall of the museum, which contained a gargantuan skeleton of a dinosaur raised up on its hind legs. "Looks familiar," Cass murmured.

I nodded. It resembled a slightly smaller version of the skeleton in the Great Hall of the House of Wenders, back on the island. As we stepped to the end of a long, snaky ticket line, I craned my neck up to see its head.

I almost missed the man wearing a dark robe, who disappeared into the exhibit hall behind the skeleton.

I jabbed Dad in the side. "Look!"

"Massa?" Dad asked.

"Where?" Cass said.

"You are too hyped up!" Aly said.

"Normal people don't wear robes!" I shouted.

I bolted toward the front of the line, barged past the ticket taker, and raced into the exhibit hall. It was a high-ceilinged room with a balcony, and in the center was a circular display of enormous elephants. The floor on all sides was crowded with families and school groups. I ran to the right, leaping to see over people's heads.

There.

I caught a better glimpse of him now, his robe swinging as he walked. I thought he was heading out the other side, but he seemed to change his mind. Picking up speed, he made a full circle and headed back out the exhibit entrance.

Had he seen me?

"Excuse me . . . sorry . . ." I pushed my way through, nearly trampling a two-year-old in my path, and stumbled into the hallway outside the room.

Elevators lined both walls, but only one car was open—and it was closing, jammed with people. I saw a bearded face, a flash of the robe's material, before the door shut.

A "down" arrow lit up. Behind me was a set of marble

stairs. I nearly fell trying to run down. I got to the next level just in time to see the door shut again. A crowd had exited, but the Massa was not among them.

I ran to the next floor. The bottom. I could smell burgers from a food court behind me. A sign pointed to the subway entrance. I heard the ding of the elevator, but it was a different door. A different car. I'd missed the one I'd been chasing.

"Pardon me, young man," said an old lady with an American Museum of Natural History hat. "Are you lost?"

"I'm looking for a guy in a robe," I said.

She nodded cheerily. "Ah yes, I just saw him."

"Do you know where he went?" I blurted.

"Of course." She pointed to a room with two wood-paneled doors, just beyond the food court. The guy was disappearing inside. I sprinted after him. "Yo!" I yelled as he entered the room. "Stop!"

A million words welled up from my gut and collided together in my brain. I was breathing so hard and fast I could barely speak. "I don't know . . . how you got here, but you . . . will never . . ."

The man turned. He was wearing thick glasses, a clerical collar, and a long black beard. "How I got here? Why, I took the C train. There is an exit from the platform— so convenient. Do you need directions, son? Have you lost your parents?"

That was when I noticed a name tag just below his collar: REV. JONATHAN HARTOUNIAN, MID-ATLANTIC ARMENIAN ORTHODOX COUNCIL. On a blackboard in the room behind him, someone had written GLIMPSES OF ARMENIAN RELIGIOUS CULTURE IN MODERN ARCHAEOLOGY. A crowd of bearded, black-robed guys turned in their seats, all staring at me with placid smiles.

"Um, sorry," I said. "So sorry . . ."

I backed into the hallway. Two kids were staring at me, holding tightly to their mom's hands. The old guide was approaching me with a curious expression.

Without a word, I turned for the stairway and ran.

I was losing it.

CHAPTER FORTY-FOUR

THE SONG OF THE HEPTAKIKLOS

"PROMISE YOU'LL STAY with us," Cass whispered over his shoulder as he climbed the basement stairs.

"Yes, Cass," I said wearily, "I promise."

"No chasing nice priests," he said.

"Ha-ha-ha," I said.

"Or being scared of beggars?"

"Knock it off!"

"Ssshh!" said Dad.

"Easy, Jack," Aly whispered. "We don't have a Loculus of Soundproofing."

We were walking fast, heading up from the lower level to the museum's first floor. At this point Cass was the only one holding on to the Loculus of Invisibility, which had hidden us nicely while the museum had closed for the night. But in a narrow stairwell it was hard for everyone to hold hands while one person held a Loculus, so Dad, Aly, and I were in plain sight. But that was fine. We'd snuck into a supply closet and found a custodial uniform for Dad. If someone did see us, Dad would say he was an employee and we were his niece and nephews from out of town, who he was showing around.

We gathered at the top of the stairs. The place echoed with the whine of distant vacuum cleaners. Just to be safe, we all held hands—Cass to Aly to me to Dad—and went invisible. We tiptoed through the empty Native American exhibit, under the disapproving frowns of dark totem poles that lined the aisles like trees in a forest.

At eight P.M., the museum had been closed for over two hours. We'd already seen a lot of the place, and I hadn't yet felt any sign of the Loculus of Healing. We were going to cover every inch until we did.

"Uh, guys, I have to go," Aly said.

"Go where?" Cass asked. "You have a hot date?"

"Go *there*, I mean." Aly gestured toward the restrooms.

As she headed in that direction, we all followed to maintain our invisibility.

We walked past a huge wooden longboat filled with Native American mannequins and a bear. To our left was a locked exit. Windows looked out to a circular driveway and a row of old apartment buildings across the street.

Aly gave us a raised eyebrow look. "Guys. You're not invited," she said.

"Not—wha?—we know!" Cass stammered. "We'll just, um, wait outside."

But then I began to feel a tingling in my feet. Then my knees. My heart started to thump.

"Wait a minute," I said. "It's here. The Loculus."

"In the bathroom?" Aly asked.

"Farther away," I replied. "But in this building. I feel it."

Aly's face lit up. "Go find it! Now. You, too, Mr. McKinley. Give me your phone, Jack. Cass and I will follow with the Loculi and catch up."

I fished out my phone and handed it to her. As Aly darted into the restroom and Cass vanished from sight, I went quickly into the next room. And the next. Dad followed close behind. Exhibits raced by us, but I hardly noticed. Rodents hanging on a wall. A roped-off exhibit in preparation. A stairway.

Floor Two. Secretary birds. African costumes. Antelopes.

The feeling was getting stronger, throbbing in the marrow of my bones, tickling the follicles of my skin. I stopped at the bottom of a dark stairway. "Up there," I said quietly.

At the base of the stairs was a sign on a brass post that said RESEARCH AREA/PERMIT REQUIRED. Dad slid it aside.

"I think an exception to the rule can be made."

We scampered up the stairs and paused at the top, staring into a dimly lit hallway with closed doors on either side. Down at the far end was a T, two hallways leading left and right.

I froze. From the left hallway I could hear the steady tap-tap-tap of distant footsteps.

"Don't worry." Dad smoothed his uniform and began whistling softly.

Whistling?

"Why are you doing that?" I whispered.

"So they know someone's here and won't be startled when they actually see us," Dad said. "It'll be less suspicious. Now come on. Look like you belong."

I tried not to feel completely dorkish as we walked up the corridor. But the Song of the Heptakiklos was screaming inside me, pulling me forward. Telling me where to go. "Go right," I said through Dad's warbly whistle.

When we turned, we nearly collided with a woman in a simple custodial uniform, with her hair pulled back into a tight ponytail. "Howdy!" Dad said, way too loudly.

"Yesterday," the woman said.

"Huh?" Dad replied.

"The song you were whistling—'Yesterday,' by the Beatles—I like it." She looked closely at Dad's name tag. "How do you pronounce your name? Kosh . . . Koz . . ."

For the first time I saw the name tag on Dad's uniform: KOŚCIUSZKO.

"Koz!" I blurted out. "Everybody calls him Koz."

"This is my, er, nephew," Dad added. "Just giving him a little private tour."

"Nice to meet you," she said, pointing to her own tag, which read MARIA. "My name's easy."

"Well, Maria, we were just heading to grab something from room number . . ." Dad said, glancing toward me. "Room number . . . which one, young man?"

I didn't know!

It could have been any of the doors. There were three of them, one on each side and one at the end of the hallway. The sound was so unbearable I couldn't believe they weren't hearing it. I staggered closer. The room numbers swirled before my eyes—B23 . . . B24 . . . B25 . . .

I could feel Maria's gaze. "Is the boy all right?" she asked.

"Fine," Dad said.

"Fine," I said at the same time.

She suspects something's off. Pick a room. Any room. "B twenty-four!" I blurted out.

I bolted to the door and turned the knob, but it wouldn't budge.

Dad forced a chuckle. "That door is locked . . . um, Josh. We lock our doors here, heh-heh." He patted his pockets. "I, er, I think I left my key in my other pants."

"Very energetic young man," Maria said, fiddling with a lanyard around her neck. She stepped toward B24, holding out a plastic card. "Maybe he'll be a paleontologist someday."

What if that's not the right room?

I knew I might need to try them all.

"Can I do it?" I said. "Operate the key. I just want to see how it works."

Lame, lame, lame!

"That's a good idea," Dad piped up. "That way you can leave us here, Maria. James can open all the doors. We'll return your key to you."

Maria looked at him curiously. "I thought you said his name was Josh."

"He always makes that mistake!" I blurted out, grabbing the key and sliding it down the slot.

The door clicked open. It was a small meeting room with one long table, bookshelves, and a whiteboard. But I was interested only in the two file cabinets along the opposite wall. I raced over and pulled them open.

Papers. Folders. "It's not here," I said.

Now Maria looked alarmed. "What isn't?"

"Excuse me," I said, backing out of the room, into the hallway. Dad continued talking, chortling, grabbing her attention, stalling.

There. B25.

The room at the end had double doors. As I stepped

closer, the Song cranked up to eleven. It was deafening.

"The Beatles' *Abbey Road*, actually, was my favorite album . . ." came Dad's cheery voice from down the hall.

I had to find the Loculus before he bored Maria to death.

I slipped the card through the slot, hands shaking. The door opened and I flicked on a light.

The room was square and huge. Some kind of staging area for dioramas. Its smell made me gag, at once musty, sweet, and bitter—equal parts rot, animal odor, chemicals. A lifelike figure of a Neanderthal stood with its back to me, half-covered with hair. African tribal masks were lined up on a table next to bottles of cleaning fluid. Some kind of deity was sitting on a table, its headdress practically touching the low ceiling. It smiled down, surrounded by goats and cattle, balancing what looked like the sun in one hand and the moon in another.

In the center was a blocky wooden table about waist-high. On it were furry hides, rocks and gems, half-stuffed bird specimens, tools, half-used tubes and jars, lengths of rope. A strange raccoonlike creature seemed to be staring at me, but its eyes were missing and the bottom half of its body trailed over a mold like a baggy dress. All around the room were shelves, open wooden cases, cabinets with big doors. I went to work, opening them one by one, pushing aside tiny heads, bushy tails, flattened birds, a box of fake animal eyes, and what seemed to be a rhinoceros horn.

No Loculus . . . nothing . . . nothing.

"Argggh . . ." In frustration I banged my hand down hard on the center table. The deity seemed to jump.

The voices down the hall—Dad's and Maria's—had stopped.

But my eyes were rooted to the deity's left hand. To the replica of the sun it was holding high. It was painted a metallic gold and it seemed somehow too big for the statue's hand. Bigger than a basketball.

And it was moving.

No.

I stepped closer and realized the object was perfectly still. Its surface—the paint itself—seemed to be in motion somehow, flowing slowly and unevenly around the sun. Light seemed to glow dully from within and then fade.

I placed my hands around it and pulled upward. I felt an excruciating twinge in my injured shoulder, where the griffin had nabbed me.

The sun separated from the deity's hands. I had it now. And warmth was taking hold of my entire body. It oozed slowly across my shoulder, tickling my skin. My body hummed with the Song of the Heptakiklos, every ache smoothing out as if the pain were being lifted out by invisible strings. I watched an open sore on my arm scab and fade.

He . . . ling.

300

I thought of Professor Bhegad, and for a moment I wanted to cry. This was what we could have saved him with. Gencer's theft from the Mausoleum ruins had cost Bhegad's life.

But I could hear the old man's scolding voice in my head, telling me that this was what he wanted. *If my sacrifice brings forth a Loculus, at least my life will have had some worth.*

We had three of them now. We were almost halfway there.

I felt an intense glow of well-being. The only thing that hurt was my face, because of the huge smile that was stretching across it.

"Eureka."

Maria's voice shocked me out of my stupor. I spun around to the door, nearly dropping the Loculus of Healing.

She stood in the door with my dad. His eyes were wide with panic. "I . . . found what we were looking for," I said.

With a quick shove, Maria sent him sprawling against a cabinet. In her right hand was a long gun with a silencer.

"You got here first," she said. "But I get the prize."

CHAPTER FORTY-FIVE

SHOULDN'TS

I HEARD THE clatter of fossils raining down around Dad. Out of the corner of my eye, I saw him covering his head with his arms. But I couldn't take my eyes off the weapon. "Your name isn't really Maria, is it?" I said. "And you don't work for the museum."

The woman smiled. "Maria is indisposed at the moment. I expect she will eventually want this uniform back. You will be considerate and avoid soiling it with your blood, won't you? Now, to business."

She held out her free hand, palm up.

The beeping of Dad's phone made me jump. Cass and Aly.

"Don't even think of answering that," the woman said.

"And don't even think of not handing the Loculus over."

"Give it to her," Dad said.

My brain shouted at me with shouldn'ts. I shouldn't have let down my guard. Shouldn't have left without Cass and Aly. Shouldn't have assumed that we would beat the Massa here.

Shouldn't have allowed myself to hope.

The phone stopped ringing. I had no choice now.

My body was strengthening by the second, but it didn't matter anymore. I moved my arms toward Maria, holding out the golden orb. "Give my regards to Brother Dimitrios," I said. "And tell him we won't give up."

"Oh, I'm not through with you, Josh-or-maybe-James." With a mocking laugh she stepped forward, taking the Loculus from my hand. "Brother Dimitrios is expecting three of these, and so now you can just lead me to the others."

"They're right here," Dad piped up. "I have them!"

I spun around. Out of the shadow came a jagged black fossil, hurtling straight for the woman's face.

She flinched, turning away. The stone caught her on the side of the head with a thud both solid and sickening.

With a tiny, involuntary scream, she fell to her knees. I lunged forward, grabbing the Loculus from her hand.

Dad was scrambling across the room. His own head was bloody. He yanked away the gun with one hand, shoving

303

her down to the floor with the other.

The rope.

I grabbed it off the center table and tossed it to Dad. Dropping the gun, he took the woman's arms and held them behind her back. She thrashed and cursed, but he managed to tie her wrists tight.

"That was a petrified dinosaur jaw I conked her with," he said, catching his breath. "Guess it qualifies as a blast from the past."

The woman kicked with her legs but only succeeding in turning herself faceup. "You won't succeed," she said. "You know this."

"That's what my high school wrestling coach said to me thirty-two years ago," Dad said. "But look—he was wrong!"

"Are you okay?" I asked him. "Your head . . ."

"To quote my favorite son," Dad replied with a wry smile, "'it's only a flesh wound.' Now let's find your friends. And be very careful. There are probably more Massa where this charming lady came from."

We ran out of the room to the sound of the woman's threats. I held tight to the Loculus of Healing. "On the way down," I said, "grab my arm. You'll feel a lot better."

CHAPTER FORTY-SIX

ANOTHER EXIT

"WHERE THE HECK are you?" was Aly's greeting to me over the phone.

"Heading to the front entrance, near the Roosevelt statue, with Dad." I held Dad's phone tight to my ear as he and I charged down the stairs. "I have the Loculus in my backpack."

"You found the Loculus?" she shrieked.

"Aly, listen," I said. "The Massa are here. We ran into one of them. She's upstairs, third floor, all tied up. But there are bound to be others, so be careful. And hurry!"

"On our way," Aly replied. "Cass says emosewa. So do I!"

Shutting the phone, I gave it back to Dad. He led the way, racing past the elephant exhibit, but he stopped short of the museum's huge entrance hall. Ducking behind the archway, he whirled around, mouthing "Police."

I ran up next to him and carefully glanced into the hall. Near the giant skeleton, two policemen were peppering a night custodian with questions. Beyond them, outside the main glass doors, I could see the flashing red-and-blue lights of their car at the bottom of the outer stairs.

"What are they doing here?" I whispered.

"We took uniforms, so did the Massa," Dad said. "The real Maria was assaulted. Anybody could have called in a report. Let's use another exit. I'll call Cass and Aly."

As he pulled out the phone, Cass's voice boomed out loudly: "Woo-hoo, we're back in ssenisub!"

I spun around, wincing. Cass and Aly were hurrying toward us. Dad waved frantically, and I put my finger to my mouth to shush them. The conversation out in the exhibit hall stopped. "Hello?" a deep voice called out.

"Go back!" Dad whispered to Aly, Cass, and me.

"We can go invisible!" I whispered. Cass started to shrug off his pack, where the Loculus of Invisibility was stashed.

"No time!" Dad whisper-shouted. "Get to the other exit—Seventy-Seventh Street, where the restrooms are. I'll stall these guys."

"But—" I protested.

"Go! I will meet you!" Dad said. "Protect the Loculi!"

I could hear footsteps approaching. Dad gave me a shove

306

and Aly took my arm. She quickly gave me back my phone and I shoved it in my pocket, stumbling back across the elephant exhibit hall with her and Cass. He led us through the museum, past the watchful eyes of thousands of dead animals.

We burst into the exhibit hall with the longboat. Standing in our path, his back to us, was a museum guard. As we stopped short, he turned around, startled.

His eyes went wide and he whipped his radio out.

"Run!" I shouted.

We made a break for the exit, going the long way around the boat. The guard was shouting into the radio now, reporting on us. The police would be here any second.

I raced to the exit. Someone in a black leather jacket and a watch cap was standing outside in the driveway. His back was to us and he was staring across the street. A guard? A cop?

We had room behind him. We could make it.

I slipped through the door with Cass and Aly right behind. The guy turned around, and the light caught his face.

He smiled, and we stopped in our tracks.

"Dudes!"

My legs locked. I blinked my eyes once, twice.

Only one response was possible.

"Marco?"

CHAPTER FORTY-SEVEN

THE PRODIGAL SUNSHINE

HE LOOKED OLDER. Bigger. But that was impossible.

Everything about this moment was impossible. He wasn't supposed to be here. He wasn't supposed to be smiling at us, like nothing in the world was wrong.

"'Sup, Brother Jack!" Marco bounded toward us, right hand held high. "Aly, my pal-y! Cass but not least! Fives!"

All three of us backed away. Cass looked afraid. Aly could barely contain the disgust on her face. "How—how did you get here, Marco?" I said.

"Clicked my heels three times and said 'There's no place like the Big Apple'! Plus Brother D has private wings." Marco slowly lowered his hand. "What, no high fives for your Prodigal Sunshine?"

"A joke . . ." Aly said, her voice simmering. "It's all a big joke to you. Well, you just laugh your head off about this news, Marco—Professor Bhegad is dead."

Marco glanced at Aly warily. "Wait. For reals?"

"Your people did it," Cass said. "They injured him at the island. We rescued him, and then he sacrificed himself so we could get a Loculus." He was looking at Marco with crazy intensity, as if he stared hard enough he might flip a sanity switch. "We almost died, Marco. Jack just had a treatment. So did Aly, and me. The episodes are coming quicker. Time's running out."

Marco looked out onto the street. Three figures were running toward us. I wanted to run, but he gripped my arm. "Dudes, listen. A couple of weeks, a month tops, you won't recognize the island. The Massa plans are insane. We throw those Locues on the Hepto? Bam, we live forever and the place is jamming . . ."

"And you will be King Marco and the sky will rain fairy dust," Aly said, nearly spitting her words out. "We've heard it already. Marco Ramsay, you are an idiot. And a monster."

"But . . . whoa . . ." Marco looked hurt and a little bewildered. "I figured by now you guys would have changed your minds . . ."

Enough.

I ripped my arm out of Marco's grip and pulled Aly up the driveway. Cass stumbled behind us. As we bolted out toward the street Marco called out once. But he didn't pursue us.

The two other figures, however, veered in our direction. I saw a taxi speeding across Seventy-Seventh Street toward the park and I waved my arms crazily to hail it. One of the figures left his feet and dived into me, smashing me against a black iron gate. The other pointed a small gun toward Cass and Aly.

As I scrambled to my feet I caught a whiff of cigar and stale cologne. A fist grabbed my collar and yanked me to my feet.

"Nice work, Brother Yiorgos," said the man with Aly and Cass.

"Thank you, Brother Stavros," said my attacker.

Marco was running up the driveway now. "Yo, Bluto, why'd you have to go and do that to my peeps?"

"Peeps?" Yiorgos said. "What is peeps?"

My chest was heaving. Brother Yiorgos seemed to have lost a tooth since we last saw him. The thatch of his meager salt-and-pepper hair waved in the night air like a clump of dying crabgrass, and his grin looked like piano keys. "We go, Stavros," he said. "Police out front."

Police.

I looked back. Where was Dad? No sign of him at the Seventy-Seventh Street entrance.

Brother Yiorgos's eyes were darting toward Stavros, his

younger, slightly smarter and thinner clone, and then back toward the park. There, another black-clad figure was waving his arms crazily as if swatting flies.

"Whoa, what's wrong with Niko?" Marco asked.

Stavros shrugged. But his eyes were cautious and intent. At the moment, none of the Massa was paying much attention to me.

I slipped my fingers into my pocket and pulled out my phone. As quick as I could, I sent Dad a text: WHERE R U?

I looked up. Marco had seen me, but he quickly looked away. The two Massa goons hadn't noticed a thing.

"Hrrrmph!" That was Aly. She stared at me, eyes bugged out, exaggeratedly looking toward Columbus Avenue. As if sending me a mental message: *Let's make a run for it!*

I glanced in that direction and spotted two hooded, black-garbed figures a few feet up the block. I sent her a message back as best I could: *We are surrounded.*

Just beyond Aly, Cass was frozen. Like Yiorgos and Stavros, his glance was slowly sweeping the section of the block between here and the park.

The door in the building across the street seemed to be moving.

And the windows around them.

I blinked. On second glance I realized it wasn't the buildings themselves. It was a weird trick of light. Something barely noticeable was moving across them, something

311

in the air. Like a giant, sheer black curtain or a cloud of smoke.

Brother Niko was running toward us now, babbling in Greek. His eyes were as bright as streetlamps. *"Skia! Skia!"*

Stavros ignored him, turning to Yiorgos with an impatient shrug. "Now. Fast. Go."

"Go where?" I demanded.

The answer I got was a sharp shove. The two men pushed Cass, Aly, and me toward Central Park, against the protests of Niko. "Meet someone," Yiorgos said.

But the strange smoke cloud was thickening. It seemed to billow toward us from across the street. "Dudopoulos," Marco called out. "It's looking like a mad crazy weather front. Or some cockroaches playing Quidditch."

I could hear a pounding, like a distant herd of cattle. The ground shook slightly under my feet. "What's that sound?" I asked.

"The subway?" Aly guessed.

"The subway doesn't run under Seventy-Seventh Street," Cass said.

Stavros lurched backward, as if something had caught him on the chin. Yiorgos suddenly screamed, falling away.

I saw the flash of two bloodshot eyes in the dark, appearing and disappearing like a phantom. "Run!" I shouted.

Cass, Aly, and I bolted in the opposite direction, past the circular driveway. Behind us I could hear the squealing of a car's brakes, a bone-jarring crash.

Ahead of us, the two hooded figures had turned. They were staring at the commotion, too. We stepped off the curb to avoid them, to circle around them, but my ankle caught on the curb and I stumbled.

My phone spilled out onto the street. Its screen was lit up. A reply from Dad. ARRESTED. ON WAY TO PRECINCT 20.

I fought back panic, shoving the phone into my pocket as I scrabbled to my feet. I felt a hand closing on my arm. With a grunt I pulled it back, trying to shake loose.

The hood fell off the Massa's head. A cascade of light-brown hair fell out.

My legs locked in place. For a moment I couldn't breathe. The woman's features were lean and sharp, the face of an athlete, a person who was prepared for anything and never took no for an answer. Her eyes, a deep blue-green that pierced through the darkness, seemed to dance in her head, and as she smiled tiny wrinkles spread on either side of her face.

"Hello, Jack," said my mom.

CHAPTER FORTY-EIGHT
MOM

"M—!" I BLURTED out, but her hand was over my mouth before I could finish the word.

Mom.

In that fraction of a second, I wished that Nostalgikos had stolen away my memory. Because if it had, I could have faced her like this and not cared that she was alive and warm and beautiful. I wouldn't have wanted to wrap my arms around her and breathe the scent of her neck. It wouldn't have occurred to me that this closeness, in this moment, could bring back six whole lost years.

All I would have known was that I was looking into the face of a killer.

And that would have been so much easier.

I was trembling as she carefully put her finger to her mouth.

I shook my head, not to disagree but because I didn't know what else to do.

Her eyes were darting over my shoulder, to the noise down the street. "I am Sister Nancy," she said.

"No!" I said. "You're not! You're—"

"Come!" She pulled my hand and began running away from the sound, toward Columbus Avenue. Cass and Aly were already ahead of us.

"Hurry!" Cass shouted.

I looked over my shoulder. Niko, Yiorgos, and Stavros were stumbling toward us, their limbs flailing. Marco was spin-kicking and punching into the thin air. It looked like some strange ritual martial arts dance.

Before I could react, I felt a bony hand around my neck. And another. I grabbed onto them and tried to pull them off. The dense blackness shifted and thickened before me. Eyes materialized out of the air, a jaw, teeth, cheekbones. Now I saw a ragged, grinning face of ripped flesh and empty eyes.

Shadows.

They take on a more diaphanous appearance when they wander the upper realms . . .

Queen Artemisia's army was here, in the living world. Howling, grunting, spitting, materializing, and vanishing

315

like the flicker of a black mist. Sucking the darkness as they floated in a current of nonlight, both solid and smoke.

How did they get here?

"Let . . . me . . . *gggghhhh* . . ." I rasped. The zombie's grip was tight.

A foot lashed out of the darkness, landing a sharp kick on the Shadow's jaw. With a muffled, gurgling squeak, the zombie fell away.

"Are you all right?" Mom said, pulling me down the street at a run, her arm around my waist. "I—I don't know what's happening."

We were running across Columbus Avenue now. On the opposite side was a busy restaurant, but no one seemed to notice us.

As we pounded down the next block, I saw Aly's feet leave the ground. Then Cass's. I heard them scream with surprise. Mom, too. We were caught up in the flow of Shadows now, surging under and around us, lifting us upward. I saw a grimace here, a skin-shredded skull there, and I prepared for another battle.

But their eyes, at least the ones I saw, were looking upward. Over the roof of a nearby brownstone apartment building. I followed their glances, but I saw nothing.

Until the sky shimmered.

I almost missed it. But the atmosphere was gathering up there, too, this time not into black clouds but an oval of dim blue light. It came toward us like a comet in slo-mo, growing larger, rustling the leaves of a scrawny street tree. It was expanding and contracting, forming arms, legs, a head. As it leveled out above the car roofs, it was the shape of a barefoot woman in a torn dress.

"Skilaki . . ." I said.

She scanned the street, scowling at the unseeable undead. Her face seemed to have lost some of its skin, and in her mouth were only two teeth. When she spoke, her voice seemed to enter my brain directly, bypassing my ears. "Whoever harms the Select," she announced, "shall receive Artemisia's wrath!"

Below us came an excited flurry of grunts and snorts.

"Bring them quickly," she continued, her bony finger pointing farther up the street, "and bring them alive, if you will please the queen."

We were borne higher and higher, flowing down the street on a river of invisible hands. The amber windows around us, the homes of brick and stone, jittered in and out of sight in the shifting blackness. I glanced around for Cass and Aly and saw them floating far ahead, almost to the next avenue. "Do you know who this creature is?" my mother asked, her voice more awed than scared.

Her calmness surprised me. My entire body was shaking. "An ex-sibyl," I said. "She works for . . ."

No. Keep it tight. Keep it a secret.

"Works for who?" Mom asked.

Could I tell her the truth? Could I ever trust her with anything again?

We were moving faster now, across one brightly lit avenue and then another. Churches, shops, castlelike apartment houses sped by like phantoms, until the light dimmed and the smell of exhaust gave way to grass and soil. We veered right, following the wide band of a moonlit river.

Riverside Park.

Now we were catching up to Cass and Aly. They looked as petrified as I felt. Aly glanced at my mom and did a double take. "Mom?" she mouthed.

I nodded. I could see her whispering to Cass.

"Where are you taking us, Skilaki?" I yelled.

The ex-sibyl turned in midair. "As you may surmise, things have not been so jolly in Bo'gloo since you left. And I had every reason to think they would get worse. So I suppose I should thank you."

"Thank us for what?" Aly shouted.

"For opening the portals of the dead, of course," Skilaki said, "so that the dead themselves may pass through."

"We—we didn't do that!" I protested.

Skilaki zoomed closer so quickly I thought I'd lurch clear out of the zombie cloud. She tapped my backpack with her bony, clattering fingers. "Yes, you did. By finding and activating this wayward gift of Massarym, you unsealed a breach that had been closed for a very long time. Ironic, isn't it?" Skilaki threw her head back into a hissing laugh. "The bauble that heals bodies is the one that gives access to the dead."

"Massarym?" My mother gasped.

My heart sank like a stone. The secret was out now.

I could hear Shadows nodding and snuffling, until Skilaki held up a rigid right arm. "Silence, you nincompoops!"

"Poops," one of them repeated, making a squeaky choking sound that I took to be a laugh.

Skilaki raised a bony finger toward the giggling zombie and I saw a wash of black careening upward. A moment later I heard a sickening smack against a tree.

"I will return Queen Artemisia's gift to its rightful place," Skilaki continued, "and, as she has been in a bit of a snit over your rude and rather destructive departure, she will be especially pleased to finish some business with you."

Aly and Cass gave me a panicked look. We were moving fast now. The wind was battering my face.

"Did she say Artemisia?" my mother said.

She knew. The Massa knew where we'd been. And they knew what we'd found.

Until today the Loculus of Healing had been lying in storage, nothing but a stone, a decoration, a sale from a crooked art dealer.

Waiting for a Select to come and activate it.

Where the lame walk, the sick rise, the dead live forever.

The Shadows were slowing now. Their voices became frenzied, excited. In the distance I saw a monument with a great dome.

"Skilaki," I said, "where are you taking us?"

As she turned, her smile ripped a gash in what was left of her face.

"Sightseeing," she said.

CHAPTER FORTY-NINE

ARTEMISIA AWAITS

AS WE SET down on the ground, the Shadows dissipated like wind across a burned field. Before us was a columned monument, glowing a pale greenish white in the moonlight. The steps were nearly obliterated by the cloud of Shadows. We were at the top of a hill. To our left, a walkway led to a fenced overlook, and beyond that the hill sloped to the river. At the bottom were train tracks that emerged from a tunnel, leading north.

"Skilaki," Cass said. He was staring at the monument, his voice shaky. "On that map of Bo'gloo you showed us? There were portals. At first we didn't know where they were—or where they led. But then Jack and I found one."

"We traveled from the underworld directly into

modern-day London," I added. "Through a replica of the Mausoleum . . ."

"Aren't they clever children," Skilaki said.

I turned my eyes to the monument. The top was a dome, which wasn't exactly right, and the columns didn't surround the whole structure, but the influence was pretty obvious—the classic details, the same squarish shape. "Grant's Tomb," Cass said. "I knew it was here. But I never made the connection."

Behind us I could hear a confused rush of oaths and shouts as Marco and the other Massa landed on the grass.

Skilaki smiled. "You know, there's an old joke. It goes like this. Question: Who is buried in Grant's Tomb? Answer: Grant. And his wife. And Bo'gloo."

"That's not even a little bit funny," Aly said.

"It kills them in the underworld," Skilaki said. "Minions, bring these children and their magic backpack to the entrance, so we may begin our adventure."

I could hear Shadows hooting with excitement. Out of the black cloud came a Shadow shape that seized me, turned me around, and reached into my pack.

"No!" Mom, Cass, Aly, and Marco cried out in unison, running toward me.

Skilaki sent them flying with a wave of her arm.

The Shadow took out the Loculus of Healing. His face was a rigid, skeletal mask, but the shreds of remaining muscle were working hard to pull his lips into a greedy smile.

I grabbed on to the Loculus, and the Shadow jolted involuntarily. The orb began to glow, its golden surface to move. As the zombie let out a surprised grunt, his hand began to radiate light. Tiny waves of crisscrossing movement passed across it, like microscopic silkworms leaving thin trails. Its parchmentlike skin was gaining color and thickness.

The Loculus of Healing was repairing the zombie's hand slowly.

"*Hmrph?*" it said, gazing at me.

"Don't ask me," I replied. As I snatched the Loculus away, putting it back into my pack, he held his hand up in the moonlight, examining it.

I took a deep breath. "Skilaki," I said, "we can't let you have this."

Skilaki stood by the entrance to Grant's Tomb. "You have no choice, my little chicken. But by all means, carry it yourself if you wish!" she called out. "Come, Queen Artemisia is waiting."

I looked at my two friends. "We got out once before," I said softly.

"We're in this together," Aly said.

"We have all three Loculi," Cass added. "That means we still have hope. Professor Bhegad would be proud of us. Let's roll."

Holding the Loculus, I walked up the steps. Aly took

my other hand and Cass's, too.

Mom ran up the steps in front of us. She stared at Skilaki, her face resolute. "No. Take your Loculus but spare them."

"She means take them but spare the Loculus!" Yiorgos bellowed.

"Silence, Yiorgos, we have plans for them," Mom said. "Banishment to the underworld is not in our best interest."

"Dudes," Marco shouted. "What about me?"

Skilaki rose above the ground again. She pointed her arm in Marco's direction and he froze in his tracks. "You would like to join them?" she said. She turned to Yiorgos and then Stavros. "How about you? And you?"

"No!" Yiorgos bellowed as he was lifted off the ground. Mom let out a gasp as she rose, too.

Cass, Aly, and I turned. "I thought you just wanted us!" I shouted.

"Well, we are in the business of souls, child," Skilaki said. "And it appears we have volunteers. My queen will be overjoyed with this abundance!"

Now a gray mist was seeping out around the edges of the tomb's front door. The door shook, at first gently and then violently. With a deep, loud crack it flew open, spewing wood splinters and paint shards in all directions.

I leaped to the side, nearly falling down the hill. Cass and Aly huddled near. Above us, Brother Yiorgos and

Brother Stavros began screaming. With guttural snickers, Shadows began pushing them in the air, sliding them toward the door's gaping black hole. "No-o-o-o!" Yiorgos shouted, bracing his arms on either side of the doorjamb.

The Shadow grabbed his shoulders and threw him into the blackness. His frightened wail diminished into silence as two Shadows jumped in gleefully after him.

Mom's face was rigid with fear. The Shadows were toying with Brother Stavros now. After him they would come for Marco, and then Mom. Marco was dancing and shuffling like a boxer, daring them to come closer. Of all of them, he was the only one who had a hope of making it back out again. The only Select.

I felt a rumble that shook the ground. A muffled whistle. *The train.*

I looked down the hill. From under the park, I could hear the squeaking of brakes, the slow chug of an engine. The northbound train would be emerging from the tunnel soon. *When?*

"Jack, look!" Aly shouted.

I turned. Mom was floating toward the Tomb, her arms locked by her side. Her face was shrouded by the moving black mist, but I could see her eyes looking at me, full of tears. And I could make out the movement of her lips forming words: *I love you.*

She was next.

325

CHAPTER FIFTY

A RUSH OF AIR

THE TRAIN'S MUFFLED blast belched up from the bottom of the hill. Its wheels thumped slowly on unseen tracks. I couldn't tell exactly where it was. All I knew was that it was closer. And it would soon emerge, heading north.

I looked back upward for Mom. She was putting up a good fight. Even though her arms were locked, she was managing to spin in the air, kicking at zombies only she could see. Skilaki laughed as she watched.

No one was paying any attention to me.

Move. Now.

I squeezed Aly's hand. She turned to look at me. So did Cass. Sweat beaded my forehead.

HOOOOO...

I let go of Aly, ran down the walkway to the left of the tomb, hopped the fence, and sprinted down the hill. The incline was steep and my knees buckled.

"Hurry, Jack!" Aly cried out.

She and Cass were behind me. I knew Skilaki would see us. I expected to feel her power lifting us from the ground, boomeranging us back to her.

There. A tugging at my limbs. A force that was pulling me backward. I could see Cass stumbling beside me. I grabbed one arm, Aly the other. "Keep going!" I shouted.

"The farther we get . . ." Aly said, "the weaker her power!"

With each inch we were gaining strength. I guess even an ex-sibyl's power isn't infinite. "Keep it up," I said. "This is distracting her from Mom!"

Soon we were running free down the grassy surface toward a highway ramp. Just beyond it were the tracks.

We hopped a barrier and sprinted across the ramp. I could hear the approaching train clear and close. The only thing separating us from the tracks was a tall chain-link fence.

"What are we doing?" Cass asked.

I whipped off my backpack and held up the glowing orb. "Destroying this," I said.

Cass's jaw dropped. "It's a Loculus, Jack! You destroy that, we die!"

"If I don't destroy it, my mom dies!" I shouted. "The

portal remains open. The Shadows can come and go. They can suck souls from innocent people whenever they want. Are our lives worth that?"

I dropped the Loculus back into the pack, ran to the fence, and hopped as high as I could. Clutching onto the links, I climbed upward. Fast.

Cass and Aly were scrambling on to the fence to my left, yelling words I couldn't hear. As I hopped down the other side, I could see another silhouette racing down the hill from the Tomb.

Marco.

The locomotive burst out of the tunnel with a sound like a bomb blast. I dropped the pack, took out the orb, and reared back with my arm. No chance to second-guess. No matter what Cass and Aly said. All that was in my mind were Professor Bhegad's final words to my dad.

I am always willing to do what's right.

I threw the Loculus as hard as I could, spiking it directly down at the track. Toward the train that was now inches away.

"He diiiives for the block!"

Marco's voice startled me. He was over my head, leaping from the top of the fence, flying over my head at impossible speed.

"Marco, don't!" I grabbed for his shirt in midair but he was already by me. He slapped the Loculus off course to the left. It thudded to the ground and rolled away from the track.

"Have you lost your mind, Brother Jack?" he yelled.

I ran for the golden orb, but it was no contest. Marco's G7W skill put him light-years ahead of me. So I did the only thing I could. I rammed into his side, hard. It didn't do much, just slightly threw him off balance. But it bought me a fraction of a second. Just enough to grab his shirt.

I hooked my leg around his, and we both fell to the ground.

Marco swatted me aside with his palm. "Sorry, Brother," he said, leaping away toward the Loculus.

The train was coming closer, moving slowly. The Loculus had stopped rolling now, about three feet from the track. I scrambled to my feet, but Marco had gotten a big head start.

On me. But not on Cass. He had run ahead while we were scuffling.

He scooped the Loculus off the ground as Marco leaped high, ready to swat aside Cass's throw. Instead, Cass underhanded the orb toward me. It spun in the air. I dived for it. Aly was running toward me, too. Behind her, a Shadow was scaling the fence.

Got it.

My fingers closed on the golden sphere and I thudded to the ground. The tracks were to my left, inches away. The locomotive was a blur of black looming closer, and my teeth rattled with the noise.

I stretched my arm out and tossed the Loculus directly on the tracks.

Marco yanked me away from behind, pulling me to safety. Together we rolled onto the gravel, huddling protectively as the hulking train sped by. The *ca-CHUNK-ca-CHUNK-ca-CHUNK* of its wheels on the track was deafening.

"Duuude, what did you just do?" Marco screamed.

His face was red, distorted. I had never seen him so angry.

But my eyes were drawing upward, to a small, fast-moving cloud of blackness floating over the fence. It was dropping fast, gaining human form.

"Watch out!" I cried as a zombie materialized, its shredded clothes flapping in the air directly over Marco's head.

He spun around, crouching for impact.

But the Shadow never reached the ground.

Instead it vanished into thin air.

CHAPTER FIFTY-ONE

ONE LAST LOOK BACK

WE STARED SILENTLY at the place where the Shadow had disappeared. The train had moved north, its rhythmic clatter mixing with the sound of cars on the highway. I couldn't see the Loculus now, but I knew it was gone. Destroyed.

I felt like a part of me had been ripped out and thrown under the train, too.

"What the heck just happened?" Marco moaned.

But I didn't answer. Instead I looked up the hill. In the darkness, at this distance, it was impossible to make out faces. But I could recognize a few shapes up there, walking unsteadily away from Grant's Tomb. *There.* I recognized the walk. "She made it," I muttered. "Mom's alive."

I felt Aly's hand on my arm. I watched Mom for a moment, not sure what to do. I noticed that she was gazing upward now. They all were, their necks craned toward the sky.

I followed their glance. The black smoke had lifted, and I could see a dull shimmer passing across the faces of the park path lights, working its way up toward the moon.

"The Shadows . . ." Cass murmured.

"That's it?" Aly said. "They're gone?"

Marco scratched his head. "That was killer, dude."

"I had to do it," I said.

"Yeah. Maybe you did," Marco replied with a big sigh. "I guess I owe you. For keeping my peeps out of Zombieland. Well, most of them. I think Stavros is going to want to kiss you."

"What about you, Marco?" Aly asked. "What about all four of us? That's the end of the game. No sudden-death overtime. I hope you're proud of yourself."

"Well, who knows?" Marco said. "Maybe Brother D has something up his sleeve. He's up there now."

Cass glanced up the hill. "Oh? Nice of him to show."

"He'll be happy to see you." Marco climbed the fence and jumped to the other side. "He likes you."

"Wait," Aly said. "You're leaving us?"

"Dudes, the invitation's open," Marco replied. "Come with me. It's never a bad idea to side with a winner."

"Winner?" Cass said. "That coward Dimitrios? What

planet are you from?"

"Dude, every game has to have a winner and a loser," Marco said. "Just think about it."

We stared at him in utter disbelief. He shrugged sadly. "Hey, I gotta have faith. I know you'll get it. You guys are too smart not to."

As he turned to walk up the hill, I could see two other figures at the top, making their way downward.

"Jack?" my mom called out. "Jack, are you all right?"

I turned to answer but stopped myself.

Mom's voice tugged at me hard. It was the voice that summoned and soothed. Encouraged and brightened. Well, it had, way back when. But six years was a long time, and she had become someone else. Something else. Something I couldn't trust.

"Jack, honey?"

Peanut butter sandwiches. Hot cocoa. Read alouds.

Fakery. Betrayal. Attacks. Slaughter.

I pulled Cass and Aly into the darkness, far from any streetlamp. "Cass," I whispered. "Give me the Loculus of Invisibility."

He looked at me a good long moment. "Are you sure?" he said softly.

"Torquin's gone," Aly reminded me. "Your dad is under arrest. The Loculus is destroyed. We're not going to live much longer. We have nothing."

"Take it out," I said.

Quickly Cass removed the canvas sack. I reached in and took out the orb. "All of us," I said.

We put our hands on it. I felt the shimmer of energy course through me.

"Jack?" Mom was nearly to the fence now, looking. Looking right through me. "Where are you?"

Her eyes were wide, and even in the darkness I could see the fear in them as she stared at the track. "Oh dear heavens, the train . . ."

She leaped up the fence, getting herself over in quick, expert moves. When she landed on the other side, she let out a sob and scrambled across the gravel. The train was long gone, its rear red lights winking distantly along the Hudson. She scanned the tracks, her face etched with horror, her glistening cheeks wet in the streetlamp light.

She was worried. About me. Convinced that since I was no longer here I must have died.

My heart was sinking. Words welled up from my gut—*I'm right behind you. I'm okay.*

Aly took my hand.

Slowly Mom walked onto the track. Jammed into the gravel in the center of the track were the pieces of the broken Loculus—dozens of them, glowing golden in the dim light. Mom stooped to pick some of them up. I could hear her crying now.

I couldn't do it any longer. Couldn't hide.

As she turned back, I let go of the Loculus. Cass let out a gasp.

Mom's eyes immediately looked up and locked on mine. In the flash of a moment I saw grief give way to shock and joy.

But before I could move, before I could do a thing, her eyes moved and her expression changed abruptly.

When she looked at me again an instant later, her intent was so strong, so direct, that the strength of her glance nearly knocked me back on my heels.

Stop now. Don't do this.

"Sister Nancy!" Brother Dimitrios's deep, unmistakable voice boomed from behind us.

I shoved my hand backward and touched the Loculus. Behind us, the tall monk was stepping awkwardly down the steep incline, eyes on his sandaled feet. In the darkness, his beard seemed to obliterate the bottom of his sallow, bony face. But as he neared the bottom, glancing toward Mom, there was no mistaking the coldness in his eyes.

"Where did they go?" he demanded. "Where are our assets?"

"You ask now, Brother Dimitrios," Mom said, "but when we were fighting the forces of Artemisia, where were you then? Protecting your own assets?"

He climbed the fence with some difficulty and fell awkwardly to the ground. Brushing himself off, he looked at the shards in Mom's hand.

"Oh, by Massarym's grave . . ." he said, his voice falling to a dismayed hush. Carefully he lifted a piece of the Loculus and turned it in his hand. "He didn't . . ."

"Threw it under a train," Mom said. "The boy did. Jack."

"So the prophecy of Brother Charles has been fulfilled," Brother Dimitrios murmured. "The destroyer . . ."

"Shall rule . . ." Mom continued.

Brother Dimitrios gazed slowly back up the hill. "I thought it was the athletic one. Marco the warrior. What an . . . interesting surprise."

"He's a strong young man in his own right," Mom said.

Brother Dimitrios shook his head uncertainly. "I suppose there is no arguing what is meant to be."

My head was reeling.

The message in the Charles Newton letter—*The destroyer shall rule*—wasn't about Mausolus. It wasn't about Artemisia.

It was about Atlantis. About the person destined to rule it.

In the new world, you can keep calling me Marco. But to everyone else, I'll be His Highness King Marco the First. That was what Marco had told us in Babylon—Brother Dimitrios's plan for him. A plan that had been misunderstood.

Mom was still holding tight to the shards. What did they say? What ruler did they predict? And what was going to happen to Marco now?

"We must convene immediately," Mom said. "Go ahead, Brother Dimitrios, tell the others we will have a very long night. I will collect pieces of the Loculus."

Mom watched Brother Dimitrios climb back over the fence and begin the trek up the hill. But she did not turn back to the track to pick up any more shards. Instead, she waited a good thirty seconds, motionless.

Aly gripped me tight. I didn't dare move.

Mom began walking, veering toward us. I wanted to reveal myself but her face was still closed up, still a mask of unmistakable *no*. As she passed, she let something drop from her hand. Without pausing, she continued on.

I stooped to pick it up.

When I finally managed to look back, Mom had turned. I realized I had let go of the Loculus and was visible again.

Mom's eyes blazed. I gave her a shrug, holding out the shard. "Who?" I mouthed.

"Acch, these miserable sandals," came Brother Dimitrios's voice from the darkness. "Will you help me, Sister Nancy?"

Mom's face went taut with panic. I reached back quickly to touch the Loculus of Invisibility, but my eyes never left Mom.

And as she climbed up toward Dimitrios, I saw her point directly toward me.

FOLLOW THE ADVENTURES OF

Jack McKinley in the mysterious, action-packed
series that takes place throughout the
Seven Wonders of the Ancient World.

For teaching guides,
an interactive map, and videos, visit

WWW.SEVENWONDERSBOOKS.COM

SEVEN WONDERS

DISCOVER
THE HISTORY BEHIND
THE MYSTERY...

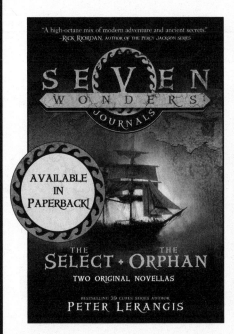

"A high-octane mix of modern adventure and ancient secrets."
—RICK RIORDAN, AUTHOR OF THE PERCY JACKSON SERIES

SEVEN
WONDERS
JOURNALS

AVAILABLE
IN
PAPERBACK!

THE
SELECT • ORPHAN
TWO ORIGINAL NOVELLAS

BESTSELLING 39 CLUES SERIES AUTHOR
PETER LERANGIS

"A high-octane mix of modern adventure and ancient secrets."
—RICK RIORDAN, AUTHOR OF THE PERCY JACKSON SERIES

SEVEN
WONDERS
JOURNALS

THE
SELECT
AN ORIGINAL NOVELLA

FREE
AVAILABLE
IN EBOOK
AND PDF!

BESTSELLING 39 CLUES SERIES AUTHOR
PETER LERANGIS

HARPER
An Imprint of HarperCollinsPublishers

SEVEN·WONDERS
of the Ancient World

BLACK·SEA

THE·TEMPLE·OF·ARTEMIS
AT·EPHESUS

ATHENS

THE·MAUSOLEUM
AT·HALICARNASSUS

THE·STATUE·OF·ZEUS
AT·OLYMPIA

THE·COLOSSUS
OF·RHODES

M E D I T E R R A N E A N · S E A

THE·LIGHTHOUSE·OF·ALEXANDRIA

THE·GREAT·PYRAMID·OF·GIZA

NILE